CONTINUUM

CONTINUUM

AL WOODS

Continuum

Copyright © 2020 by Al Woods. All rights reserved.

No part of this publication may be reproduced, stored in a retrieval system or transmitted in any way by any means, electronic, mechanical, photocopy, recording or otherwise without the prior permission of the author except as provided by USA copyright law.

"Birds Piranhas & (and) Corporate Thieves , The Raven's Story's" Bio
Copyrighted- Published 2002
"Continuum"
Copyrighted - Published 20 ~ Fiction
"Hap Jos'e and (&) Slick"
Unpublished Fiction
"Shoutout Windshield"
Unpublished Bio
Author Al C Woods additional Bio Info 8-1-2019

The opinions expressed by the author are not necessarily those of URLink Print and Media.

1603 Capitol Ave., Suite 310 Cheyenne, Wyoming USA 82001

1-888-980-6523 | admin@urlinkpublishing.com

URLink Print and Media is committed to excellence in the publishing industry.

Book design copyright © 2020 by URLink Print and Media. All rights reserved.

Published in the United States of America

ISBN 978-1-64753-377-9 (Paperback)
ISBN 978-1-64753-378-6 (Digital)

28.05.20

INTRODUCTION

This book is about a man named Gerald Kanin—his immediate family—and a rivalry that started to develop first between two brothers and then later, their sister.

Chris—Gerald's first-born was very humble and had a kind and considerate personality early on. But to many observers without ever revealing the reason why, his father was horribly strict and began scolding him while he was quite young.

Gerald seemingly was aggravated at what life had to offer him during such a period; the early forties-onward.

Soon he started scheming—thinking of a way he could get out of the situation he was in; a horridly, impoverished one.

Praising the son next to Chris—for any small thing he ever managed to accomplish, after the death of three of his other offspring he began to show complete favoritism toward his second eldest child whom was named Marcus.

Gerald boasted loudly about Marcus and never once did he ever acknowledge that Marcus never deserved such proud recognition.

Chris however remained obedient, and always showed concern. And deep within his heart he loved his family very much.

Yet, the tragedy that took the lives of three of his boys, Gerald blamed Chris for such an occurrence.

His mood was awful towards his victim son and occasionally he would aggravate his wife Elmira to the extent of her just wanting to scream often.

Chris dropped out of school and worked side by side with his dad at his construction company giving whatever job he did his greatest effort.

As a result, of Chris' aggressive labor Gerald was able to expand his firm.

Regardless of how much his eldest son gave of himself, Gerald made more concessions for Marcus. Simply overlooking the talent that Chris possessed as a building tradesman. And not even noticing—at least publicly—that he also had a daughter that then existed.

He pursued and made it possible that Marcus and Pitney—the daughter could attend a top rate school. He did just the opposite in Chris' case. Nothing was ever mentioned about him attending a school to possibly further advance himself.

Elmira eventually began to suffer under such pressure that Gerald had inflicted upon their family.

Gerald was quite vindictive and invoked revenge on those that he disliked as he existed on a daily basis.

Soon his wife began to suffer tremendously.

It was a constant challenge for him to play mind games with Chris and his mom (Whom was his only comfort.) Mind games which led to aggravation and torment in their lives.

Desperately seeking help—trapped in chaos, without her soul mate reaching out to her, his wife was driven to become a boozer.

There at his home Gerald permitted a jealous atmosphere to exist.

More and more he showed favoritism. Choosing Marcus—even over his daughter Pitney.

He became promiscuous; chasing young females.

Chris worked hard to make sure that their business succeeded. But he didn't hang around Gerald too long while at home.

Marcus showed disdain and contempt for Chris and other individuals he grew up with.

Gerald raised him up even higher on a pedestal.

Just those two: Gerald and Marcus. Enjoying everything that life had to offer, the deuce, all along together, in their little private clique.

There was sibling rivalry.

Marcus always feuded with Chris, putting him down constantly.

It appeared he was Gerald reincarnated while Gerald was still living. Before Long, Elmira succumbed.

Still yearning to love all his kin during the course, Chris had to distance himself from them. And if one wanted to mention such a weird group loving each other, there was only two in such a family whom truly understood what such a word meant.

A while went by, then Gerald passed.

He showed his contempt for everyone during the reading of his last will and testament.

Thinking often while he existed that his son Chris might've possessed gay tendencies but not divulging as much to anyone, Gerald verbally blasted his son saying that he thought he was a weakling.

Gerald sent a thunderous jolt through the family members gathered when he in so many words, left Chris out of the will he'd drawn up.

Strongly put, the empire which Chris had worked hard to help his dad establish, was handed over to his two siblings on-a-gold-platter.

Gerald showed that maybe he also had a humorous side whereas, he occasionally joked with individuals in his will.

Moving forward, the next chapter tells of Chris first becoming a criminal and how he associated with a band of hoodlums whom would help propel him in the direction of him becoming a wealthy man.

Chris would even involve himself in the practice of espionage in an attempt to succeed.

All along, Marcus enjoyed life to the fullest at the expense of Kanin Enterprises.

There was a robbery at a military base which caused a series of events, whereas Chris would be involved as either the person who had done the crime, or he was a co-conspirator to such a crime.

Agent Dan Throbs and other agents from The Pentagon and their pursuit of attempting to solve such a caper would lead them to many cities—and countries—and it would take a few extended years for them to even get close to the main suspect(s) whom were involved.

During the course, Chris' approach to starting out on his own landed him in deep doo doo. He didn't have enough street smarts, nor simple wisdom to know how to associate and deal with master crooks and killers like the ones he'd recently linked up with. It almost seemed?

Somewhat afraid, yet determined to move forward in life, he had great self-esteem while seeking a prosperous future for himself.

Later Marcus would become involved with a female singer, then bring her into his family and the duo would engage themselves in numerous business ventures.

After committing illegal acts in Mexico, Chris sets up shop in Paris, France. As a service industry, meanwhile his sister Pitney contacts him and buys goods from his operation below import clothing prices.

All along, agent Dan Throb's clique set in motion a search for him in Tel Aviv, Italy, Columbia, the U.S. and France.

Chris gets in trouble and is asked to leave the country he'd grown so fond of.

Still seeking a fortune in cash as he leaves France for a new territory, an expert plastic surgeon performs a highly professional job on him—leaving him sporting an apparition that would help him to act normal and remain stable, while venturing to, and existing in a different land.

After Chris travels to England, he not only meets, but gets connected to a party who helps him get inaugurated again in the building trade.

Chris consequently finds unreliable good fortune. And as time elapses, such a corporate action as the one he was involved with expands, prompting him to have hope that his constant dream of becoming a success in life was being fulfilled.

He felt reassured that eventually he'd excel to an even greater height than the point he'd reached while working—during that period— side-by-side with his father.

Darn it. As fate would have it, back in the U.S., trouble arose. There was a serious predicament that his immediate family was in— that needed attention.

Chris, unhesitating, resolved their problem and immediately won their favor again. Or did he?

Consequently, again Chris was faced with a weighty circumstance. Which, for the first time in very many years, since his self-imposed exile, he comes in contact with his cunning rival, his brother Marcus.

Once more, Marcus was vibrant with hostility towards his kin. His reason for such was that Chris was "so unrecognizable" and "out of touch with reality with the real world", when he did surface.

The final episode climaxes with all three of the Kanin extended family members embroiled in contention and psychological stress— bidding against each other on a multi-million dollar building launch; a project that was to be built in the U.S. and Mexico.

Because of their ongoing lack of respect—contempt, disdain, and scorn directed at each other—a lamentable fate awaited them.

Their awful bickering continued and consequently an unfortunate crime occurred that was the eventual solution to their whole-heartedly sad, distressingly troubled, demented family ties.

There is violent intrigue as one ventures to recapture how the Kanin's co-mingled as young adults there in the environment from which they sprang. And how they continued to relate—disrupting each other's sanity—from childhood throughout their entire life span together.

If either of the perpetrators of disaccord would have been considerate enough to take into account the honest and good things that the best member of the Kanin clan had done over a period of time —promoting goodwill in the family, in compromising during their final heated moments of feuding with each other, then was the time they should have taken the gamble to try and smooth the troubled waters— wherefrom one probably could've prevented the ominous tragic drama which occurred next.

The tighten bolts that holds a sane person's mind together can on occasion become weakened by demons whom inhabit the earth seeking to destroy kindhearted human life forces.

While trying to find sedulous space during his immortality— it seemed that the pendulum of bad luck, or evil portion, kept on swinging Chris' way.

CHAPTER ONE

Carson City, California—Autumn 1950

Inside the small five room brick stucco home on Cloverlawn Street, the aroma of fresh garden vegetables and beef stew that was cooking filled the air.

Seated at the dining room table terribly neurotic after retiring from a twelve hour shift, performing strenuous labor at the Millerkin Construction Company, Gerald Kanin asked in a weary voice, "How's Chris and his teacher getting along hon'?" he was speaking to his wife who stood in the kitchen preparing his special dish for their evening meal.

"Fine. I would imagine." There was genuine dread in the young woman's voice.

The note that Chris brought home with him. Should I mention it to Gerald? She pondered quietly to herself.

"Honey, I insist that you inform me. Has Chris gotten himself into any more trouble lately?"

"Well—I hope what I'm about to tell you doesn't upset you."

"Besides his recent low grade average, what else has he done that could possibly upset me?"

"O.K. here goes. Chris got expelled from school again today."

"What," Gerald seemed annoyed. "What has he done now? Did he break a window… Piss in that agonizing broad's flowerpot? I know," he hesitated. "Maybe he screwed her cat. Please forgive me darling," he quickly interjected. "You don't have to respond to that.

Obviously the lady is a thrill seeker, and the only way that she can get her balls off, is by ridiculing my son."

"I beg your pardon dear," his wife's composure darkened.

"Are you deaf?" he raised his voice a note.

"Only when you're yelling at me," she muttered, then hurried across the room over to the stove where she stood momentarily trying to ease the tension that gripped at her mind.

"Apparently you didn't hear me the first time, sweetheart," Gerald persisted, "so, I'll ask you again. What reason did Chris' teacher give for sending him home today? And this time I demand a fucking response from you."

"Calm down, dear. Calm down," she pleaded with him. "There's no need for you to get upset."

"Upset," Gerald retorted. "Who's upset?"

After pouring her husband a cool drink, Elmira took a seat and elaborated further on the subject. "Chris told me that his teacher doesn't like him, but I find that hard to believe."

"Why?"

"Because he's a little bit stubborn at times; just like his dad."

"You think he's like me, huh?" Gerald seemed offended by such a remark.

Abruptly there was silence.

After Elmira had stopped shaking she went on, "Gerald Chris obviously has done something terrible. Why would any adult want to expel a child for nothing?"

"You tell me." Gerald looked at her astonished.

"Written on the note that Chris brought home with him, Mrs. Farantino said that it was urgent. She wants to meet with us to discuss what she senses is a serious problem Chris is having when it comes to trying to learn. She says that when she confronts him with the issue he develops a temper and shouts that everyone is against him. When she tries a kinder approach he just sits and stares at her closed- mouth.

All the other students tackle their binding loads and are attentive. But, Chris has been caught sleeping during class and he's also been caught goofing off more than once: sailing paper airplanes across the room.

Mrs. Farantino frankly admits that she's left devastated by his exorbitant attitude. Since school started he's been given several assignments and not once has he completed them. She speculates that what's causing Chris to act so abnormal is that he's having serious difficulties when it comes to absorbing class information."

"Class information," Gerald appeared highly irritated. "What gave her that impression?"

"I don't know," Elmira earnestly admitted.

"Maybe, I know," Gerald said emotionally, his voice barely audible. "The lady is trying to tell us that our son is a slow learner."

"Chris said he explained to her that most of the subjects that she was teaching he already knew, but she refused to put him in a grade higher. He also feels that there is a language barrier between the two of them. You know, with her being Italian and all. He says that it is very hard for him to comprehend what she relates to the class because of her confused, American-Italian diction.

Maybe they shouldn't let people with foreign dialects teach our kids. I mean at certain levels of learning."

"What about George's kids next door? Or Mrs. Vigilottos' kids down the street? Has there ever been a rumor of one of them being sent home—for acting weird I mean?"

"Not that I know of."

Unwilling to tolerate the subject further, Gerald's voice erupted quickly, "That's it. I've listened to enough of this nonsense. Where's Chris now?"

"The last I saw of him, he was fooling around in the backyard."

Gerald's face contorted with repressed violence. "This is insanity," he mumbled, then raised his voice, "fucking insanity. Wait until I get my hands on him."

Despite her worry, suddenly a chilling wave of fright crept over Elmira. "Gerald—" her voice trembled.

Seemingly transformed into another being, Gerald turned and stared at her defiantly. "What is it? What the fuck do you want?"

"Forget, it," Elmira said unhappily. "Just forget it."

Around in the backyard, inside the garage sat Christopher Kanin. He was playing with a large pile of blocks that were stacked to resemble a building. Each section was enforced by cement to keep it solid and held neatly in place.

"Chris—What in the hell are you doing?" Gerald shouted frantically at his son. "And why were you sent home again today?"

Staring, confused with tears building up in his eyes, Chris started to explain to his father. "I was—"

Without allowing the youth a chance to communicate further, Gerald yelled angrily, "So you don't have an answer huh? Get your rear-end inside the house."

Chris tried to move as swiftly as possible, but suddenly Gerald was provoked into an uncontrollable state of anger and he began brutally striking his son with a homemade whip that he had hidden behind him.

While fighting an impulse to attack her husband, Elmira said uneasily, "Gerald, why punish the child before you allow him a chance to defend himself?"

"I wear the pants in this house. You understand?" Gerald's voice rang with authority.

Elmira stared at him defiantly.

He continued brutally assaulting Chris and after he'd seen that the youth was putting on a wild tantrum, he then backed off.

En route to the dining room, Elmira tried again to reason with her husband. "Gerald—the child must have had a reason for—"

"Reasons. What reasons?" Gerald said hastily blocking his wife's attempt to try to communicate further with him on the subject. "That damn kid is nuts. It's as simple as that. And you," he stood pointing his finger at Elmira all the while fighting an impulse to punch her out cold, "you've been dragging your ass. So shut the fuck up."

Instantaneously, Elmira grew quiet.

"Each day I'm up at four o'clock in the morning punching that clock." Gerald grumbled irately. "Working like a damn slave. Twelve to fourteen hours a day. Breaking my back for a corporation that earns millions, while all I earn is just enough to pay the bills. So what. No one around here gives a shit whether I live or die. Then, after trying to cope with the pressure of my job, I come home and find out that my dinner isn't ready. When did you start cooking Elmira—I ask, two o'clock this afternoon? Damn-it, here it is seven o'clock in the evening, and you're still cooking. For Pete's sake. How much can a man take? Not a whole bunch of what I've been taking that's for sure. Then added to my anxieties is that ding-dong in there, whom I have constantly tried to persuade to keep his rear-end in school. I tell you, if I don't get some help; I mean psychiatric help, the both of you are going to drive me totally insane."

He hushed momentarily waiting for Elmira to respond. Any kind of response from her whether negative or positive would be welcomed at this moment.

Once dinner had been served and Chris hadn't come to eat, Elmira decided to go and have a talk with him.

"How do your feel, son?" She sat his tray on the lamp stand beside his bed. After Chris didn't reply, Elmira then took a seat beside him.

"Listen," she gently stroked his hair, "you probably feel that your punishment was cruel and unjust, but put yourself in your father's place. What would you have done if your son had been kicked out of school twice in one month?"

"I don't know. But I wouldn't have tried to beat the hide off my son's back like he did." Chris seemed bitter. "I hate him."

"Sh-h-h. Don't say such horrible things about your father," Elmira warned him.

Immediately Chris appeared withdrawn.

"I believe what upset him most Chris, is when he was told that you weren't participating in your class studies," Elmira continued. "Boy, was he upset by that. But no matter what kind of predicament you've gotten yourself into, your father still loves you."

Chris wondered momentarily about her last statement.

Elmira continued, trying to convince him.

"Gerald has always let it be known that he doesn't want his son to be just an average person when he grows up. He wants his kid to be beyond average. He wants him to be a highly successful person in life. Someone with a sense of identity," Elmira paused.

"Am I getting through to you, son?"

Chris nodded his head hoping that she would quickly end the little pep talk that she was having with him.

"You see Chris, your father is a very highly skilled man. But, no matter how much he knows about his trade, his poor educational background has limited him to working as a common laborer—and it's very hard for him to identify with that. Knowing that with such skills he might have to work for someone else for the rest of his life. He doesn't want the same thing to happen to you."

"Nowadays, a man's son is the light of the world. A fostered soul. And dummies," she hushed, "well, they get the boot. We're living in a world of automation; a world where education plays a very important role in an individual's life. Not only will you need an education to get a job, you will need one just to survive. And a final reason that he wants you to be smart is, he wants you to be prepared for the future.

The only way that you can prepare yourself for the future is by attending your classes. Staying in school, and learning the things that your teacher teaches you. Don't argue with her. She's there to help you learn. And when the time arrives that you've learned enough about a subject—regardless of what that subject is—Who knows? You might one day become one of our country's greatest innovators. A person like Mr. Henry Ford the automaker. Or you could grow up and become another Thomas Edison—the gentleman who made the light bulb.

By accomplishing such things son, you could then pave the way for your children to become important when they grow up. Now does that make sense to you? When you grow up, wouldn't you like to become an important person in life? Someone like Mr. Ford or Mr. Edison?"

"Oh mom. I don't know." Chris answered dismally. "I guess so."

Please try to understand Chris. Most of our schools have their own comprised systems of learning. Try to adjust to your teacher's way of instructing a class; and in the event that it ever becomes too hard for you to understand, call her off to the side and explain to her that you are not absorbing the information that has been related to you. Then ask her could she please help you out. Even a teacher who acts tough can be kind. I'm sure that yours would sing praises if such a handsome kid like yourself asked for her help. Don't you know how to smile at the girls, boy, to get what you want?" Elmira tapped him.

Without answering her, Chris sat staring bluff into space.

Through ponderous fear Elmira wondered if the nine-year-old had understood what she had just related to him.

In addition to the children that she already had: Chris, Pitney, and Marcus, within the next six years, that went past, Elmira gave birth to three more offspring. They were all boys, whom she had the pleasure of naming—Aaron, Jerry and Karl, the last of the Kanin Clan.

A young headmaster of his own future state, Chris now shunned demand. He managed to stay in school and out of trouble, with the exception of one little freak incident. It happened about six months ago. He was caught inside the garage playing with this stack of blocks.

When Gerald asked him in a stern manner what he was doing, he replied very cautiously, "I'm trying to build a school dad."

CHAPTER TWO

1956

As time passed, Gerald's home was becoming too much. Moreover, he was being physically drained, tolerating internal pain.

My kids are growing up so fast. He said in alarm to himself, thinking that he had seen another gray hair suddenly grow on his head.

Soon, my youngest will be starting school. How can I provide for such a large family? A question he had asked himself a dozen times but one he now pondered very seriously. Each week there's never enough money to go around. How long can a person survive like this? I've got to find a way....

Like many men during his time Gerald dreamed of becoming successful and one day owning his own business. Yet he pondered at the moment. Would it be wise for him to pursue such a svelte notion during a period when America was in the process of trying to rebuild it's economy after participating in World War II.

To own and operate a construction company could be a big challenge. Gerald sat thinking of all the strenuous labor that he'd performed while working for the Millerkin Construction Company.

But, so can life. Face it, Gerald, he deliberated the subject further; you are not a young man anymore. It would be wise to make your move now. Simply, because you won't be able to pass up many more chances in life.

Immediately Gerald discussed his plan with a psycho-graphist. After reading Gerald's palm and explaining to him that the cards wouldn't lie about him soon becoming successful, the homely automatist convinced Gerald that the time had indeed arrived that he should go into business for himself. Even though he had seen it in the cards, en route home, Gerald began to be plagued by questions that needed prompt answers. One was, how long had he held his present job?

How well was he established within the community where he lived? Did he own his own home? Did he attend church? What school did his children attend? Did he have any character references.... .

"Darn." He took a deep breath, then exhaled heavily. "Why does life have to always be a problem for the poor man?"

Maybe I should try to establish a relationship with someone who has the finances to back me. Gerald pondered a few alternatives. In the meantime, try to establish some credit with a bank. Eventually, if I work hard, and save up enough cash, some lending institution out there might loan me enough capital to get my business started? Geez, how can a person be so unfortunate? But, one day....

Gerald labored for three more years before he finally became brave enough to approach a lending institution with his business idea. He almost passed out when the First Federal Savings Bank of Carson City told him that he qualified for a one hundred thousand-dollar line of credit.

Gerald seemingly adored his second eldest son Marcus. He taught him to be firm and cautioned him not to let anyone infringe upon his rights.

Maybe Gerald taught Marcus with his best interest in mind? One would have to judge that for himself.

Consequently such teachings resulted in Marcus believing that it was fine for him to infringe upon the rights of others. He lived with such a fury inside of him as a youth. He continued to behave in such a manner as an adult. He was rude to almost everyone.

"He's a genuine nut," is how Pitney viewed her brother when he grew older.

"Insensitive. Very insensitive," is what Chris observed.

"Now there's a kid who really has guts," Gerald was always extremely proud of Marcus. "He's never going to let anyone kick him around...."

"Marcus. Marcus. Marcus." Gerald tried in vain to convince his family members that he had a vision that Marcus possessed great qualities. When speaking of great qualities, Marcus truly possessed some alright. He had perfected the skills of an amateur con artist by the time he reached the age of ten. Oddly, his friends thought that he was a patron saint. Marcus seemingly respected such friendships.

He never hesitated to share anything that he had with any of his coalition: money, food, clothing, whatever. But whenever he wanted to borrow something from one of the combination, he would ask them for a loan that would equal five times the amount of that which they'd borrowed from him. After one of them had sworn to it that they would never let Marcus use them in such a manner again, he would approach one with a proposition and would end up swindling them out of their very last dime. Such devilish characteristics had won Gerald's heart and he was driven with great pride proclaiming that Marcus was one of the most gifted kids that he had ever known.

"When my son goes off to college, he's going to be an ingenious, talented person who will serve mankind in some great capacity."

Chris flunked twice in the twelfth grade. Computable, tellurian, he knew that the time had arrived that he had to make a decision to either stay in school and look stupid or go out and find himself a job.

While observing that Pitney and Marcus were doing super in school, Chris thought that if the time was ever to come that the Kanin family could benefit from what he learned over the years, it was now.

"The eldest child should be the one who should set the pace for the younger members of the family." Such teachings were what his father tried to instill in him since he was a child.

Chris got hired as a construction worker at Kanin Construction Company. He was thrilled; overjoyed. It didn't bother him at all when he found out that for the first few years he'd be employed by Gerald's firm that he'd have to work for free.

Unlike Marcus, whom Gerald admired, Chris was very obedient to his father. He tried to prove how much he also cared about his family by working ten and sometimes twelve hours a day out in the field, holding on to his dream that Kanin Enterprises would one day succeed and make him and his entire family very rich.

Chris' aggressiveness often made Gerald upset. He looked upon his son's greatest achievements with contempt. Chris was unmoved by his father's insane moods and as things would turn out, his contributions towards Gerald's business would make it soon become a very highly successful enterprise.

CHAPTER THREE

Mid-year 1968

Nine and one-half years passed and Gerald's business contracts were piling up. Orders were pouring in from cities like San Francisco, Los Angeles, Oklahoma City, Chicago and even New York. Meanwhile the outside competition was simply astonished. They could not believe that within such a short period of time Kanin Enterprises emerged as a competitor which now ranked as the second largest building development firm in the world.

Recently, Gerald had achieved many successes. And all the while pursuing his goals, not once had he ever encountered trouble along the way. However, one hot day in June while he was performing construction work on an auto trim plant, an accident occurred which caused a series of events that would lead to human exploitation, mental suffering, financial wreckage, and death in the Kanin Family.

Up fourteen stories high, on an already established slab, Gerald stood welding an incinerator set. Both Gerald and Chris were in an area where there was open-faced construction in progress.

Instead of going home that day after school, Jerry influenced his two brothers to take a hike over to the job site where Gerald was working to see if he would be interested in letting them earn a few bucks to buy clothing to participate in their class play.

After informing the crewman that Gerald was their dad, the boys persuaded the operator of the access elevator shaft to loan them a buggy and shuttle them up to the slab where Gerald was working. When they reached him, Gerald paused for a moment and thanked his sons for wanting to lend a hand. Then firmly his voice echoed to them, "Old men, the job I'm doing could only be performed by a skilled welder." And he joked, "After you two attend college, and trade-school, and get some on-the-job-training, come back and see me. By then, I doubt if you would even think about doing this kind of grubby crap."

Next he warned them, "Don't you go around playing games at the worksite. My insurance company will not cover you if something happens. Nor is it safe for boys your age to be in an area where there is open faced construction work being performed."

Suddenly Chris was jolted by the unknown. Instinctively, he moved from where he was standing over near the edge of the building. When looking down beside the chute for concrete access he observed that Jerry was moving the controls on a loaded crane. Fearing what might happen, Chris quickly raced toward the elevator shaft.

It seemed like a halo of darkness had covered Jerry's face as he shifted the leverage of the machine into operation. The crane's carrier began gliding freely in an easterly direction toward the slab where Chris and Gerald were working.

Hastily, Chris raced against time. The controls that operated the machine were as alien to Jerry as a three-dollar bill. To his amazement, when shifting the leverage again the crane's carrier speeded up and before he had realized what had happened, he had dumped thirty tons of concrete and steel onto the foundation where Aaron and Karl were standing.

There was a loud noise. Then upon impact the slab beneath the two boys began to fall. Instantly there could be heard what seemed like endless moments of terrified screaming. Intense moments passed. Then the echoing of the high pitched shrieking voices began to fade away.

Absolutely in shock, Gerald experienced a disquieting uncomfortable feeling.

As he stood there in silence awaiting the outcome of the tragedy, he suddenly began to shiver. Then loud thuds of pain seemingly pierced his heart after he realized the accident had caused his sons to be seriously injured. Their bodies could be partially seen lying sprawled on the grown crushed beneath a large group of beams.

With incredible speed Chris reached the crane quickly shoving Jerry from the controls. Momentarily as he sat quiet, dreading the aftermath of the incident he gazed over his right shoulder and observed that Jerry wasn't moving.

After seeing blood gush out of a wound of Jerry's head, he'd sustained during the accident, Chris quickly panicked. "Oh my god. What's happening?" He checked Jerry's pulse. It had stopped. He then tried to do mouth to mouth resuscitation. Jerry didn't breathe. He raised Jerry's body and held him in his arms, all the while pleading with him to speak; only to find out that Jerry would never be able to converse with him again.

Suddenly, the world around Chris began to grow hazy. He was petrified and in extreme shock.

With his torch still lit, experiencing the agony that one experiences when a loved one has suddenly died tragically, Gerald stood staring in sad disbelief.

All the while, Gerald was becoming successful, there had been numerous stories printed about him in the news. What manner of man was this Gerald Kanin? "Quite baffling." said the chief editor of The Carson City Daily Newspaper. He was simply astounded on the one occasion that he had gotten the chance to interview him. He learned that even though he had heard negative information about Gerald, seemingly none of it was true. When he met Gerald in person, he was kind, polite, astute and also seemed to be a person who was well informed about his trade.

Gerald was quite fond of the way the editor had portrayed him during his coverage of him in the news. There had been other stories that had been printed about him that individuals portrayed him as being an egocentric person who acted extra ordinarily weird at times. Such stories made him highly upset. He felt that they were quite demeaning to his character. Such news report coverage, however, landed with great effect. Three months after the stories were printed Gerald went into seclusion.

Was Gerald being temperamental? Maybe so, maybe not, but while defending their position none of the reporters ever bothered themselves to find out whether Gerald had a personality disorder.

Stuck alone, not gratified with his wealth, yet commanding a proud ego, his abnormal behavior was simply his way of not revealing the real side of his personality to the public.

One must wonder now did Gerald have any friends. Sure, there were individuals who were fond of Gerald. For a man who seldom smiled, most of the females who worked for him thought he was rather handsome. They adored his thick, white, curly hair and there were those that marveled at his overly tanned complexion and captivating blue romantic eyes. "His protruding nose and untamed mustaches adds excitement to a sometimes gloomy face." A constant female companion of his, during separate occasions had uttered such affectionate words about her beau.

Born ten or twelve years before the depression in Pittsburgh, Pennsylvania, Gerald was the son of a Pennsylvania steelworker. Gerald's mother ran off with another man when he was five, leaving his fate and that of his sisters and two brothers in the hands of their father. Nearing his sixteenth birthday, Gerald's father died of alcoholism, sadly leaving the grim choice up to his kids to raise themselves alone.

As a youth, Gerald performed numerous jobs that involved him working in the steel industry. Soon he became restless with his trade. He then became a hobo. Hitchhiking rides to New York and Miami. On his twenty-fifth birthday he arrived in Carson City. During his stay there he landed his first secure job, working as a laborer for the Millerkin Construction Company.

All during his teen years and early manhood, Gerald was a fragile and undernourished person. But, after settling down and trying to raise a family, over the years he had grown into a huge six-foot-two, two hundred and ten pounder. As mysteriously as he'd grown structurally—less being in deep daily pain—he also had grown tremendously in spirit.

He'd only been self-employed for a short while and the competition quickly labeled him a person who was obsessed with a vision to succeed. Their assessment of Gerald's hidden ambitions however, were true.

As a child, he tried to express to his father what he dreamed of. Such behavior continued into his adulthood with him trying to convince anyone who would listen that he had foreseen the day that he would become a success among the top ranking building developers of the world. Even though he encountered many failures while he tried to climb to the top, he still refused to let his dream die.

Meanwhile Gerald mastered in the fields of welding, carpentry, heavy equipment operations, surveying, masonry, blue prints, architectural design, and business management. He acquired such skills knowing that he could always use them whenever he became successful in the building trade industry.

But with the recent unspeakable tragedy hovering over him, an incident that he would endure deep within his heart until his death, Gerald pondered at the moment would any of his ideas ever materialize.

While finding himself extremely bereaved over the death of his three youngest children, he began directing his vitality toward mentally punishing Chris, blaming him for the tragedy that had occurred.

During his outbreaks of anger he violently referred to Chris as being the person who invited them over to the construction site that day.

Gradually Gerald was abandoning what little love he had left for his eldest son. Also during this time, Gerald gave up hope that Chris would ever amount to anything. Quickly there was a mood of despair that developed between Chris and Gerald.

While at home and on the job each day that went past now seemed like a month to Chris.

Soon the nimbus of darkness that overshadowed the feelings between the duo became obvious to their family and friends.

Elmira, Pitney and even Marcus called Chris and Gerald together for a talk trying to get the two to absolve their differences.

After their little chat, Gerald stood numb for a while and when his paranoid mind began functioning properly again, he quietly held Chris in contempt.

Chris tried several times to make friends with Gerald, but on each of his attempts Gerald was vindictive toward him.

Week after week, Gerald gave Chris the cold shoulder and when Chris couldn't stand it any longer, he left home.

During one supper after she hadn't heard from Chris for more than eight months, Elmira spoke furiously to her husband concerning their family matter.

"It's not fair," she said nervously with tears building up in her eyes. "It's just not fair. This is nonsense. I can't stand it any longer." She began yelling, "How in the hell can you sit there and pretend to be so preoccupied, so calm, and so relaxed, and not worry about the welfare of our son? How can you come home day after day 'attending to what's wrong at Kanin Enterprises,' and do nothing to learn of his whereabouts?"

She lowered the tone of her voice. With a trickle of a tear streaming down her face she spoke as if her vital force had been broken, "Gerald, he's our son. You have to get rid of that hatred you have embedded in your heart for him. You can't keep burying your thoughts in that awful tragedy that happened. Be it an act of the devil, aliens, or whomever, they are gone. Our children are gone. Fate moved it's dark hand, and you, me, nor anyone else could have had the power to save them from such a tragedy. That period of blackness is all over in our lives. Let's not create new problems for ourselves. I don't think that I could live through another tragedy like the one that took the lives of our boys."

They each were silent for a moment.

"Put yourself in Chris' spot. The anguish, the guilt, and the pain that he's feeling. Even at this very moment, he could be thinking of committing suicide. Please Gerald, please try to find out where he's at."

Elmira's benevolent speech quickly drew ineffective results.

Gerald responded by angrily tearing up his newspaper. It appeared that he'd momentarily witnessed some kind of guilt feeling about his abandonment of their son.

A couple of weeks went by with Elmira contacting Chris' friends. Of the four he had, she found out from the most interlocutory person in the ring, Augie, that he had gone to Southern Texas where he was working as a ranch hand.

In Texas, at the Blass Ranch, Elmira had a hard time trying to persuade Chris that his father wanted him back home. After she called Gerald up and begged him to differ, he promised their son that the two of them would be friends.

Motivated by observing him doing such a cavalier job at their ranch, The Blass', gave Chris a brown pony whom he named Shining Star.

Hence, Shining Star and Chris would share many precious moments together.

CHAPTER FOUR

April 1973

Suddenly Kanin Enterprises had become a threat toward the economic stability of the only other top ranking building firm in America. This was fine with Gerald, simply because he felt their loss was his gain.

Meanwhile the building trade industry was rapidly changing. The town where Gerald now did business was indisputably getting too small for Gerald. He needed to be able to purchase more advanced materials and in the meantime keep abreast of the newer developments that were taking place in the building trade industry. Gerald pondered at the moment how would he be able to accommodate such a growing clientele like the hundreds whom he presently had lined up requesting his prompt services.

Would it be feasible for him to move Kanin Enterprises to a large urban community and in the meanwhile maybe expand it. He reassured himself that once he relocated he was certain to gain new customers. He was also in dire need of an architectural firm and an outside contractor. Such a move he knew would put him in close contact with both enterprises whereas they could help him finish the huge backlog of work that he needed to get done for his clients.

He contacted a building firm analyst to study such a move. When the study was completed, Gates Associates was in favor of Gerald expanding his firm. They recommended two cities of which he could choose from: New York or San Francisco. The idea was brought to the attention of his family and after discussing the issue for about two weeks, they voted unanimously that San Francisco would be the city where they would live and a prime city where Kanin Enterprises would grow into an even greater success than it currently was.

"Wow, San Francisco." Pitney said daydreaming. "A friend of mine said that it could also be a very exciting place to live."

Pitney was envious of Marcus since it had been decided that Marcus would venture to the east coast where he would attend Harvard to major in law. "Why does he get the opportunity to go to the top rated school...." she quizzed her dad, pretending to be joking.

Gerald had also seen to it that "soon after" they'd become organized in San Francisco, Pitney would get her chance to attend school at U.C.L.A. While there, she would major in marketing. The only interest shown towards Chris getting an advanced education would be Gerald's offer to him to consider staying with the company working as the firm's chief engineer.

Once settled in San Francisco, Gerald bought a home in an affluent neighborhood that was housed at the foot of a mountainous area west of the Bay Bridge.

Within a short period of time, Gerald's firm had accumulated three subsidiary firms: The Hackeet, Goldstein, and Webster. Of the four businesses that he now owned, Gerald Kanin was slowly merging his business interest with the constant thought in mind of making Kanin Enterprises a corporate giant.

As a young adult Elmira Kanin could have been described as a female who was plain and simply beautiful. She was a slender, but shapely, five foot seven brunette who had curly brittle hair that reached below her shoulders, and medium violet blue eyes with pretty teeth; mouth and dimples.

Born in 1927 in Boston Massachusetts she was the daughter of a prominent doctor whose name was Paul Lagemess. He and his wife Jennifer were a family who was dedicated to having strong moral values. And to prove to Elmira how strong their moral pageant turgidity was, after she'd become sixteen and had eloped with Gerald, they denounced their only offspring and immediately warned her:

"Until you get rid of your boyfriend Gerald, we'll have nothing else to do with you."

A few years prior to her running away Elmira had the pleasure of meeting Gerald at the home of her cousin Delores. Gerald had visited

Boston with a friend of Delores' who had come to Boston in search of work. Eventually, Elmira would refer to the day that Delores introduced her to Gerald as being the day that she fell in love with Satan and swiftly sold her soul to "That Devil."

Obviously stressed, before her forty-seventh birthday Elmira had started to grey at a rapid pace. She'd also began to detach weight and would casually hold conversations with herself.

It was quite confrontational to her immediate family why she'd impulsively commenced acting so odd. Gerald, Pitney, nor Marcus were concerned with Elmira's problem; simply because, they were hung up on self. A very—to the far left—self.

If either of them would've extended their hand in acknowledgment that she was growing sick, they would've discovered that it was the present, that she was beginning to lose her sanity.

There were voice's talking to Elmira. Excruciating voice's that quickly changed her whole free will. She was altered into a being who was very recondite at times. There were even moments when she was wretched; thinking about committing suicide.

From the start of their relationship, Elmira's life with Gerald had always been twisting. Even though he constantly treated her cruel she had extreme respect for him. She never spoke an afflictive word about her husband. She was always there when he needed her.

Seemingly settled with a multifarious person like Gerald, the average person would've shot him while living under such a tremendous strain. But, not Elmira. She was permanent. She'd remained strong by holding on to a hope that she would be able to raise her children proper. Maybe teach them the principals of correct behavior that her loving parents instilled in her.

She had an exceptionally great relationship with Chris.

"Chris and I are the only one's in this family that have any sense." She'd occasionally express with bitter discontentment in her voice to Gerald whenever he became infuriated with jealousy over how close the two were.

Elmira was growing wearier by the moment now.

For extended hours somehow she managed to keep busy. Her garden was so well groomed she won a neighborhood award for her efforts. The grocery pantry and shelves were fully stocked. And the clothes that her family had discarded were spotless; ready for the salvation army whenever they wanted to come by and pick them up.

At a certain time of the morning she'd take a break and sit in the den by the telephone waiting for Gerald to call her. "I've sat here for over an hour today and answered ten calls that weren't important—at all. Business. Business. Business. That's all anyone ever wants to talk about…."

Distinctive, Elmira at the moment, highly furious, protested vehemently to her maidservant, Marsha one humid afternoon. "And, my husband, "The Patron Saint", Gerald," she was crushed, then quickly tears came trickling down her face, "he could call me… communicate to me what's wrong with our relationship."

Marsha comforted her; hugging her, all-the-while shedding tears with her.

Seemingly time passed with great speed and the communication that Elmira yearned to have with Gerald never took place.

Even Elmira, who professed that she understood her husband, found Gerald to be an alien creature occasionally. She knew of several events recently that Gerald had attended: business meetings, luncheons, and parties—along with his business associates and their wives, but never did he ask her would she be interested in going to such events.

Momentarily she desired a tolerable answer. Yet in her heart, she knew, such a response most definitely would have to come from a stainless life force.

For some extraneous and incurable reason it now became apparent to Elmira that next to Chris' name, she too had been placed on Gerald's list of individuals to persecute whenever he wanted too.

It quickly became a habit with Gerald that whenever he was in Elmira's presence he began to act extremely odd. Elmira didn't know how to respond to his weird behavior so she became unbelievably jealous hoping she could get Gerald's attention.

Months went past and upon realizing how dumb her jealously act appeared, she unloaded it and began drinking heavily.

February 1976

Within a while Elmira became an alcoholic. Gerald reacted calmly to her present state of affairs. She's near the brink of self-destruction. He pondered deceptively quiet. How can I rescue her? Is she worth saving? . . .

Finally he decided to summon to her aid, a gigolo; whom he told Elmira that he was to be the head butler. He informed her that the hired help duties were to help her keep the maidservants in line. And to help her out with any additional work that she had to do around the house.

"Once he balls her real good she probably will forget all about his assignment around the house." He once confided in Harry Stemphel his only male friend.

Usually a kind and socially well-behaved individual, Elmira now sensed that she was losing her grip on reality. Seemingly more of her thoughts were vexatiously overcrowded with inner voices deforming her as she went about her daily activities.

May 1977

While feeling greatly stressed she hired a celebrity psychiatrist to assist her with her newly acquired illness.

One squalid series of events led to another in her life. Then suddenly she found herself occupied with her therapist in an extramarital relationship.

July 1977

Dr. Tatleman assured Elmira that there was a report done recently "which confirmed" that sleeping at least twice with your therapist is definitely a cure treatment for alcoholism.

Gerald's indifference was frequent toward his two principal enemies, Chris and Elmira. His newly meretricious praxis was to try to ascertain any kind of potential talent each of his children had; and in the final analysis, he would choose which of his offspring would become the heir of his estate.

He professed that Pitney was the chosen one. But whenever a person would relate to her becoming the heir, face-to-face, Gerald would express to them with vague discontentment in his voice, "My heir will be the offspring whom I think possesses the greatest skills in the family."

Quickly Gerald began to speak poorly about Pitney's achievements and began shining the spotlight on Marcus. The person whom he'd always had in mind of becoming the heir of his estate.

The foregoing was proven rudely. When Marcus was home from school, Gerald would take off during his work hours and angle backward trying to develop the potential builders talent he imagined his son had inside him.

Nevertheless, such a relatedness would soon lead to his dismay. Simply because Marcus' only interest would be to jump in and out of bed with different females.

In small lengths of grief this weighted on Gerald very much. But regardless, he still held on to the impossible dream that one day his well-educated son would learn his trade and become wealthy. And as a result of his ambitions he would fill his shoes and make something good out of the Kanin name.

But what was quite disturbing now was the fact that all the while Gerald pursued Marcus' interest, none of his effusive vigor was ever steered in the direction of his eldest son Christopher Kanin. An individual who now had chosen to be a loner.

Torn with bitterness and anger Christopher worked long hours at the construction site hoping that when his day ended and he went home he wouldn't have to encounter his dad. Now it suddenly didn't matter to Chris whether he possessed any talent. He simply devoted himself to what he was doing. He was the relentless force that was behind seeing to it that Kanin Enterprises remained strong and continued to be as profitable as the other prominent builders of the world were.

Elmira was sitting near the pool one afternoon writing her memoirs, when suddenly she experienced chest pains. As she sat grasping for air, Georgio phoned Dr. Tatleman who advised him to administer CPR until he could arrive. When Dr. Tatleman arrived at the Kanin Estate he immediately began cardiovascular testing on Elmira and found that she had suffered a mild heart attack.

A call then went to Gerald where he was attending an important business meeting being held in Las Vegas. When he was informed about his wife's grave condition, Gerald related to it as being another ploy Elmira was using to get attention. His insensitive response and lack of concern over his wife's welfare is what broke the last straw of their more than twenty-eight years of marriage.

Immediately after Elmira was able to move about, she hired a private investigator to spy on Gerald. Her prompt concern was to find out if Gerald was having an affair with anyone. It took the investigator only two weeks to confirm the notion Elmira had about Gerald cheating on her. It was revealed that he had been sleeping around on numerous occasions during the past five years. He had been observed dating a couple of blondes, a brunette, a redhead, and on one occasion even a black female. All of whom were young females between the ages of twenty-four to thirty-five.

The estranged couple had two violent arguments and when realizing one of them might soon end up on a slab in the morgue, they quickly settled their feud and entered into a mutual agreement that it would be in their best interest for them to share separate sections of their spacious mansion. Gerald would reside in the east wing section and Elmira would have the west.

Now entangled in a web of suspicion Elmira fought desperately to control her emotions.

From a distance Gerald watched her as she struggled to free herself. His wife, who was in a cave of despondency with an alien disease which tormented her mind, heart, and eventually it would torment her soul.

September 1977

Elmira had Dr. Tatleman increase the number of nerve pills that she was using. While trying to rid herself of the agony that her husband had bestowed upon her, she flaunted her relationship with Dr. Tatleman in the public eye. And meanwhile, being involved with Dr. Tatleman she also committed herself to sleeping around with at least two other men.

Time went by fast. Elmira felt that she now was constantly battling with a dark force while she steadily and persistently tried to win Gerald's affection.

Not particularly pestered by the serious problems that his wife was having, Gerald continually did whatever made himself happy.

Mid-October 1977

Elmira was in critical agony. Whom could she turn to? She asked herself but found no answer. She induced Dr. Tatleman into increasing her dosage of pills.

After living in a paranoid, delusional, and drunken world, Elmira finally gave up the desire to live.

On the day when the entire family was to be home sharing their first Christmas together in over three years, Elmira died of an overdose of pills.

December 31, 1977

You could quickly count the mourners who attended the graveside services of the recently departed. Of the twelve individuals present, what was peculiar was that Chris was absent. Chris, Elmira's favorite child did not shed a tear when the doctors told him his mother was dead.

Chris remained calm simply because housed deeply in his heart, he knew Elmira loved him dearly. He also was comforted knowing that she no longer had to be in bondage, nor, be a prisoner or a slave. Nor would she have to suffer any more of the inhumane things that she had endured while living with his father. Her passing away and going to heaven, (a place where one should find peace)—Chris felt it was mercy granted by God. By her wanting to die, to rid herself of the many evils that tormented her life for so long, there was nothing sad about that.

The day following the funeral Chris had his pony transported to a warmer climate. For six weeks he and Shining Star were inseparable again.

CHAPTER FIVE

April 1978

After his mother's death, Chris yearned for love in his relationship with his family. But, for some odd reason their efficient services were unattainable.

Of the three family members that he now had left, Pitney was the only one whom he could relate to. He and Marcus could never communicate. They were always at each other's throats. Whenever he tried to discuss his anxieties with his father, Gerald's advice to him was, "You should do what your mother did when she was having problems. Seek help from a psychiatrist."

Each day Chris would take on numerous challenges. He found no work too hard for him to perform. Whether it was snowing, freezing, raining, or humid, he worked diligently out in the field helping his father's firm build newer and larger projects.

Even though he'd been discredited many times, Chris was very talented. Although his manhood was on trial, he was truly a born genius. Within just two years while performing the duties of a surveyor and engineer, he could have been considered an expert in either field. Sensing the many hidden qualities that Chris had, Marcus did everything within his power to defeat any of the growing attributes his brother had to offer and lend to the Kanin name. It also was to Marcus' advantage that by him holding a position on the Board of Directors at Kanin Enterprises, he was in the drivers seat to scheme and cover up any particular job that Chris might ever have had the guts to complete. Taking credit for many of his brother's ideas, Marcus was congratulated often for jobs that he would have never been articulate enough to have created.

Added to his skills, Chris was also an architect. In his private quarters he designed modular buildings. He'd show them to Marcus, seeking his guidance along with his approval, but almost always Marcus would discourage Chris. Later, Marcus would present the same concept to the corporate architects. Conspiring together they would make minor changes to Chris' designs and use the prints as their own; hoping Chris was too dumb to know that they had copied his work.

When seeing a building completed, one which looked like a twin copy taken from his prints, Chris would smile to himself. A warm feeling and a sense of accomplishment would creep over him. He took pride in knowing that the real loser was his brother. All of the hidden irony, the yearning, and his longing to reach a goal had momentarily vanished. On each occasion he also bowed his head and gave thanks to God for the moment of sunshine he'd brought into his life.

When home from school, Marcus had a habit of sneering at Chris, often implying that he was gay. One holiday he asked Chris to join him and his friends on a date and when Chris declined the invitation he added insult to injury. "A famous gay poet once said, 'in every affluent family, there is a fellow with pudding in his pants.' I must say, yours looks awful shaggy back there."

The main reason for Chris' abandonment of the "smartest" member of their family was that he couldn't stand his brother's constant boasting about his attending school at Harvard and how "he" had helped their father become a success story. And an added reason was that Marcus would bring up conversations involving their family member's personal lives. He felt that if Marcus had any pride, he wouldn't have ever dared to stoop that low.

Chris said to his brother one day, "I would like to think of myself as being a real decent human being, but very few men I communicate with can attest to that fact. There are many bright con men whom think that they have class. To an individual like that," (All of Chris' huge frame was blocking Marcus' view by now.) "I say that he's a pompous ass. Like you, a baby piece of shit, who shows very little respect for anyone. What animal compound did you learn your manners from, Marc?"

Marcus stared at him speechless.

Pitney soon got married and moved out of the Kanin Mansion. While feeling awfully wary, Chris thought that it was in his best interest that he should do the same.

Once speaking to an associate of his, he defended his actions with discontentment in his voice. "I moved out because it was necessary," he yelled. "If I had chosen to stay around Marc and my dad any longer, there's no doubt I would have ended up in a nut house somewhere."

A year later, Marcus graduated from Law school. Gerald gave a party for him and bought a cake for him that read, 'In Honor of Marcus' Successful Achievement at Becoming an Attorney....."

After having a few drinks that evening, Gerald aroused his guest's admiration by predicting that Marcus would probably become one of the United States' most respected attorneys—a powerful individual whom he believed would one day work his way to the Supreme Court bench.

Many whimsy, rich, 'love to rump in the sack crowd', attended the 'cool' bash that real estate tycoon Gerald Kanin was having in his son's honor. And to add to the excitement of things happening all too cozy, was the fact that a large number of females who were present were lively members of Marcus' sex fan club.

Throughout the night, in an orderly manner, they waited their turn to have a chance to show off their pretty white teeth while being detained by Marcus, their "man of honor."

During the festivities, Chris seized a moment to congratulate Marcus on him becoming a part of the team at Kanin Enterprises. Abruptly following his acknowledgment of the super job opportunity that his brother was about to receive, Marcus surprised Chris by making a bold public statement about the recent position that he held at the firm. Slurring with a drunken stupor on his face, he boasted about what a huge success he was. "I out-rank any engineer, surveyor, or marketing analyst on our staff... And furthermore, my contributions made Kanin Enterprises what it is today."

In reference to Marcus, Chris would often try to erase the fact that he ever existed. He first discovered how merciless and odious Marcus could be, during their early childhood.

One day, the two had a horrible fight, and lucky for Chris, he won.

Otherwise, Marcus might have been happier with their fight ending in one senseless tragedy.

While continuing to be angered, Marcus waited until Chris went to sleep and hit him over the head with a baseball bat.

Such an incident confirmed Chris' belief that Marcus possessed an unmistakable boldness in his character. As time passed, Chris would relate to this brother as being a divine demon who was conceived with the special determination in mind of one day being his executioner. Luck was also in Chris' favor that Marcus' bat was only plastic.

Often Marcus' personality reminded Chris of his father. No matter how crudely he'd achieved many of his goals, he was always lacking in compassion or maudlin emotion for those whom he'd injured while en route to his fame.

Ruthless, manipulative, and arrogant—all of those traits made up Marcus' character.

"Long range planning. That's the key to becoming successful," was the business slogan that he constantly used. "And while you're trying to accomplish your goals," his voice was strong when he spoke of his philosophical approach to life, "a person should first seize the opportunity of making money anyway that one can. By any means necessary." Occasionally, he created a stir when making the latter statement, (particularly with his girlfriends). Even though they were destitute and simply clearly at his mercy, they couldn't understand why a gentleman who was from such a rich family always demanded money for the sexual services that he performed for them.

Quickly Chris had a temper flare and counter-attacked his brothers remarks, "Your con-tri-bu-tions," he protested fiercely. "What contributions? I'm amazed that you expect someone to believe that incredible bull. That which you have contributed to the firm can be quickly found in the public relations department indexed under the title of Theft."

"Theft?"

"Yes, theft. Why is it so hard for you to relate to being a thief? Everyone at the firm knows that you are a pro when it comes to stealing another person's ideas. You are an engineer of deceit. That's what you are."

Chris now stared defiantly at Marcus. "It's your turn to speak. Go ahead. Deny my accusations."

For a moment, Marcus' customary popular voice was hushed.

"Face it Marc, you are a person who has illusional aspirations. And, be warned, you're skating on thin ice. Your contributions to Kanin Enterprises—that's a laugh. How could you deliberately mislead your friends. Filling their heads with such lies? Deceitful, despicable, lies. You lie for the fun of it. And I have to be defamed because of such stupidity. I can't match wits with you in such a field. I doubt if anyone can box with a liar whose been out of touch with reality as long as you have."

Chris now directed his attention to the guest who had gathered around them to listen to the two men feud. "I would like to apologize for my brother's audacious and personal behavior. But, as you can see, he's not quite the same after a few drinks. However, I caution you. Don't be misled thinking that it's the liquor that's causing him to look down his nose at others. He can portray the role of a typical ass, drunk or sober. And even though sarcasm, criticism, and harassment is a chronic illness with him, I forgive him for the way that he has acted here tonight."

For a moment Chris stood choking back tears.

"Don't let your sudden rise to success influence your duty to be fair to others, Marc," he managed to continue. "Every person that was born, I believe, has a talent."

"It would appear to me if you did have such a talent you would have succeeded at something by now," Marcus interjected. How horribly odd that all the while listening to Chris defend himself—Marcus could be so insensitive toward his feelings.

"Seemingly some individuals are more fortunate than others." Chris told him. "But regardless, I'm no different than you or anyone else who possesses a skill. And like you, I am too obsessed with a vision that, one day I will become important.

Stop your ridicule. You're not a psychic. You can't predetermine what destiny has lined up in store for me. You've realized some of your dreams," he paused, "and I'm happy for you. But, don't count me out. Simply because I'm one of those individuals who has the will to succeed. Your attempt to try to persecute and dishonor me in front of these people will never change that."

"An excellent statement Chris. Excellent." Bang. Marcus plowed on determinedly to further insult his brother. "I have this friend whose a prominent and well respected gynecologist, and he is also remarkably good when it comes to lip surgery. Here's his card. Maybe he can be of some service to you...."

As Marcus continued to make a fool of himself, Chris quietly excused himself from the room.

Two years later Gerald became terminally ill with a serious case of pneumonia. While on his deathbed he summoned his personal attorney to have his last will and testament drawn up.

Weeks later he died.

On a humid afternoon in August, in San Francisco, California, the Kanin family was gathered together for the reading of the will of business tycoon, real estate developer, and father—Gerald Kanin. The Kanin children found themselves highly suspicious when Gerald's family came from as far away as Florida to see what Gerald may have left them in his will.

Standing inside the private library at the Kanin estate was Pitney Dominique and her husband Salvo. The Dominique's owned two small clothing store chains. Seated was Sarah, Don and Todd Kanin, sister and brothers to the tycoon. Sarah and Todd are beverage plant owners and Don's business is prostitution and loan sharking as well as a producer of X-rated films and distributor of wholesale sensual sex products. Leaning up against the wall near the doorway in the back of the room stood Christopher Kanin. Minus the grey hair, he looked identical to his father. Being the lone pioneer who helped Kanin Enterprises become a success story, Chris had great respect for himself and his work. But because of his shyness and peculiar behavior, his father despised him. "He's an underclass." On numerous occasions Gerald had spoken poorly of his eldest son. "An extraordinary weirdo. That's what he is. He has no guts...." Gerald was provoked into saying such horrible things about his son because Chris was never able to live up to his expectations. There was also something else that bothered Gerald very deeply about his eldest child. The rumor that had been spread around their immediate social circle that Chris appeared to be gay. This information was highly embarrassing to Gerald. He often wondered what was his son's preference. Unlike all of the classy females that his brother Marcus dated, Chris showed an interest in just the opposite. It appeared that he was only interested in women who were the partying type and females that worked at restaurants, or those that were on state aid.

Chris' most constant companion was a plain and simple blonde whom he had met while vacationing at Newport Beach. But because of her below middle class background and zest for having fun, Chris' father looked upon him with contempt and denounced him whenever "Blondie" was in his presence.

Soon there was an incident which occurred that quickly ended their relationship. It happened when Chris wasn't home that "Blondie" came around looking for him and encountered Mr. Kanin. Gerald, "the devil," furiously and abusively insulted her in the presence of a few of her friends. Four days later they found her washed up on the beach. Without it ever being revealed what really caused her death, through a public statement made by Gerald, Chris, and the San Francisco coroner, her death was ruled a suicide by the over indulgence in cocaine.

Chris mourned for his dearly beloved for nearly a year, then his guardian angel blessed him with another companion. But his newly found friend was in a class all by herself. She was a person who would not have been intimidated, scared off or subjected to abuse by business tycoon Gerald Kanin, nor by any of the members of the Kanin family.

After befriending and confiding her life's story to Chris, he swore not to ever introduce his girlfriend to his family; simply because of her past. A past that would unveil graves of shocking episodes. She was an encyclopedia that was filled with stories of crime. Stories that would make your skin crawl just by listening to them. An unlawful person whom only an open-minded person like Chris would have accepted such a notorious character as being his friend.

Since achieving the ranks of a planner, architect, surveyor, engineer, and while on the job, a powerful, one-man workforce, Chris also had good advice to share with those that were underprivileged. He stated in his philosophy that, "Insight, dedication, and perseverance is the key to success. First, spend a little time researching whatever it is that you are pursuing and when you become familiar with the basic fundamentals of your occupation, have enough cash on-hand, or be able to borrow enough capital to start the ball rolling in the right direction. Then become totally committed. Be energetic and occasionally move on impulses. Regardless of how impossible things might seem from time to time, stick with whatever it is that you are trying to accomplish. Such an effort," he maintains, "could put the wheels in motion that could produce an abundant lifestyle for one who sought it."

Grinning and smoking an extra long cigarette Marcus sat reared back in, a large leather chair observing the mood that his kin folks were in, as they sat conversing in a low tone of voice—"About his father's money," is what he figured. Renowned as a swindler since he was ten, he had worked painstakingly at winning a place in his father's heart. He was also an individual that wanted everyone to look up to him. However, it was apparent that even though he had graduated from Harvard, he wasn't highly intelligent. He lacked possessing one little small thing many individuals possess. It's called wisdom.

Nevertheless Marcus did specialize in one field. He had charm that mesmerized affluent women into bed with him.

During the years it had been his trade secret that he should keep a low profile while having a fling with such prestigious females. However, it turned out that he had done such a great work for them that soon his popularity as a glamorous gigolo was too hot to keep undercover. It was after his secret was made public that it established him as being one of the most sought after pimps in and around the bay area.

"In the presence of the family, Mark Chatman, the president of Security Pacific Bank, which holds the bulk of Gerald Kanin's and Kanin Enterprise's assets, Dr. Jake Tatleman, the family's private physician and close friend... I, Martin Goldstein, Executive lawyer of The Kanin Estate, disclose the last will and testament of business tycoon, Gerald Kanin: To Pitney, my beloved daughter, I bequeath to you my controlling stock shares In Kanin Enterprises and the home estate. With such tokens of appreciation, you should have enough money to keep you secure for a lifetime.

Now a brief digression from the will. As you know, each surviving family member has the rights and privileges to use the family synagogue whenever they want to, but I'm issuing an order that on the day of my funeral, it be closed. My reason for such, is for you, Pitney to use it to pray constantly during the services, that my condemned soul might be forgiven once I land in hell. Yes, hell. You heard it right. Its a place where evil saints go.

To Sarah, Todd, and Don, I bequeath to you my Doberman dogs, and as an extra gift, I'm throwing in my pet rattlesnake Jacob. In the years to come, may each of you share warm, loving and tranquil moments together. For "you all" highly deserve each other."

Instantaneously the three-some turned pale. Such small tokens that were left to them from their rich brother wasn't at all what they had expected to receive from him.

"To Marcus, my smartest and most faithful son, I leave an account entrusted in your name with a hundred million dollars in it. You are the chip off of the old block. A man who has wisdom, knowledge and insight. You have the skills and ability to be one of the world's greatest builders. You and Pitney are to share ownership in my Realty Development firm. You two also will retain the right to have control over all subsidiary shares of stock. You are to hire a private master trainer that will teach you all there is to know about the business operations of the building trade industry. Marcus, you will be tested as a businessman for the period of one year. If you prove yourself to my appointed board of trustees, you will then have the legal right to become Vice Chairman of Kanin Enterprises. Consequently, upon termination of the years trial period set forth in this contract, and the board finds that you have been placed in an unqualified position, you are at that time, to transfer to Pitney all of the firms stocks. Think about the task that you have ahead of you, son. Simply, because if you do not perform up to standards you could find your bank fund in jeopardy. Martin Goldstein will act as an overseer of both your accounts. Take this offering and along with it, my blessings son, and accomplish what you will."

Suddenly a loud thud ripped inside of Chris. He stood momentarily experiencing the agony of what seemingly felt like a thousand heartbeats pounding inside his body. As tears welled up in his eyes he quietly excused himself from the room.

"To Dr. Tatleman, I leave to you a charge card which can be used internationally. It has now been made more convenient for you to buy larger quantities of drugs direct from your wholesaler in South America. As a sentimental offering, I'm throwing in my wife's false teeth, Bible, and girdle. In the future, I hope your adulterous practice flourishes and your earnings decrease by ten-fold. To Mark Chatman, I give to you my 920 A.D. Scroll. Read it, and in the event you're able to interpret it's mystery writings, who knows, maybe your reward will be millions.

To you Cecelia, Marsha, and Anna—when sober, a cheerful group of maidservants. I leave to you the guest rooms in the maidservants quarters, and as an extra gift I'm throwing in my beloved wife's waterbed, Cocaine bowls, and medicine prescriptions, (Bless her soul), and a charge card each. See, I kept my promise. It has been made possible that you all can now have a lifetime membership at any wholesale liquor dealer in the state. You three were also great in bed.

To my butlers, John and Thomas. I leave to you the keys to the guest rooms in the maidservants quarters and my 1948 Buick. Please share your gifts equally and without squabble. Thank you for your devoted services.

To Martin Goldstein, I leave to you, your law firm—paid off in full. My cigars and a new case file.

With these tokens of appreciation, I do hope that all of you are well off."

Moments passed. As a few started to talk, Goldstein interrupted. "Oh, I almost forgot this folks. I now read to you the information concerning the new case file."

With painful emphasis and a saddened tone of voice he began to solve. "To my eldest son, Christopher: I leave to you my case file numbered 196-692. It tells of all the hardships that I've had on my rise to success and my belief in you. Of which, I'm greatly disappointed. I feel that you have a chronic illness when it comes to you accepting the responsibility that goes along with being an important figure among the great builders of the world. Drowned in that pity alone, you will never succeed at anything. How could you have been such a hopeless case? A demon must have possessed your most divine spirit. In all of my greatest attempts to try and acquaint you with different aspects involving the building industry, you have failed me. I waited patiently over a period of years hoping that you would show some improvement. But nothing happened. I'm now convinced that you are a loser. A person who is not able to stand up in his own shoes, let alone fill the ones that his father has stepped out of. Being considerate, and you should be thankful that I'm not disclaiming you as being my son, I've given the power of attorney to the Board of Directors to keep you on the payroll as an Assistant Vice-President in charge of the subsidiaries and new venture divisions, as well as Field Operations Manager in charge of surveying. Within the one year trial period set forth in the agreement made between the board and I, you are to get private help in each of these departments. Maybe with Marcus' super ingenuity he can help mold you into being a businessman. I also leave to you a ten-thousand dollar bank account. See, I did appreciate your efforts. God be with you, my son."

Suddenly eyebrows went up. It was truly a shock to all concerned upon hearing the last will and testament of entrepreneur Gerald Kanin.

"It's not fair. Dad's will... How could he have excluded Chris?" Marcus appeared sad, all the while feeling a warm sense of triumph inside.

He spoke to Pitney, who at the moment sat staring through a purple haze. Her mind was clouded with all sorts of thoughts. How is it possible that father could have been so cruel? . . .

"Boy what a tremendous shock," Marcus almost smiled. "Where did Chris go?"

Sarah pointed, "He's outside on the patio."

"Maybe I should go and console him. He probably needs someone to lean on at a moment like this," Marcus said saintly, in a parting shot.

"I wouldn't dare if I were you," Pitney tried to remain calm; but suddenly she began yelling, "you lowly conniving bastard. Who knows better than Chris and I, the evil that lurks behind that dark heart of yours; a person whose all for himself; a person who could sit there comfortably and accept a business that was passed on to you on a silver platter. You are a damn leach. That's what you are, Marc. And, no. I wouldn't try to console Chris if I were you. You. An individual whom a person could easily despise. For him to accept compassion from you, it would be like accepting sympathy from the devil himself."

Looking like a hound who suddenly became ill with his sickness, prompted by the taking away of a flavor filled bone, Marcus grumbled, "Gee sis', how did I suddenly acquire such a bad rating? Me, your brother Marc, a low life?"

Pitney stared at him defiantly.

Marcus sensed her anger. "Maybe you're right. He probably wouldn't care to hear anything that anyone had to say to him right now."

"If you'd just experienced such a painful blow," Pitney said firmly, "would you want to talk to someone who you considered at the moment to be your enemy?"

In the meanwhile, through grimaced smiles there were greetings, compliments and congratulations shared among the group that were gathered for the reading of Gerald's will.

Outside on the patio, standing in a lifeless pose, Chris tried not to think about the depressing truth of him being left out of his father's will. "Chris I'm sorry. I'm so sorry." Pitney lamented sadly while taking a seat on the banister. Instantaneously, there was a moment of silence. "I can imagine that you feel deprived."

"Deprived?" Chris shouted. "I feel greatly tormented. A torment that's almost too painful to bear."

Pitney paused momentarily waiting for Chris to let out all of his frustrations. "I realize that you're not in the mood for conversation right now. Anyway, I would like to express my feelings about what has happened here today."

An acute quietness overcame Pitney as she stood watching tears flow from Chris' eyes. As she stood in silence momentarily, she must have experienced what Chris was undergoing, because suddenly she broke down in tears.

"Marc could never measure up to being your equal," she said after their brief cry. "Nor does he possess your qualities. It's not fair what dad has done. How could he have chosen Marc to be the Vice-President of the company, after all of the back breaking work that you've put into it? You deserve some kind of reward."

Pitney stared down at the porch all the while shaking her head in disbelief. "What has happened here today was inconceivable; and even though dad despised you, nothing justifies what he executed to you in his will. How could he do such an unjust thing to you? I mean, how could he have overlooked the potential that you have as a building tradesman and give such a prestigious business to a person with Marc's background? Just because you don't have the first class education that he has, in no way does it justify this action. Outside of father, everyone else knew Marc bribed his way through law school.

It was highly impractical for him to have learned about the functions of the construction business there."

With a calming tone entangled with anguish and bitterness Chris' voice quivered, "Marcus' inheritance doesn't matter much; simply because it was all a part of dad's fantasy. Pitney," he sobbed, "I've contributed so much, but regardless of how much I gave of myself, father was ungrateful. He never bothered himself to see if I was capable of performing any of the administrative tasks of the business. Nor during his entire lifetime did he ever bother himself to see if I was capable of performing any function at all."

"I'm so sorry. I had no idea that if dad had suddenly passed his will would have been drawn up like it was," Pitney exclaimed. "If there is anything—anything within my power that I can do to make amends for this awful thing that has happened, believe me Chris, I will do it. If you want, you can have my share of the business."

Pitney Kanin was an exquisite woman; so delicately constructed. She had violet blue eyes with large black pupils featured on an almost perfect face. Sometimes impetuous like her father, she could be better described in the likeness of her mom. A young noble and emancipated female who had the heart of an angel. She loved both her parents very much, and yet she could be rational and sympathetic toward their differences of opinion when the duo would occasionally argue blaming each other for the tragedy that killed her younger brothers. It only happened once that she was provoked into choosing sides. Naturally, she sided with her mom. But it was after she had learned that her mother was ill and would at the time become enraged and violently opposed to Gerald's personal vengeance aimed at Chris. Because of what she had done, certainly Gerald communicated with her less. But in spite of his ill feelings toward her, Pitney still held a special place in her father's heart.

Pitney also loved and respected both brothers. Chris and Marcus responded with mutual affection toward their sister. It was always obvious to Chris—the alert member of the Kanin clan, that Marcus was faking his affection.

"I wouldn't think of it," Chris sounded displeased with the idea. "I rank much higher than being a vagrant in this family—whose given handouts. I've also been out in the field too long. With Marc as Corporate Executive, he would do everything within his power to send me back and have me stuck out there."

"My understanding of the way the will is set up, Marc and I are to share the load as Corporate Executives. You two could work side-by- side. He could teach you the functions of the corporation, which you already know, and in the meantime you could show him how to operate out in the field."

"I doubt if that's possible," Chris pondered his reply, then a harsh note crept into his voice. "Nor will I accept charity from anyone. Dad gave the business to Marc. It's his. The other half belongs to you. The offer that you made me, sis' sounds great. And I truly appreciate your concern, but at the moment, the way I feel, this family owes me nothing. Nor do I owe it anything. From this day forward, I have no family."

Even though there wasn't very much that mattered to Chris at the moment, long afterwards he would remember the words that was stated in Gerald's will with bitterness and anguish.

Shaking her head in sad disbelief, Pitney stood closed mouth as she watched Chris walk with his head hung down slowly toward his car.

More than three thousand mourners visited the church where Gerald lay in state. Both dignitaries and laymen came from near and far to see a man whom many adored as being one of the first successful early pioneers who helped steer the construction business in the right direction. Such a man's just efforts, many of Gerald's observers concluded at the time, seemingly brought new insights to the building trade industry which resulted in it rapidly becoming a fast growing and very rewarding industry.

Regrettably the offspring of Gerald's who helped him design and lay the foundation to build his projects into such well adored building complexes, chose not to attend the funeral services being held for his father that week. He was in the process of transacting a deal. A deal that would steer him off course of being a common laborer for Kanin Enterprises and lead him in the direction of achieving a few of his own goals. But to do so, he needed someone near; or force to be tough in order to embark upon such a task as an individual whom would try to control his destiny.

Such strength would ignite his imagination and set fire to an impacted adventure that would eventually lead to his rise to success.

CHAPTER SIX

Feeling horribly drained, somewhat sick, also highly depressed, Chris sought refuge at his girlfriend's dwelling.

During her romance with Chris, she would've introduced him to some slime underground thugs whom were dying to be involved in coded—evasive and threatening activity continually.

These soon to be associates of Chris would paddle the sanity of many law enforcement officials in several countries, while they pulled of all kinds of legal tender endeavoring illegalities.

Indulging in such a social circle there was a successful northern California stock-broker who loved intrigue—playing the game of middle-man whom sold arms—valuable secrets, etc. to the highest bidder.

Perry White and Gregory Steward, both retired mercenary soldiers who served two tours of duty in Vietnam, and a tour of duty working as paid soldiers with the contra in Nicaragua.

Even though their lifestyles had now changed, they both dreamed that they'd one day enter into a scheme—or business transaction—that would net them enough money for them to retire on.

However, unlike Greg, Perry had a philosophy that he illustriously made legendary.

He impressed his investigative datum on a small congregation of followers.

Publicly, arguing his cause he believed that if a group of individuals were to massively employ their mind power, provoking an attack from within the ranks of their present system of government, they could defeat it. By accomplishing such a goal, it would place them in a position where they could form their own body of government. A government that would enable them to move toward a socialist regime. He had confidence, real confidence that, "If a number of individuals owned a share in the profits of the goods and services that a corporation in America produced, the people would contribute more to a system that one had private ownership in."

Stephen Blass, a wealthy Texas rancher's son, who held a degree in industrial engineering. His minor was the medical profession, mainly surgery.

It was a simple task he undertook just to prove to himself that he was mentally acute enough to complete the course.

He chose to further his interest by employing himself as a demolition expert. A person well acquainted with sophisticated weapons and explosives.

Stephen contracted out his services when a customer had a bank job and other unlawful crimes to be pulled off.

Hausan Sabb, a Lebanese professional soldier, once a powerful figure with the Shiite Muslims, turned terrorist. He'd indicate unmistakably that he alone had destroyed two American Embassy's by bombing them to pieces. One Embassy was in France and the other one was in Germany. He took official credit for a siege of territory in the Mecca Valley; and the hijacking of a British airliner which exploded in mid air killing all of the passengers whom were aboard the flight.

Patricia, Newmar, Hausan's girlfriend, a fearless individual whose interest was in computers. After graduating from the University of Southern California she quickly became an expert schemer who would occasionally lock into a bank's computer system and spy on rich account holder's assets. It certainly wasn't a secret to her co-workers when they learned from the FBI that she'd been singled out by the ABF Communications department as being the individual who, when it was expressed, was intelligent enough to plan, set up, and activate her own computer during a bank heist where she worked. In exile, enjoying the cities of the French Riviera, Patricia was thrilled;

feeling a sense of excitement when reliving how she'd been able to scam the bank triumphing, pulling off such a very sensitive crime.

This licentious, suasive, ducket endeavoring clan of professional dangerous criminals would soon be Chris' secret confined friends.

For the first time in his life Chris drank liquor. He smoked dope. After twenty-four hours of listening to voices cheer leading him to commit suicide, such anxiety drove him to break down and cry for an extended period of time. His girlfriend comforted him. She consoled him like an angel would watch over and protect an individual that was a saint in the eye sights of their elite elected group.

Immediately when it seemed like the proper time she began grooming Chris—coaching him to maybe view life from a different prospective.

Finally she encouraged him, "I feel that you're at the point in life where you must confront the things that's tormenting you. And fight back."

Chris quickly understood that she held his best interest at heart; by advising him so direct and proper.

On that Thursday evening as the funeral motorcade procession that was carrying Gerald's body entered Forestlawn Cemetery, Chris and his lady love sat discussing what a promising future he could have.

". . . . I agree with you. I do have certain strengths. However, with the small amount of money that I have saved, it's not enough to get started in the kind of business that I would like to pursue. It takes huge capital to get started in the building trade industry. I don't have a college education. Therefore, I can't get a job doing some administrative task somewhere. Let's face it. I'm doomed."

"What you're saying is very true," she went along with him. "But, you must remember, 'only the strong survive.' Maybe, just maybe I can be of some assistance to you."

"Can you?"

"Would you like to make some cash?"

"Cash? Certainly. You know that I'm in desperate need of money. Do you have a plan? A business scam? What? But, before you answer—Ms. Secret Agent Blaze—be specific. And tell me exactly what it is, that I've got to do, to earn this money?"

"Buy weapons—and pass on secret documents."

"Buy weapons—and pass on secret documents?" Chris seemed terrified over her request.

"Are you insane? A person could get life in prison just by attempting to pull off such a risky crime."

"How true." She agreed with him. "But there really is little danger involved in the job we have to do. If it's any consolation to you, any individual that we employ always gets the opportunity to work in a well kept secret environment. You will be surrounded by people whom you can trust. And if you find that there are any very serious risks involved, our agents will immediately order someone to do the job for you. Understand?

"Proceed." Chris said in deep thought.

"We have this contact who lives in San Francisco. You'll meet with him. He'll give you instructions as to what you have to do."

"San Francisco. Instructions from a stranger. God, how fearsome."

"No one said that life would be easy Chris." She tried to ease his fear. "My motto is always be curious when greeting a stranger, and without a doubt never trust one."

"Why can't you accompany me on this trip? I'm sort of shy when it comes to meeting strangers."

"I'm sorry love, while performing such a mission, you will just have to be brave. And even if I wanted to accompany you on the trip, I couldn't."

"Why?"

"The American authorities have had me under surveillance for over a month now. That's why. But, if you do run into any problems, our man who will be tailing you will intervene and handle things from there."

"If such an intervention does take place, should I phone you from home—or Roselawn Cemetery?" Chris joked with her with innocent terror on his face.

"When I depart tonight, I'll leave you a hundred and fifty thousand dollars in the top drawer. Upon contacting our friend, he'll introduce you to those who have access to the information that we'll need. They will be a group of specially selected personnel who will steal the documents and pass them on to you. Once you obtain them and the necessary risk has been taken to have them secured, your role as an espionage agent will then be over."

A chilling wave of fright crept over Chris as he agreed to accept the job that his girlfriend was offering him. "I should be able to accomplish such a task."

"You look pale." He quickly digressed from the subject. "Is there something else that's worrying you?"

She stared bleakly at the floor. "I have a job to do in Mexico," she replied sounding as if she had a horrid feeling about her new assignment.

"Mexico?"

"So how does that create a problem for you?"

"How does it create a problem for me," she shouted frantically. "Have you ever had to kill someone?"

"No. I haven't. But if I had to, I seriously doubt if it would bother me very much."

"You don't know what you're saying, Chris. Believe me, it would bother you. Each time you kill, it gets worse. So worse that there are moments when there is no feeling left inside you at all. You sometimes go through periods of deep depression.

It's true that after you've killed someone there is a strange kind of numbness that persists in your body, and as time passes, you soon become a very empty person. You can also find yourself being afraid to fall in love with someone. Simply, because you never know when the time may come when you have to do something that might place that person's life in danger causing them to get hurt; or to be killed. Suffering from those kind of anxieties can also cause a person to disrupt very easily.

You often have problems with insomnia. You'll encounter moments when your past history seems to haunt you. You lie awake reliving the tragic episodes; hallucinating. Viewing the drastic violence that erupted while you were engaged in such a demented frenzy to take the life of a fellow human being. Each day that goes by, you live in the constant fear that someone's out there lurking in the dark who at any moment, when your back is to them, they'll try to take your life. There have been times when I wanted to take the weapon, put it to my head, and pull the trigger. For me, it could be the simplest way out."

She now began to sob. Unable to offer his friend advice, Chris held her gently in his arms. Approaching the end of the month Chris drove to San Francisco. Past the city limits he headed West, then East to 10467 E. Circle Drive. There he met with a wealthy retired stockbroker who used the alias of Mr. Renaldo Fabrejii. When greeting the stranger, Chris' alias was to be a Mr. Dewey Taubman.

While taking the mail out of the mailbox Mr. Fabrejii extended a warm welcome to his new guest. "Come in Mr. Taubman. Come inside." Then suddenly without anything provoking him he kicked his wife's poodle off the doorstep. As the feeble pup groaned out loud Chris stared at him with distant admiration.

Once they had been seated in the lavishly furnished living-room of the Fabrejii mansion Chris' host offered him a drink. "What will it be my friend? A martini; Tequila sunrise; scotch on the rock; or a dynamite joint?" The fat, short, slightly graying man coughed while puffing on what smelled like cocaine rolled up in a cigar.

I'll take a joint; if you don't mind." Chris replied.

"Wow, what's this fucking world coming to?" Fabrejii seemed offended. "Here—I've purchased the best damn liquor in town. It's imported you know—and there you sit asking me for one of those cheap get highs. I only offered you the drugs as a fit analogy, you know. I had no idea that you were actually a pot head. I certainly conveyed the message right. Personally, I don't fool around with the stuff myself."

"How hospitable," Chris remarked scornfully, then he uttered in a low tone of voice, "you fucking snob."

"Here—" Mr. Fabrejii passed Chris a potation, all the while, he was trying to force Chris to devour his special brand of liquor.

"Thank you," Chris politely accepted the dram—then bang. He was preheating. Breathing—listening to inner voices encouraging him to dash it in the snob's face.

"I thought that we would see eye to eye," Mr. Fabrejii chuckled with his nose in the air.

Soon after dinner had been served Chris roost lidless. After all, his only purpose for visiting with this oddball who called himself Renaldo, was to gain access to the documents.

Fabrejii grinned rather sheepishly babbling about subjects that weren't very important. It seemed that at the present moment the stir of espionage was the farthest thing away from his mind.

As the servant cleared the table, Chris spoke, "Mr. Fabrejii, I came here on an assignment to discuss business."

"Can't you see that we're joined by outsiders?" Mr. Fabrejii shouted in a rude tone of voice. "We'll discuss all business matters in private."

He's an indignant bastard. Chris thought quietly to himself. I can't understand why do some people have such wicked personalities? Especially the little short ones.

That post meridiem, at a posh supper club on the south side of town the ever changing personality of Mr. Fabrejii revealed yet another side of him. Surprisingly, he got out on the dance floor and got into the groove of things. After dancing more than three times with a female who had arrived at the club with a black couple, while feeling exhausted, he then decided to come over to the table and let his disenchanted friend Mr. Taubman borrow his exercise partner for a while.

When Chris joined the young woman in a dance, Mr. Fabrejii then secured himself, his female companion and Mr. Taubman a seat at the table where the newly arrived black couple were seated.

Once the long playing record ended, Chris went over to greet his new associates.

"Mr. Taubman this is Mr. Steward. Mr. Steward, Mr. Taubman." Mr. Fabrejii introduced the two men. "Hi." Chris spoke.

"Evening." Mr. Steward said.

"Mr. Taubman, this is my wife Maria. Maria, Mr. Taubman."

"Hello."

"Hi. Welcome to Northern California." She said.

"Thank you."

Immediately Fabrejii and his friends began to babble about subjects that didn't pertain to why Chris had come to visit them at all.

"Are we going to sit here all night and admire whose the best dancer around town?" Chris interrupted angrily. "Or are we going to talk about business?"

Erratically, Mr. Steward sped off with his wife onto the dance floor. For he too seemed annoyed just as Mr. Fabrejii had acted when Chris wanted to discuss business at what obviously seemed like an improper moment for them to discuss such a topic.

Chris sat for a while playing their strange game. Around one o'clock a.m. as it had suddenly become apparent to the men that Chris was about to dissolve their pet doings, Fabrejii quickly gave in to Chris' feelings.

He compromised by enticing a female who he often dated while frequenting Touche's place to be Chris' companion for the evening.

After the young woman and Chris appeared to have been communicating with each other Mr. Fabrejii boasted to Chris, "I bet this here pile of dynamite will make you forget all about discussing our activity—huh partner?"

Tune after tune, Chris and his charming lady friend danced and danced until the club owner announced to them, "You, two clubby patrons it was a good party, but if you look around, you will see that this one has ended."

Hours later, feeling ecstatically thrilled, Chris forgave his recent business associates for their odd behavior during their first meeting.

7:45 p.m. the following dusk-tide on the northwest side of Berkeley, California, in a group assembled at the apartment of Greg Steward, we learn that during a brief talk Greg has already described to Mr. Taubman the doctrinal work he must perform at Armsted Development Center, a nuclear arms plant just outside Richmond, California.

While Greg talked to the men present, his wife Maria had to excuse herself from her duties of serving their guest food and drinks and go into the bedroom to try to find something that would maybe calm her down. She quietly became terrified upon overhearing at the beginning of the scheme that her husband and his friends were plotting a very risky crime against Uncle Sam.

Mr. Steward, formerly Army Captain Gregory Steward, had also related to the duties of that of two other Officers who along with himself would be in charge of a convoy transporting a shipment of military weapons and nuclear devices to his home base the following month. The officer's duties would also entail acting as a guard unit escorting two Generals and a Major who would be carrying an order of secret documents that were being sent to an official at Armsted.

"When reaching the security checkpoint, hastily immobilize the security guards, because we'll be doomed if one of them makes contact with the base… Be very cautious. Make certain you spray them with enough insomnious gas vapors to keep them knocked out until your chore out there is finished. And Perry, please see to it that your men have their disguises in order. We cannot take chances on anyone being able to identify us. That would make the CIA's job too easy for them. When their investigative team comes poking their noses around the base looking for clues, we want to make their job almost impossible. We don't want them to be able to point their finger at anyone who was connected to our crime. Also, if they encountered a lead that it was mostly black men who ripped them off for those documents, they could make my life at the base a living hell. Inspector Bob Nem wouldn't be able to converse on the subject 'until they brought a coon in.' And it wouldn't matter 'who' such a person was. His rank would not hinder them.

Certainly while engaged in the formalities of trying to find a suspect, they'd impose their most violent form of interrogation when questioning me about what had happened. And such an alarm would be warranted simply because they only have two black officers on staff there. I'm the only officer of the few ranking officers who knows their plan. Oh incidentally, Perry, please try to persuade your men to perform their assignment without doing bodily injury to anyone."

"Are you serious man?" Perry seemed outraged at Greg's stance.

"What you demand of me and my men is really asking too much."

"Why?"

"Only a fool would flirt with such danger. And flirting with a couple gung-ho Captains and highly trained truck drivers who will be carrying loaded weapons could spell danger."

"On this mission, even if they are allowed to carry weapons they are not allowed to fire them."

Perry interrupted quickly, "Think for a moment Greg. If you yourself had to approach those vehicles, would you risk the serious possibility of going out there getting your fucking head blown off? Even an amateur stick up artist would have better sense than to attempt to rip off Uncle Sam without engaging in some kind of fight."

"I agree with you," Greg replied. "But aren't you hip to the element of surprise?"

"Surprise." Perry stared at him amazed. "How in the hell do you surprise someone whose protected by armored steel and bullet-proof glass windows?"

"Why don't you be cool for a minute; mellow. And let me rap." Greg stared defiantly at Perry.

Momentarily Perry grew quiet.

"I indeed have a surprise for them," Greg continued. "And you Perry, will have a hand at pulling it off."

"How?" Perry was curious. "Please inform me."

"You know how it can be in certain establishments; relatives using their influence to get another relative a job. Well, just by coincidence, General Thornwell's son and General Scott's nephew will be scheduled to drive on that day. If everything goes according to our plan when you attack, General Thornwell's vehicle will be the first one that you'll come in contact with. I'm willing to bet you that when seeing an automatic weapon pointed at his kin's head he'll be simply thrilled to see things our way.

"What about their CB's?" Mr. Taubman asked.

"Perry and his men will have in their possession, equipment that will distort any signal that they can try to send by radio," Greg replied.

"How unique," Mr. Taubman thought aloud.

"So far," Perry interrupted, "the plan sounds good. But again I ask you, how does one pull off such a crime without engaging in a fight?"

"I'm not the only person whose in charge of this meeting tonight." Greg spoke frantically. "Nor am I, the only person who will determine whether or not we should use acts of violence when pulling off the caper. 'Anyone' whose present, could make that decision. Right?" He pointed to different individuals.

No one responded. A brief second or two passed.

"Perry, since you're the one whose doing all of the bitching, in what manner then do you suggest that we go about taking that shipment of goods? Would you begin by going on a shooting rampage. And murder such high ranking military personnel?"

"No. That's not at all what I'm suggesting," Perry exclaimed. "The most un-briefed criminal would realize that to murder such important people would put themselves in a dangerous position. But, you have to analyze things realistically man."

"That's swell, Perry. Since I haven't at this point analyzed things realistically, please inform me. How would you go about pulling off the robbery? Would you begin by violently attacking the men in charge of the security check-point, and then launch an assault on the vehicles carrying the high ranking personnel—behind all that bullet proof glass?"

"I don't know man," Perry answered, uncertain. "Maybe."

"Come on," Greg screamed. "You're the person who has all the answers to our problems."

Perry pouted momentarily.

"If we use those kind of dumb tactics while attempting to pull off the caper," Greg assured him, "Uncle Sam would have all of us thrown in the slammer within a week. How could anyone profit from such a move?"

Suddenly an acute quietness overcame Perry. He sat pondering different alternatives as to how his men could safely approach pulling off the crime.

As Greg was about to continue talking, Perry interrupted, "Greg forgive me if I sound rude," he said flinching his eyelids, "when did you become such an authority on crime? You've never committed one. You've always been afraid to. Remember? As a kid, when you tried to steal candy from the neighborhood store, I had to steal it for you. The same was true during the war. I had to make decisions for you there too. But, since you've become a Captain, you feel that I'm not qualified to make decisions anymore."

Suddenly Perry had made a personal issue out of things. He was referring to the advice he shared as a Sargent in charge of Greg, when he was a specialist in his Platoon in Vietnam. And also his coaching when the two of them were paid soldiers in Nicaragua.

"I'm sure that everyone whose in this room has an idea as to how we could get the job done, Perry. But when concluding such an opinion, can we truly say that he has used the correct logic in his approach when pursuing whatever the task might be?"

"How about this guy?" Perry talked dumbfoundedly to the group. "You take a high school dropout, and train him to be an Officer; a person whose in charge of men, and he turns out like this: an asshole who dictates solutions to crime like he's reciting it from one of his training manuals."

"You can save your little innuendoes, Perry, until our job is finished at Armsted. Afterwards, you'll have plenty of time to examine my credibility as being a leader."

Instantaneously, a moment of silence fell.

"While Perry was babbling I was pondering certain alternatives as to how we could set up a trap. Something which might lure the drivers of those vehicles to us. And what I came up with is, and you guys tell me if my plan sounds dumb to you, as a diversion, you know; something that might steer their minds away from a possible robbery; we'll steal a vehicle from the Officers in charge of the security checkpoint. Dress two of our men in their clothing. Create an accident along their route. And have it appear that one of their men has been injured. I'd lay odds on it, that such an incident would bring those drivers to a halt. And they'd get out of their vehicles to investigate what happened."

"While doing so, we'll capture them. And at the same time we'll rush the vehicle that will be carrying the high ranking brass. Upon holding them hostage I'm almost certain that the individuals who'll be driving the vehicles carrying the weapons will be willing to cooperate with us."

Suddenly Greg's mind focused on an additional scheme.

"And how does this sound to you? In the midst of the confusion, why don't I attack the leader of the pact. I'll act super courageous in attempt to try and save the documents belonging to Uncle Sam. But before I can inflict bodily injury to anyone, during the course of action Perry will let me have a round in the upper shoulder."

"What." Perry screamed. "Are you nuts, man?"

"Nuts? No way." Greg assured him. "Nor would I chance such a suicidal attempt unless I knew that you were an expert with a firearm. I would be a damn fool to let someone shoot me who has no background in marksmanship."

"Okay, it's fine and dandy with me if you want to play John Wayne or The Lone Ranger out there." Perry said. "But I'm not going to be the one whose gonna have your blood on my hands."

"Well, if that's the way you view things. I'll take my chance with another member of your group. Since I'll be the person whom will be in charge out there, I feel that it would be my duty to try to save Uncle Sam's goods. Such an effort might also convince the Battalion Commander that I acted as a gallant soldier; a true fighting man. Even though I had no chance to win. I would've acted, to prove that 'you just don't mess with Uncle Sam.' Perry, is there anyone other than you who might be able to pull off the hit?"

"Yeah. I can arrange it." Perry answered reluctantly. "My partner Rick can pull it off. He has a pretty keen eye."

"Now that I know who the trigger man will be, please inform Rick that I don't want him shedding any tears when the time arrives for him to burst a cap on me. This lad can take a bullet like Larry Holmes can take punches in the boxing ring." Greg chuckled.

"Also, my getting zapped could steer the suspicion away from me having involvement in the crime. And as an end result, it could protect me from receiving a general court martial. So, now do you see why I feel such an action should take place?"

"Once everything has gone according to our plan, take the documents and rush them to Mr. Taubman. Do you need further briefing concerning the drop Perry?"

"No. It's all stored in my memory bank."

"We always welcome the input of advanced technology," Greg joked.

"How grave is the danger of us encountering other military personnel while we're out there?" Perry asked curiously.

"I doubt if you'll be paid a visit by anyone from the military while you're there," Greg replied cautiously. "Traffic is very light during those hours of the morning. Oh," Greg suddenly remembered something, "as I recall, there are a group of secret service men who occasionally take laser gun training at section D. It's about five miles east of our target area. But we'll just pray that they're not taking training on that morning. If so, it could mean disaster to our plan."

There was a pause.

"So, looking at things on the positive side," Greg concluded, "all you and your men have to do, Perry, is be at the location that I detailed to you; drawn up on the map—at the set time. And taking those documents will be a cinch. Now that we have everything in tact, how does the plan sound to you guys?"

"I believe that it'll work," Fabrejii was for the plan.

Mr. Taubman also nodded his head in approval of the plan.

"Remember Perry, you and your men attack from the gorge around first dawn. After securing the weapons then unload the ammo onto our truck. You got that?"

"You can count on me partner," Perry nodded his head in full confidence that he and his comrades would get the job done.

As the conversation neared its peak, with a baffled frown on his face, Perry sat thinking quietly to himself. If I don't get busted while pulling off this job, I'm gonna take a long leave of absence from crime. God kept a watchful eye over me while I was in 'Nam. I barely escaped death in Nicaragua. And now I'm home and safe—and have the nerves to be fucking around with trying to rip off the United States Government. Only a fool would live so dangerously. It would be more than a miracle if I come out of this one unblemished. Man, what a helluva way to make a dollar. And what happens if we get caught? It could mean twenty years in Leavenworth. Or maybe life without parole. You're too old to do that much time. And the peanuts you'll be getting out of the deal, ain't even worth it.

Perry, how in the hell do you always get yourself into these kind of predicaments? Yeah, you know you shouldn't have fucked off Mr. Fabrejii's dope money. Wise up man. It's your life that you're playing games with. Stop trying to always take the shortcut to success. Simply because such a route has occasionally been known to have landed many of your associates in the graveyard.

Around four a.m. that Thursday of the following week, in Washington D.C., Three Star General, Marshal D. Thornwell and Brigidere General, Avery Scott prepared to load up two tractor-trailers with nuclear arms devices, military weapons, ammo, and an order of secret documents. Such a shipment destination was Armsted Nuclear Base in Northern California.

In charge of the convoy were Officers Gregory Steward, 1st Lieutenant Patrick B. Thornwell, and 2nd Lieutenant Harold A. Scott.

After the trucks were loaded and Captain Steward had briefly yelled out harsh words concerning safety precautions to the group gathered, the early formation was dismissed and the unmarked military motorcade began rolling.

Zero five hundred hours, three days later…

Rolling along at a cautious speed the unmarked vehicle carrying the two Generals neared the guard post entry that led to Armsted Nuclear Plant.

Once there, Captain Steward checked in at the security check point.

Quickly the officer in charge okayed the group's clearance papers and the convoy was ordered to move on.

The small motorcade drove along at a normal speed down the coiling private highway, nearing a thick wooded area.

Across from the target area, hidden in a glen over behind an embankment, Perry and his men waited patiently on their prey.

Unaware that they were soon to be confronted by bandits, the drivers of the military vehicles rolled along approaching the robbery site.

Nearer to the thicket, adjacent to the robber's tractor-trailer there sat an overturned vehicle blocking the roadway.

As the driver of the lead tractor-trailer got out to investigate the accident, the surprise attack revealed itself.

Brandishing silencer automatic weapons, Perry and his commandos rushed over the embankment and began violently attacking the military personnel.

Rapidly, there could be heard numerous outburst of gunfire. Then suddenly all grew quiet.

Generals Thornwell and Scott, along with their driver was almost in a state of shock as they crawled out of their auto pleading for mercy.

Inside the bullet riddled guard vehicle, Lieutenant Grane lay slumped over in the corner of the backseat.

Lieutenant Thornwell cried out in pain while trying to pick bits and pieces of shattered glass out of his eyes.

All the while, Captain Steward laid still, waiting for things to quiet down. He'd dove for the floor board of the vehicle, seconds before the horrifying ordeal had occurred.

In the midst of the confusion, Perry stood with his weapon pointed towards General Thornwell's head.

Quickly he ordered the military personnel out of the vehicle.

While standing guard over the soldiers, the attackers began assaulting their victims; ordering them to order their men behind the bullet proof glass to unlock the doors to their trucks.

Momentarily frightened and all the while having second thoughts about wanting to play the role of a hero, Greg inched nervously toward one of the attackers who had their back facing him.

Anticipating that Perry had informed their comrades about his attempt to play such a role, Greg began acting out his heroic fantasies by grabbing the gunman from behind.

With a quick, sudden move, the bandit swung around to face him. Instantaneously, cold chills raced over Greg's body.

A few horrified seconds passed, then the robber anxiously squeezed the trigger.

The world around Greg seemed to have exploded, as the bullet from the light fire-arm pierced his neck.

In rapid succession, the crook let off a second round, then a third, until the weapon was empty.

What a shock to Greg, for it was a woman who'd just shot him. A dreadful individual who appeared as if she was immediately engrossed in some kind of demented frenzy, laughing savagely over her recent actions.

Moments after her deranged act was over, she stood weeping as if she'd suddenly felt downcast over what she'd done.

But what was even more peculiar was that, it was after Greg had began to cry out Perry's name that something happened; that seemed to have continually triggered Pam's unconscionable slaughter of him.

Momentarily Perry's mind went out of focus.

Then quickly, a wave of anger rose inside of him.

Violently, like a raging bull, he came charging towards the unsuspecting female.

Instant horror quickly spread throughout the corridors of the frightened woman's mind.

Unlike the shocking chills that'd made her shiver from head to toe, rapidly there came convulsive pain that slashed through her head after Perry had severely crushed the butt end of her weapon to her face.

Perry continued his crude assault on Pam by bashing her brains in.

Quickly, he then ordered his men to dump her damaged body onto their semi-tractor-trailer.

Perry grew angrier. Seemingly with an enraged vengeance he began chastising the soldiers for the incident that had occurred.

After kicking a few rears and punching one to the face, all the while hollering at them in a disrespectful manner, for a job that normally would've taken their workforce a half-hour to finish, Perry had gotten it done in twelve minutes.

Before leaving the crime scene, the gas crew was called into action again.

With an unearthly look pasted to their faces, they went onward spraying each military personnel with enough thickset insomnious smudge to keep them knocked out for an extended period of time.

Preceding the robbery Chris began to work diligently at having his crew form pre-cast sections of concrete slabs that were to be used in Italy for bridge projects.

Within two laboriously filled nights, he'd accomplished storing neatly inside the group of slabs, the weapons, ammo and the order of secret documents.

Mid afternoon Friday, two days later… At Armsted Medical Center, Maria sat weeping while watching her husband cling to whatever little breath of life he had left in him.

Around 5:00pm the attending physician removed the respirator that was attached to Greg's nostrils and inserted his case in the files of the other disastrous victims of circumstances there at the hospital.

Immediately after Greg's death, the Feds announced that they would initiate an investigation that was to try and help solve the mystery surrounding the weapons caper and meanwhile, capture Greg's assassin.

When overhearing this news, suddenly Perry panicked. He dialed Greg's number.

"Hello." Maria's voice quavered.

After holding the phone momentarily and no reply came she spoke again. "Hello."

"Maria, this… This is Perry."

All the while trying to suppress her anger, after holding the phone for an extended moment, Maria managed to speak. "Why are you calling, Perry? You've succeeded at getting Greg killed. Just what is it that you could possibly want now?"

Perry became speechless. Moments passed with Perry sitting, holding the phone.

"Come on, Perry." Maria screamed. "What is it that we can do for you now?"

"Maria, I… I… I'm sorry."

Click. The phone buzzed in his ear.

Sensing Maria's dreadful mood Perry decided that maybe tonight wasn't the best time to talk her.

Around 10:30pm the following evening after getting geeked up off a bottle of liquor Perry felt that he'd built up enough confidence to talk to Maria.

Again, he dialed Maria's number, but this time before she could speak Perry began talking. "Maria," His tone of voice was a little louder than normal, "listen to me for a moment. Please hear me out. Greg's death was an accident. A weird accident."

"An accident?" Maria screamed murderously. "My husband's been murdered by one of your goons. And… And…" She fought desperately to try to catch her breath "And you have the nerves to call it an accident?"

"Maria. Maria, please. Will you listen to me for a moment? Please listen to what I have to say."

Maria held the phone.

"What Greg attempted out there was suicide."

"Suicide? Greg would never. And you know as well as I do, Perry. When you last saw him he acted totally sane."

"That's true. But do you remember overhearing the part of our conversation when Greg talked about he wanted me to shoot him, to make things look good?"

"I vaguely remember overhearing something like that," Maria lied about being orientated about what was going to take place during the robbery.

"That's what he wanted. It all happened so fast. As he was reaching for his pistol, Pam shot him. But, that wasn't enough to satisfy her blood crazed thirst for vengeance. She continued shooting him until her weapon was empty. Poor Greg. He never knew what hit him."

Instantly cold chills raced over Maria's body.

"But Maria, you know as well as I do, that when Greg first made the suggestion I was against it. I didn't take him seriously about him wanting to get shot. And I certainly wasn't in favor of me being the one who'd have to do the actual shooting. So when the opportunity presented itself, I took charge of unloading the ammo truck. Once the shots had been fired and I'd witnessed what'd happened, I stood helpless."

"Then came my first reaction. I bashed that bitch's face in. After that, there really was nothing else I could do to her. But I do admit that I might've failed in one response to act. Just like a dumb soldier, I had to pursue our mission. I remember being afraid, or quite paranoid. In the midst of all of the action it was very easy for one to panic. That's exactly what I did. My only thought was to get the job done and save the mission. If I'd only let the medivac attend to him, Greg might still be alive. Oh God, Maria. I… I cannot talk about it anymore." Quickly Perry hushed.

"I believe what you're telling me is true," Maria sighed. "Please forgive me, Perry. I didn't mean to direct my harsh feelings towards you. I'm just not myself tonight. Oh, Perry…" She began to cry aloud.

"Everything's gonna be alright. It's going to be alright." Perry comforted her.

"I wish that there was something that I could do to help make up for this awful tragedy that has occurred in your life, Maria. Maybe I can be of some financial help?"

"No." Maria said soberly. "I can take care of things."

"I tell you what, I'm gonna come over and give you some moral support. I'll also bring you a relaxer. After all. That's what friends are for. To be by your side when you need them. I'll be over in a half-hour, okay."

"All right." Maria said. She was in such a drunken state of grief that she'd unknowingly invited Perry over.

Once over to the apartment, Perry was in the process of consoling Maria.

"Here. Drink this." He poured her a drink. "Maybe in a while you'll feel better."

Maria meditated for a brief period.

"Everyone who knows Greg has been expressing their bereavement over his death," Perry said. "And I'm terribly bereaved myself. His sudden death leaves a deep dark void in my mind, as though his passing was just a dream and not a reality. I feel that one day I'll wake up and there he will be—alive. And we'll be friends as always. Here. Let me pour you another drink."

While listening attentively to a gospel record playing on her cassette deck, Maria become emotional. For nearly ten minutes she cried uncontrollably. Perry helped console her by forcing her to drink.

Within a while, she appeared no longer grief stricken. She was suddenly feeling that everything was okay.

With a friendly gesture, Perry coached her into lying down. And while relaxing her onto the bed, he relaxed beside her.

Maria's head was spinning.

Endless moments passed, then suddenly she realized that Perry was seducing her. As he continued his seduction, she laid paralyzed with her eyes staring fixedly on the ceiling.

After he'd finished, her feelings underwent changes of indecency, disgrace, and repentance.

Momentarily she envisioned herself alone; someplace on a dark and desolate island. Intensely she felt her body temperature rise. And as tears quickly flooded her eyes she raced into the bathroom and slammed the door shut behind her.

She stared at the mirror that hung in front of her, but for some strange reason she could not see herself.

Her face contorted with repressed violence as she tried to bring her mind back into focus.

While lying in bed in an alcoholic lethargy, suddenly Perry's sixth sense alarmed him. He awakened quickly, only to panic and go into shock when he saw an enraged emotionally disturbed female rushing toward him with a knife.

Like the pressure force of an air hammer, the glittering blade came down powerfully finding the mattress.

Enveloped in a palpable state of fear, swiftly Perry grasped Maria, pulling her down onto the bed.

Aggressively he was attempting to defend himself, when suddenly Maria's body went limp.

She'd used such violent force in her attempt to try to stab Perry that when he had grasped her, she was thrown off balance, seizing the knife the wrong way, and as a result, she accidentally stabbed herself to death.

Momentarily all sorts of thoughts began racing through Perry's mind. Sitting, experiencing heart pounding shock waves, he tried to convince himself that the blood that he saw seeping from Maria's stomach wound wasn't real.

Oh my God. What's happening? Perry's conscience tormented him. First Greg, now Maria. It's such a bad omen. Someone has put a curse on me.

Drinking. Now you see what kind of trouble it has gotten you into. Oh man, are you in trouble, now?

Think.

Use your head.

Think.

Go to your place.

No. People might become suspicious.

A moment or two passed.

Call Mr. Fabrejii.

No. He wouldn't help.

I know, I'll call Mr. Taubman. He has influence.

Suddenly, the voice quieted down and Perry's mind began functioning properly again.

Quickly Perry moved about the apartment wiping away as many fingerprints as he could find.

Then quietly, he left the building making sure that no one saw him as he was leaving.

When phoning Mr. Taubman, Perry was told by a recorded message that no one was available to talk to him at the moment.

I know, he thought to himself, he's probably at the mixing plant.

An hour or so passed with Perry driving out to the plant, then waiting 'til Chris sent his work crew home.

When it was safe to go inside, he approached Chris and told him about what'd happened at Greg's apartment.

Chris explained to him that after they'd completed the robbery, he had been informed that he was to have no further contact with the individuals whom were involved with their crime.

This aggravated Perry very much.

What am I going to do now? He asked himself.

Before Perry's visit tonight it was the weekend that he was to have received his payment in the mail for the job that he'd performed at Armsted. But for some odd reason, it hadn't yet arrived. Being in fear over the accidental death of Maria, he became panicky and thought that it would be the proper thing to do if he confronted Chris, demanding that he speed things up.

"I've already sent the money in the mail," Chris shifted uncomfortably. "Just as Mr. Fabrejii had instructed me to do. The letter was addressed to him. He was to pay you guys off. Not me."

"Sure. You guys worked out the details, right," Perry said critically bemused. "But, I still don't have my money. So, I demand that you pay me right now."

"I'm certain that your money is in the mail," Chris said in a trembling voice.

"I had a personal friend check it out for me. Nothing, came man." Perry seemed enraged.

"Now let's look at things realistically Mr. White. It's a fact that the mail doesn't always run on schedule. It could be a day—sometimes, two days late."

This honky's trying to pull a fast one on me. Perry thought angrily to himself.

"My girlfriend carries the mail. She also works our route. She said that no mail came for me today. Could it be possible that you never mailed a letter to Mr. Fabrejii?"

What Perry didn't know was that the payment had arrived for him in the mail that morning. But his well trusted girlfriend had heisted the package.

Since she'd sorted the mail on the day before, at the post office, it was an easy job for her to swipe the loot.

Presently by him not having the money on hand, Chris found himself fumbling for the appropriate words to say that might satisfy his angry partner.

Perry gritted his teeth, then hastily with all of his six foot two, two hundred and ten pound frame, he let go a blow to Chris' head.

Stunned and weakened by the blow, standing with blood dribbling from the cut on his face, Chris pleaded with him, "I don't have your money Mr. White. Isn't it possible that we could work this out some other way?"

Again Perry swung on him.

Not realizing that Chris had done many menial jobs centered around construction work, Perry continued his violent attack thinking that it would be an easy task beating up on him.

The fight had went only a minute before Perry had been knocked flat on his face.

After coming back to life Perry searched for his gun.

Hastily Chris reached inside a desk drawer that sat near him and pulled out his weapon letting it go off several times into Perry's body.

Engrossed in fear, Chris lugged the heavy stiff across the floor over to one of the mixing molds.

Then tiredly he dumped Perry's corpse over into it.

Within a few moments, cement had slowly began covering up one of the recent mistakes that Chris had made.

Quickly realizing that he had no knowledge about how to sell stolen weapons, Chris contacted his girlfriend and asked her to help in dumping the stolen items.

She set up a meeting with a contact. Such a meeting would set into motion a second adventurous crime ordeal for Chris.

Off the pacific coast highway, at one of the summer resort homes owned by the Kanin's, Chris and his lady friend greeted a Mexican gentleman and two of his associates.

The men present tried to restrain themselves from constantly staring at the beautiful female who Chris introduced to them as Uritla Giastrenko—a name which was only one of the woman's recent aliases.

"I can tell by her accent she's a foreigner," Rodriguiez whispered to Betiz. "But from what country is she a native of—it's hard for me to identify."

"Uritla has informed me that you're interested in purchasing some diamonds," Estrada inquired.

Chris opened a briefcase that had one hundred and fifty thousand dollars inside it. "Yes, that's what I'm in the market for," he said calmly.

Estrada's interest was peaked. "If you don't mind me asking, how much dough do you intend to spend?"

Confident, Chris beamed, as he responded to Estrada's question, "Before we discuss money, Mr. Delgrecco, first you must let me see the diamonds?"

Delgrecco pointed to one of his men to bring the attache case over. Upon opening it, there was a large cluster of diamonds in the center of the case, surrounded by a large number of different uncut stones. "Does this satisfy your curiosity?" Delgrecco asked.

Chris responded with a nod of his head.

Uritla gripped her Uzi making sure it was secured in her hands.

Since meeting with strangers, Chris was somewhat uncomfortable, but he was compelled not to let them know it. His heart pounded with fear as he stood realizing what could possibly happen to him while being engaged in such illegal activity.

Delgrecco, looking intently in Chris' eyes, said, "Now my friend, before we continue, how large a quantity of these beautiful jewels do you seek?"

"A very large quantity. I want to open up my own boutique. A posh one. Somewhere in a foreign country, where the diamond value is higher than it is in ours." Chris explained.

Delgrecco was thinking of all the profitable possibilities. "Such an acquisition, my friend could cost you a very large sum of money."

"How large a sum?" Chris waited attentively for his response.

"One million dollars."

"One million dollars? You're joking. I don't intend to open up a business that caters to royalty."

"The affluent are the only ones who can wear expensive diamonds, my friend. Or do I have to remind you of that?"

Chris' face turned deeply red.

"I apologize if I offended you Mr. Cohen," he called Chris by his alias. "Such sarcasm was to enlighten you. The group of diamonds that you see before you are indeed very rare. In order to purchase them, one must be willing to pay the price. Since you are a jeweler yourself, you must also realize that one can reap an enormous profit after the stones are cut and sold at retail value?"

Estrada momentarily stared at Chris to see how vulnerable he appeared while he was working his intended con on him. Chris remained silent.

"Before I waste any more of my time, can you afford the jewels?" Estrada asked.

"The price you just quoted me is simply ridiculous," Chris roared.

"Okay. Calm down. Don't lose your cool. Maybe we can work out a deal. And as someone once said to me, there's more than one way to skin a cat."

Chris suddenly was puzzled. *I wonder what this swine is conjuring up? He's definitely out to trick me.*

"A deal? What kind of a deal?" Chris asked him in an intense voice.

"You do have weapons to sell?"

"Yes. That information is correct."

"Fine. Opportunity knocks on your door. There's a way you can earn the diamonds you want and in the meantime, sell your weapons too."

Estrada hesitated. Chris waited in anticipation. "You have the green light Mr. Delgrecco. Please continue."

"I have this friend who lives in Columbia, whose in desperate need of what you have to offer. However, before I introduce you to my associate, I must ask you, would you be willing to trade your weapons for something quite more valuable?"

"Trade. Hmm." Chris pondered. "Maybe. Keep talking."

"My friend would take the weapons off your hands and in return you would get from him a package which you would transport back to me."

"This package of yours, what's inside?"

"Drugs."

"Drugs. You mean transport drugs back to the U.S.?"

"Yes. The U.S."

"That could be very risky. Wouldn't you think so?"

"Waking up each morning is risky, Mr. Cohen. However, if you're one who cannot do a little time in prison, then I suggest that you find a more legal line of work to engage yourself in."

Chris' eyes flinched.

"Like you, my friend is also in the construction business; and into shipping international cargo. Therefore, your task should be quite simple. I'll leave it up to the two of you to figure out how to ship such a package."

Chris didn't hear Estrada's slip of the tongue.

Quickly ideas began forming in Chris' head.

"You're asking for two hundred and fifty thousand dollars for the weapons, correct?"

"That's my price."

"To be honest, Mr. Cohen, at the moment I do not have that much capital on hand.

But as you can see, I do have two hundred and fifty thousand dollars worth of diamonds. When the drugs have been safely delivered to me, the diamonds are yours. And for the risk that you'll be taking to smuggle the drugs, I'll give you an additional hundred and fifty thousand dollars in cash. How does that sound?"

Chris' heart pounded with excitement as he thought to himself. Wow. Two hundred and fifty thousand in diamonds, and a hundred and fifty thousand dollars in cash. I never anticipated making that much money on the deal.

"I guess it's a fair amount of Cash," Chris pretended to be dissatisfied with Estrada's offer.

"Fair?" Estrada laughed. "You're getting the deal of the century my friend. We'll finalize our bond in Mexico City. Is that agreeable with you?"

"You have a deal, Mr. Delgrecco." The two shook hands.

"I think I'm going to enjoy doing business with your friend here," Mr. Estrada smiled deceptively, while addressing Uritla. "He has a great business sense. Definitely, a person that knows a good deal when he's been presented one."

"Right on for the deal of the century," Uritla joked. "Let's smoke to it." She inhaled a long puff of her joint.

"Are you coming along with me my love?" Estrada's penis became erect while examining her buxom shapely body from head to toe. Simply the thought of making love to her once again drove him temporarily insane.

"Making love to a renown gigolo sounds exciting," she said to him with a sensual smile. "And I'm sure there are many hidden secrets to passion that one could discover with you. But tonight, I prefer having sex under the moonlight with my friend Chris. He's going to need someone around to help him figure out how he's going to spend all of that cash that he'll soon be making."

"Ah, sex in the moonlight," Estrada remained a gentleman. "It sounds simply beautiful. You two enjoy it while you can. Because when one gets my age, the thrill of making love becomes wishful thinking. Va con dais."

Once the tense transaction was over, Uritla exhaled a deep breath. "Whew, I'm glad that's set at rest," she said with ease and relaxed back onto the sofa.

The task of performing guard duty against Estrada's bodyguards had been a frightful experience for her. It also dawned on her that during the moments while Chris was attempting to make a deal with Estrada, someone could have made a wrong move and bang. She could have become another casualty whom one read about in the obituary column of the Southern California daily newspaper.

"I think I'm loosing my nerve doing this kind of work. Now, I know that I should have taken my mom's advice and went to school to become a Home Economics Teacher."

"I don't understand," Chris gave her an odd stare, "such activity should have been amateur work for you. The job that you do as a means of survival is really the one that should bother you."

"That's strange," Uritla said wondering. "I find myself more relaxed while being engaged in my real line of work."

"Relaxed. How can a person in your line of work be relaxed?"

"I guess it's the money. I've always liked to maintain a high standard of living. The only way that I can continue to live good is by going out and earning some bread. But tonight, the money didn't seem important. It was my performance that counted. Once realizing the job imposed danger, not only was I afraid, but there were moments when I doubted myself. I mean, what might have happened if I was provoked? There you have this person whose armed staring at your every move. One stupid mistake and boom. Your life has ended."

"I can't really believe that you're serious. That little guard post that you pulled this evening couldn't have been the reason why you're so upset. Now come on, tell me what is it that's really bothering you?"

"Are you really interested in what my problem is?"

"I wouldn't ask if I weren't concerned."

"The Body has ordered me to perform another hit for them."

"Terrific." Chris now appeared puzzled. "You speak as though your job consists of pulling off one hit after another. In between murders, don't The Body allow you enough time to cool off?"

"There's very little time for leisure in my line of work," Uritla said with a note of dedication in her voice. "I'm employed by them constantly, day and night. However, unbeknownst to them, I do find time to relax. Right now my safeguarding you is one of those moments."

"Fine. Whose your target? I pray to God it's not someone that I know."

"You might know them."

"I do."

"Yes, it's you."

Chris looked bewildered. "Me. Come on Uritla," he said with an overtone of fear in his voice. "Enough of this nonsense."

While sitting experiencing strange vibes, Chris' conscience tormented him. Murdering diplomats has really gotten to her.

"When did your organization suddenly choose me as being there target?" He asked almost losing his voice.

"Our organization has no interest in you," she told him earnestly. "I was only joking to get your attention."

At once they were silent. They sat with each of their minds straying off into deep thought.

A minute later she continued. "I'm scared, Chris. Really afraid. Being a professional doesn't relieve the stress when being told that you have to assassinate two top officials in the same city."

"Two top officials." Chris' heart pounded in fear. "For Pete's sake, are you crazy? The authorities would be looking for you underneath every rock in Mexico. How could you get away with such a crime?"

"By being a master of disguise—I hope." she told him. "Other than me doing my job the way I was taught, I have no other skills to use."

"You'd better use your brains. I've never questioned or interfered with what you're doing, until now. I'd like to think that we're friends. So, I'll address you as being a friend. You're an individual— underneath your coarse surface—who has the heart of an angel. You've been both kind and considerate to me. And I admire that in you. Why don't you... when this mission is over... and I'm hoping that you'll live through it... Why don't you take a leave of absence from pulling off hits? Maybe attend church. Or even visit a wildlife refuge in a foreign country? Anything to steer you in another direction."

She laughed. "At least by attending church maybe I can be forgiven for the horrible things that I've done in the past, right? The wildlife refuge. I don't know. It might not be the right place for me to go visit. It might end up being a disastrous setting with too many 'king of the jungle' beasts co-mingling in the same environment."

At port, using the Kanin Firm's shipping merit, Chris had loaded onto two ships: forty 12 by 14 by 2 foot and a half inch in depth, sections of pre-cast concrete slabs. Their destination would be Italy and Columbia. Then after selling the load of slabs in Italy and making a sale in Columbia, Chris was to pick up a shipment of slabs from there and return with them to the U.S.

After transacting tense business in Palermo, Chris flew to Medellin.

Upon receiving the shipment of goods, Chris then advanced to the warehouse where he along with his contact would dispose of the weapons. Also during the process they'd store inside the slabs the shipment of drugs.

Mexico City—The Holiday Hilton—Chris moved about nervously in his room anticipating a call from Estrada.

He waited.

And waited.

But ironically, such a call never came.

A few days went past then Estrada contacted Chris, "How did everything go my friend?"

"Everything went smooth," Chris replied.

"Do you have the package?" Estrada inquired all the while, plotting quietly to himself. If my sense of evaluation is correct, he's a newcomer to this business. I'm a pro when it comes to preying on the intelligence of newcomers.

"Of course, I have it," Chris answered reluctantly, then thought to himself. Estrada's up to something. But what?

"Is the package there at your hotel room?" Estrada plowed on determinedly.

"It's here. Stashed in a safe place."

Hmm. I wonder where he has the stuff hidden. Estrada pondered quietly to himself. Because earlier that day he'd ordered his men to search Chris' room, but they had left empty handed.

"You stay put. I'll be at your hotel in twenty minutes," Estrada said quickly, then hung up.

At the Holiday Hilton…

"You've been quite inquisitive about the drugs Mr. Estrada," Chris said politely. "But, if you don't mind my asking, where are the diamonds? And did you bring along the cash that I'm to get paid?"

"Our agreement remains in tact, my friend," Estrada assured him. "I have never breached on a contract with anyone. I am a man who has integrity. Also, my reputation would be at stake if I did something so foolish. You agree?"

Chris didn't reply.

"Where are the drugs? Do you have them in your possession?"

"Yes, I have them." Chris reached inside his briefcase and pulled out a white powder substance then passed it onto Estrada for him to sample it.

"Yes. Yes." Estrada said gleefully while testing the cocaine. "This is the real stuff. Okay." He paused after testing it once more. "Let's continue with our business deal. The diamonds that you will get have to be taken care of by a fence."

"A fence?" Chris look bewildered.

"Yes, a fence. He's the person who sees to it that you can get your jewels sold. He's also an individual who buys them. And the individual whom the dope belongs to. And the person who'll pay you the money that you have coming to ya."

"I thought that I'd be dealing directly with you?" Chris was now confused.

"I'm sorry that I gave you that impression, my friend." Estrada said to him. "However, you must understand Mr. Cohen when dealing in such a trade as international gun smuggling, there'd have to be someone whose involved that was very influential; powerful; has a lot of contacts. And a person whom also wants to remain anonymous. I myself do not have such power." He now stared Chris directly in the eyes.

Is he buying this? He asked himself. Yes, He's buying it. Estrada assured himself.

"When can you be ready to travel?" he asked.

"This afternoon," Chris stared in space.

"Have the package ready and we'll leave for Guadalajara immediately."

"Why so immediately?" Chris asked him. "I have other business to take care of."

"How about 3:00 p.m. tomorrow then?" Estrada asked him.

"3:00 p.m. tomorrow should allow me enough time to take care of my business here." Being a person who took very few chances, Chris quickly phoned Uritla and told her about how he was going to approach handling his present situation.

"Hello, babe. How are you?"

"I'm fine," Uritla said. "But what took you so long to contact me? I've been pulling my hair out hoping that we could finish our business and leave Mexico."

"I'm sorry about the delay. Everything is falling into place now. It's just a matter of time before our business here will be over."

There was a brief pause.

"Have you been screwing any of your arch enemies in the political arena lately?"

"No, they're too afraid to visit my neighborhood," she said jokingly as she stood staring out the window observing the run-down environment surrounding her.

"They're probably better off," Chris said. "Because the kind of sweet luring bait that you use to get men hooked, then boldly rid yourself of them, shatters ones dream of having an everlasting relationship with you. But as a reprisal, I must admit, your leaving them with cold feet is truly a sympathetic compromise."

"What do you mean by that?" Uritla at the moment became irritated. "Sometimes, I cannot tell when you're joking or being for real."

"Ah—I didn't mean to aggravate you. And I definitely did not intend to make you angry; not when our moment of glory is so near. Playfully, it was just conversation that I use to entertain you with."

"I find your playful humor sometimes disgusting," Uritla sounded angry. "You always seem to say insensitive things to me."

"I'm sorry if I offended you Uritla. Can you forgive me?"

"Maybe."

"Please try." Uritla was silent.

"Tomorrow morning could you bring the drugs over to me," Chris asked.

"Why the rush," Uritla inquired.

"Estrada wants me to accompany him on a trip to Guadalajara."

"Guadalajara, why there?"

"Because his fence lives there."

"His fence. That's odd. Why would he need a fence?"

"His conversation dawned on me strange too. Somehow it doesn't sound right. He explained to me that the fence is the man in charge. And that he would not give me the diamonds—nor pay me—until the delivery of the drugs had been made."

"It… His story could be legit," Uritla said. "But if I were you, I wouldn't take any chances."

"Chances? Hell no. I'm not stupid. I wouldn't dare travel alone with an estimated two million dollars worth of drugs on me. In a foreign country? With complete strangers? People whom I know nothing about? How dumb do I appear?"

"I never thought that you were a dumb person Chris."

"I know babe. I've always been a person who believes in positive thinking. And such positive thinking assures me that it would've been such a waste—father purchasing that beautiful plot of land in Roselawn Cemetery where the family could be buried, and I had to be put away so far from home. Somewhere in a desolate area with an unmarked grave."

Momentarily straying from what Chris was saying, into Uritla's mind crept terrified thoughts from the past. "I know," she said speaking momentarily in a daze. "One does get a horrid feeling when involved in mischief in foreign lands. A person can not be comfortable when the welfare of their life has been entrusted into the hands of another. And certainly not someone who's a complete stranger." She'd suddenly reminisced over how close she'd come to having her disguise revealed prior to her completing the murder plot of an African diplomat. She had to react immediately and with absolute accuracy when a fellow agent recognized her and knew of her working as a double agent.

"To be honest Uritla, I am afraid," Chris said. "I wouldn't want to be alone with them too far outside Mexico City. Now, more than anything, I realize that the ten thousand dollars that I paid you isn't really enough for protecting me, nor my interest. But, if you could stand guard over me until we reach Guadalajara I would make it more than worth your while."

"To accompany you on such a dangerous mission. Yes, I would need more money. Ordinarily I wouldn't charge a double fee, but in your case, it's different. How much dough will you pay me for the extra job?"

"You mean in cash?" Chris pretended to be stupid.

"Yes. Cash."

"Thirty thousand. Is that enough?"

Obviously listening to the conning overtones in Chris' voice Uritla decided to use the boomerang counter con to find out how much of a potential crook Chris was.

"I'm altogether in a different field. Remember babes, I'm a person who carries out political missions. Not private ones. Would forty-five thousand be too much?" She asked quickly. "Plus a five thousand dollar bonus if we come out of this thing unharmed?"

"Fifty thousand dollars." Chris began to perspire. "How preposterous."

"Since I'm going to be out there endangering my life—and at the same time—risking my position with The Body—such an amount doesn't seem to be too large."

Chris pondered her request.

I'll profit handsomely when I make the delivery of the drugs. Dads firm paid the cost of having the cargo of secret documents and weapons transported. And any proceeds from this deal will be mine to share alone. I'll have mega bucks to spare even if I choose to stay in California. There shouldn't be a problem paying her what she has demanded. But are you using your head Chris? Regardless of the amount of money that you'll make on the deal, would it be wise to pay Uritla that kind of loot just to accompany me on such a short trip? It would be dumb. What are my chances of taking care of this business on my own?

Seconds passed. Then quickly, after thinking about all the risks that he saw involved, to contemplate making such a trip alone, could have easily meant his doom.

Hastily without further thought Chris made Uritla an offer of fifty-five thousand dollars to be his guard on the trip. Simply because he knew with a professional soldier like Uritla guarding his back—and at the same time protecting both their interest—the odds on him getting injured were fifty-five thousand to one.

Without bickering further, Uritla accepted his offer.

Mid evening the following day Chris, along with Estrada and his henchmen began their trip to Guadalajara.

Minutes later Uritla, accompanied by a male companion merged safely into the traffic behind them.

Rolling along at a careful speed Estrada's group drove hard until around 11:00 p.m. only stopping once for water. They'd been thoughtful to bring along enough gasoline for their extended journey.

Upon arriving in Morelia they made a stop for food.

Inside the diner Chris sat experiencing strange vibes.

Estrada's up to something. He thought quietly to himself. This route seemed to have taken us off the main road a bit.

As they drove onward about a half an hour outside the city limits, Pueblo whom was driving pulled off the road slowing to a stop.

While observing that there was no rest area where they'd stopped Chris became very uneasy.

Suddenly he experienced a strange fear. One that could've been described as absolute terror.

Unaware of what was taking place next, he turned his head to be stunned by Estrada's gunmen, who sat with the nozzles of their large barrel weapon pointed towards his head.

Chris's voice quavered. "Now, I know what Uritla meant when she said, always be careful. And not to ever put all of your confidence in a stranger."

Estrada appeared amazed.

It was impossible for him to believe that he's caught such a shrewd businessman like Mr. Cohen off guard. Because Chris always seemed so in control of himself.

"Mr. Cohen, how unfortunate for you that you feel that you can not trust me. Such words have shattered my integrity." Swash. He spat a large gush from the tobacco that he was chewing in Chris's face.

Sparked by revolting madness, Chris reached for him.

Very quickly his head exploded, as Pueblo bashed his head with the butt end of his rifle.

Estrada kindly helped him back up on the seat.

He paused momentarily; staring mischievously at Chris.

Then he said deceptively while holding Chris' chin in an upward position. "Sometimes it doesn't pay to act vengeful my friend." Spontaneously the barbarian imposed violence on Chris, smacking him to the face.

After inflicting pain to Chris' body he suddenly gained control of his brute, force-like actions.

Sitting, staring sadistically, he now began to harass Chris.

"Smile my friend. Death isn't so horrible. Actually, some consider it a new beginning."

Through ponderous fear Chris wondered whether Uritla would be in time to prevent—what at the moment, seemed like his tragic end.

Defiantly, Estrada slammed Chris' face up against the passenger window, and ordered his gunmen to assist him out of the vehicle.

After the men had escorted Chris about sixty yards, a light scuffle began. A loud thud could be heard then very quickly a person fell to the ground.

Stephen Blass, who was on a private mission in Mexico was the henchman who'd been hired by Uritla to help protect Chris.

He'd quickly killed Pueblo by using a rope with an attachment that had metal spikes implanted around the end of it.

First panicking, then trembling in fear, the other gunman tried desperately to fight his attackers off.

Within a few intense moments he keeled over.

Uritla stood tightening her grip on the coarse rope she was using; squeezing it; until she'd drained all the signs of life out of him.

For a split second it appeared that an undercurrent of excitement flowed through her veins as she prolonged tightening the rope around the neck of the now stifle bodied gunman.

Totally engrossed in shock, Chris slumped downward.

Quietly, Uritla crept slowly toward Estrada's truck.

Without alarming his suspicion she waited for the right moment to make her move.

Waiting in fearful curiosity for his henchmen's prompt return Estrada suddenly panicked and ordered his other loyal crooks to go and investigate the men's whereabouts.

With their weapons ready, the young men trembled in a palpable state of fear as they led off in the direction where their partners had went.

A few horrid filled moments had passed, when suddenly Morez stumbled over what seemingly felt like a body.

Quickly shivering in ultimate fright, he felt someone grab him from behind.

Chris fought aggressively, quietly punching, hoping inside that he wouldn't alarm the gunman's friend. During the chaos, Stephen attacked the other gunman.

Immediately after he'd broken his victim's neck, Stephen offered to lend Chris a hand. He done in his intended victim for him.

Very bravely, Uritla leaped inside the truck with Estrada and suddenly had him pleading for mercy.

Instantaneously as she was about to off him—Chris cried out, "No." he yelled quickly.

"Don't shoot him. We need him alive. He's the only one who knows who our contact is, in Guadalajara. After we meet with his silent and invisible partner in crime, the fence, he'll be all yours."

Upon hearing the stranger's voice who'd yelled out in the dark, suddenly Stephen lit up a match.

He had to make certain that it was not coming from the same modest and shy person whom the two of them had worked together back in Texas—on his father's ranch.

After seeing that is was Christopher Kanin he cussed, "Well, I'll be damned. Am I seeing this? You? A thug? Creepy."

"I know," Chris said. "Don't ask me what I'm doing out here in the middle of nowhere; and in trouble. As a matter of fact, the last time you saw me, I had problems then too huh?"

Without revealing Chris' identity Stephen burst out in laughter therefore ending the subject.

"I guess we'll save this pig and slaughter him later, huh?" Uritla asked abruptly while poking the nozzle of her weapon in Estrada's side.

"For a while," Chris said. "Just for a while."

Guadalajara—inside a vacant house Zorbou, Estrada's boss, measured and tested the quality of his shipment of drugs.

All the while Estrada sat pondering schemes that might save his life. But even though he was faced with a grave problem, he dared not to direct suspicion toward his recent partners in crime.

After they'd closed the deal and had secured themselves a hotel room, Estrada thought that it would be wise to discuss the matter on whether he would receive an equal share of the loot they'd made.

"It's really been a long hard week of work for us. Huh, mon?" he spoke to Chris with a disturbed look on his face. "I know that it's not possible for you to share with me, a part of that money, right? Here, Estrada goes through all the trouble of getting you the jewels. You must have something for him?"

Totally making an idiot out of himself, he begged only to find out that his words landed upon deaf ears.

Sitting, paying very little attention to him, Chris pursued paying Uritla and Stephen their loot for standing guard over him.

Out of hidden fear, Estrada continued talking. After babbling for a period of time his world of reality revealed a sense of loss. Each word he now drone, sounded strange and alien as though he'd finally lost his mind.

Staring malignantly, all the while, fighting an impulse to cut his throat, Uritla extended her sympathy towards his pleas. "Would someone please take this greedy beast out back and dispose of him?" she protested heatedly.

Instantaneously, upon hearing those endangered words, Estrada began to perspire. He spoke as if he'd now regained his sanity back. "Think nothing of what I asked you, my friends. I'm a strong believer that opportunity knocks more than once in a person's lifetime. All Estrada really wants is his life. One can steal some more jewels, right?"

"Having your life placed in the hands of such notables as those whom are gathered here tonight, Mr. Delgrecco, should indeed by an honor for you." Chris began to enlighten him. "Simply because, it isn't often that a criminal like yourself, gets an opportunity to share in the company of three of the most sought after individuals in the world. What I mean by sought after is that organizations everywhere are looking for men and women with unique talents, like those that we possess. Mercenaries, like Ms. Vladimir there..." He paused momentarily looking at Uritla.

She stood staring at him with a murderous frown pasted to her face.

Such a frown was provoked by Chris clearly divulging to individuals present, what her true identity was.

"A person devoted to help rid the international continents of their many corrupt heads of government. People like our friend here, Mr. Blass, a highly trained demolition expert."

"Then there's me: son of one of the richest realty developers in America. I'm the lone member of the family who was forced to be an outcast. What shit luck. It was after I'd helped make my family millions, that I was banished from the only home that I've ever had. You must be awfully thrilled to know that your life is entrusted in the hands of a group of people with such acquired popularity."

Sitting with a bewildered look on his face, Estrada pursued to lie his way out of his ordeal. "I do not understand your words," he said.

"You will. Smart dud." Chris spoke as if he'd been filled with some over powering force that was coaching him to maybe threaten malevolence toward their helpless friend.

Uritla had quickly become highly upset with Chris. She felt that he had no right. "No right at all," to expose her real name—and line of work—to the out-laws whom were present.

"One should never confide secrets to an idiot," she said with the overtones of hostility in her voice.

"There's really no need for you to get all upset," Chris said. "Our friend here won't be spilling any information about us."

Instantly cold chills crept over Estrada's body.

Sitting with enlarged eyes suddenly he began pleading with his business associates to spare his life.

Stephen and Uritla wanted to murder Estrada and leave his remains to rot. However Chris convinced Stephen, "If you tap into the knowledgeable things that you've learned while studying the medical profession, I'm sure you could find a way to keep him from exposing what we are up to while visiting Mexico."

Stephen's heart pounded with excitement. The thrilling thought of reaching into his diabolical bag of practicing medicine—and medical surgery, exuded his normal way of thinking.

Later that night he blindfolded Estrada. Strapped his penis closely to his body. He began by lacerating his tongue cutting it, as such, it would leave him unable to speak for an extended period of time. He only branded Estrada once with a hot branding iron—leaving the initial S on his rear. Sadly the branding came after he'd broken his left ankle. The consequences of how he left poor Estrada stranded, burdened him to be unable to speak, walk or sit on his backside.

"Professional maiming while letting your victim live," is how Uritla described her friend's brutal act.

"Such is done to a co-partner to crime—who doesn't play by the rules," is how all three of them viewed the light maiming of Estrada.

Momentarily Chris had distanced himself from periods of agony plaguing his being. For the first time in quite a while, he showed a sigh of relief. Relief that was brought on by him knowing that he would no longer have to make deals in a foreign country with a group of aliens whom he'd never met before.

Hours after the torture, Chris, Stephen, and Uritla boarded a private plane headed for Los Angeles. Soon thereafter, they were en route to France.

CHAPTER SEVEN

1982

During his first six months at Kanin Enterprises, Marcus performed jobs which consisted of him working in the field of office management. Gretta Sands, an elderly friend of his—whom just happened to be a member on the board of directors at the firm—had been instrumental in finding the qualified personnel to assist him with his work.

The other ranking officials were terribly shaken by Marcus holding a position that was equal to that of theirs on the board, but their grievances were quickly hushed after Gretta had mentioned that she was going to sell her enormous amount of stock shares to an investment broker. Such a threat convinced them that it was in their best interest to accept Marcus as being one of their fellow executives.

Each day in his office it became a routine that Marcus would find his desk over-crowded with stringent workloads.

Each night his private tutors would attend to the chores and the following morning he would be happily ready for the next assignment.

To sum things up, Marcus found his new occupation 'rather exciting....' He'd occasionally boast with his nose in the air. 'It's rewarding.... it's really a piece of cake.'

Boldly ignoring the fact that Marcus had failed his course at becoming an executive, a month before the deadline that he'd been given to prove himself to the board at Kanin, they voted unanimously that he should become president of the firm.

In defending why Marcus had moved up the ladder so fast they stated that 'never since the forming of Kanin Enterprises, had an executive pursued his duties with such brave courage and conviction.' Such courage convinced them that Marcus was the right man for the job.

1983

As of now, Chris has engaged himself in a booming business. Linked in partnership with a clothing factory owner named Monsieur Jacques de la Camille, he'd included in his business interest a fashionable boutique in the comfortable shopping center at Les Hall Forumn that catered only to the elite of Paris.

Outside of his business dealings in garments, as an extra hustle, Chris also had going for himself a private deal that he'd made with his sister Pitney. 'As a favor to Chris,' she would order garments from his clothing outlet at import wholesale price and would sell them through her chain of businesses at American retail price. Within the months to come, her orders would be placed so constantly they'd be too much in demand for Chris to fill.

Also being sold in his shop for an exclusive price was the diamonds that he'd taken from Mr. Delgrecco. They were a special attraction that helped him sell his most expensive attire.

During any of his busiest weeks Chris would gross more than seventy five thousand dollars. Therefore, as a result of his quick prosperity it encouraged him to open up another store.

Suddenly in addition to the patronage who bought from him elaborate garments with miniature jewel settings, once he added the star trek and yuppie fashions to his line of goods, his clientele grew from the aristocratic to the very average working citizen.

One busy day in mid April as Chris stood verbally chewing out a saleswoman he became alarmed—and almost driven to an outspoken state of contempt—when the lady that he was chewing the saleswoman out—about, stood up in her defense.

He'd only been in the intrusive lady's presence for a few moments and consequentially he found himself apologizing to the overwhelmed young madam, about his quick temper flare. "My actions Madame," he told her, "were untimely—ill mannered—and totally out of order...."

His composure then returned to normal and he became an aspiring businessman glowing with flattery, and at the same time, honored that his business was being patronized by The Prime Minister of Great Britain's daughter. She'd visited his shop that afternoon 'to purchase a dashing evening attire' to be worn at a bash being thrown in her honor at a renown nightclub there in Paris.

Chris quickly earned the reputation of 'a businessman who was going places.' Eager to please his peers he suddenly began to involve himself in many social activities. He attended Parliamentary banquets. Went fox hunting with Royal Officials. Entertained show biz people. And on one occasion he was invited by the Prime Minister's daughter —to dine at their castle.

But while there—and in the company of a gay Chief Official named Lord Blakely—when becoming too friendly with him while measuring him for a fashionable gown—was when the Prime Minister's daughter circulated the rumor 'that Monsieur de Masi acted queer.'

Oddly the latter statement was true of Chris. It was his way of not becoming too involve with people. He feared with the utmost precaution that if he chose to be friends with even the richest of people, things concerning his past would inevitably be made public.

Eventually to those whom at one time questioned Chris' sexuality they'd be in for a devastating shock. For yet to their surprise the quiet gentleman whom they'd labeled queer would be a greater threat to their homes than any nuclear disaster could be to their country.

CHAPTER EIGHT

At a capital nightclub in New York City, Marcus—accompanied by Pitney and her husband Salvo—was out partying.

Constantly chuckling in and about the crowd they were cool jerking —surfing—striking a pose dancing—and having a farcical good freaking time.

While dancing with a female whom he had met at the club, Marcus was eyeballing every mini-skirt, half-nude bottom female that danced next to him shaking her hips to the energetic sounds being played from the DJ's music control station.

Before long he had become unwanted by his lady friend, so with the remainder of the quart size drink that she was drinking—she threw it in his face—and in a quiet and sophisticated manner she excused herself from the table.

To ease his embarrassment Marcus—passed—then flew to another dance partner and disappeared into the crowd that was momentarily dancing sort of dirty out on the dance floor.

After cheerfully returning to his booth, Marcus clasped his beverage and shut his eyes.

He focused his attention on it for a few seconds then he purposely spilled it on the floor.

Abruptly he portrayed the role of a complacent drunk—immediately proud—with a nonchalant smile pasted to his face.

He managed to contain his gentleman like poise until suddenly his legs gave away sending him crashing hard down onto the floor.

Weakly he searched for the leg of his chair.

In order to avoid complete embarrassment, Pitney quietly excused herself by latching onto a passing gentleman and convinced him to dance with her.

Because of his yearning to have fun after sitting at his table experiencing a long period of agony Marcus appeared to have said to himself: "Aw—the—fuck with being a nice guy...."

Like any intoxicated nightclub bully would act, he avenged his misery by joining a sexy female who stood dancing beside the patrons seated at the cavity adjoining his.

For an extended ten minutes or more while constantly grooving to the wild sounds they freaked out on the dance floor.

Suddenly the music changed to a rhythmic beat. A group who called themselves Blade, was now laying down the funk.

As the dance crowd got more funkier and the song and music became more rhythmically moving, Marcus became more stimulated.

Examinatorial and highly interested, he danced scanning the female who was on stage, sensual, body. She was the band's lead singer who by now had the nightspot patrons geeked while she sang a tune titled, "Sexy. Sexy. Sexy."

Dressed in a lavender mini-skirt, she wiggled her hips very X-rated from one end of the stage to the other.

Momentarily there was no other female present whom had such exquisite charm.

Marcus wanted to possess her.

He wanted to love her.

Maybe even own her?

Upon returning to his seat he began to fictionalize that she was fast in his arms.

While his sister and brother-in-law sat talking about different subjects, Marcus sat in a daze; so coolheaded, with his mind occupied wholly on her dancing.

The band continued playing their highly controversial tunes.

On and on went Marcus' illusions. For he was now alone—in his own private world viewing pictures of himself and the songstress paired and winding up honorably in love.

Once the band had taken a break and was awaiting their final set for the night, Marcus' inhibitions became public. "You know what Salvo," he slurred tipsily.

"Yes—." Salvo looked at him with a drunken smile on his face.

"She's fucking lovely," Marcus' eyes glittered mischievously. "Imagine sticking your tongue inside her gash; how, sweet."

"A beautiful woman like her, you don't eat it," Salvo commented. "You grasp her by her big wide bottom—and drive her all the way up the wall."

"No—Salvo; she wouldn't like that—at all," Marcus reassured him. "She's in show biz: show biz people like to be en-ter-tained. With her, you have to tease—the vagina. You know; pretend that you're licking your guitar. That's how she likes to burst her balls."

"Oh, my goodness. How gross." Pitney spoke as if she were melting with embarrassment. "If you don't respect me as being your sister, you could at least have the common decency to respect me as being a lady. What kind of person are you," she smirked. "A guy who exposes his sex habits to the public. You're ill, man. Ill."

"I apologize sis'," Marcus said smiling. "It's my little worm that's causing me to clown around. You see," he gripped playfully at his abdomen area. "I'm holding on—to—it—as tight as I can. I can't help it, if it likes to make whoopee. It has a mind of its own. Um-m-m. Oh-h-h. Oh-h-h. Aw-w-w."

Momentarily it seemed that Marcus' fantasizing had suddenly become a reality.

Pitney's composure darkened as she shamefully embedded her face over into her hands. "Oh—are—you—sick—man. You're really sick."

"Gee, why didn't I think of this sooner," Salvo said, "my friend Abdullah owns this place. I'll ask him if it's okay for you to visit her dressing room. Maybe you two will have a chance to talk?"

"That's a swell idea, Salvo. Anything to meet her."

"Say—Salvo," Pitney raised her head, "While you're away, I know that you won't forget to lick your tongue out and wink your eye at the beautiful ladies. You—go—for—it—boy. Pinching those girls on the rear—and getting your balls off. But if it's not too much bother, feel a penis for me. And darling, please—be choosy. Any prick under ten inches long—will only upset me. Ha-a-a ha ha ha-a-a."

"Aw—fuck off." Deaf during moments when Pitney would rock his consciousness indicating to him that she wasn't a square, impervious Salvo bolted.

Within a few minutes, he had returned with some good news. He had arranged for Marcus to meet the singer after her last show.

During her next performance the outfit that the entertainer wore seemed like it had been personally designed just to satisfy Marcus' lust for her.

"Wow. Is she curvaceous," he drooled. "She's a living portrait of the perfect female."

To Marcus the twenty minute set that the band played seemed like days of waiting.

After her performance the singer went to her dressing-room and just as she was about to take off her attire there sounded a knock on the door.

"Come in," she said softly.

As she sat smiling, happily anticipating meeting her handsome guest—suddenly she became raving mad.

Dreadfully, after Marcus had walked into the room and began to introduce himself, he emptied the burning contents of his stomach over onto her lap.

Sitting with a murderous frown pasted to her face, she began to yell, "I'll just, be—Oh—Aw-w shit. My dress. My dress. My beautiful, dress. I just bought it."

Marcus began to apologize, "I'm sorry. So sor—." "Get—out—of—here." She screamed. "Go—. You; you; you, puking invalid." Slam.

After the door went shut behind him, smelling very rank, Marcus staggered quietly out into the hallway where a security guard latched on to him and rushed him toward the exit sign.

CHAPTER NINE

Sparsely operant while sticking in France, Uritla and Stephen would be the able public thugs who had been involved in several unsolved robberies that had plagued the garment wholesalers in the district where they lived.

Anticipative, their feloniousness would grieve many and their few offenses would get the attention of the Prime Minister whom eventually would strike down their bad doings.

Uritla's identity would surface with her being noted as Mademoiselle X—the invisible conspirator whom was believed to be the mastermind behind the garment thieves' operation.

Alias Uritla Giastrenko: Now Mademoiselle Chauntii de Maurepas, age thirty-six, was born Klara Frehauf Vladimir to the parents of Mr. Lawerence Frehauf and Frieda Vladimir in Furth, Germany.

Lawerence was a young German officer during World War II whom had collaborated with the enemy. Before the war ended, he defected. In compensation for his treason the Soviets offered him asylum in their homeland.

Later he was an inspiration, instilling in Klara—his only offspring— that she should carry on the tradition 'working for the K.G.B.' "Think— as I speak," he verbalized to her one day, "how you might one day gain your freedom from the dominant forces here... ."

It certainly was because of his corrupt background and constant persuasion that Klara involved herself in such dangerous work.

Klara was reared in the Soviet Union. At age sixteen she defected. Clearly her defection was faked by the Russians. She attended college in the U.S. and while doing so, she also graduated with high honors from the K.G.B. Secret Services.

Unlike many secret agent killers, Klara is strikingly beautiful. She has dyed, thick, wavy, brown hair and a full face, marbled brown eyes, tanned skin, and a perfectly shaped nose. One whom always maintained a cool image, she was gifted with a tongue that spoke fluently in more than fourteen languages.

She'd briefly met Chris during the Olympic games.

Their friendship was sparked after she accidentally bumped into him while exiting the aisle-way where he was seated.

All-the-while Klara tried to apologize to him, Chris sat mesmerized; blushing at her beauty.

Then unexpectedly, as she was about to quietly rush away, Chris grasped her by the arm and wouldn't let go of her until he persuaded her to give him her telephone number.

She was in such a nervous state, unintentionally she gave him the correct number.

Moments following her fast disappearance in the fans, Chris noticed swarms of security personnel had crowded the area around him.

When the commotion died down, he could see them carrying off what appeared to have been someone's body.

The next week Chris contacted Klara.

Their friendly little communication soon led to a love affair. An extremely hot—when they were together—romance that has endured until now.

After they had know each other for a while, one day while talking, Klara confided to Chris her life's story.

Chris listened in shock as she told him of her many experiences.

During the Olympic games she had succeeded at pulling off a hit on one of the most deadliest spies who ever shared Russian secrets. She had completed the job very quiet like by shooting the agent in the side with a poison dart. Once the crowd had stood up and applauded an event, by being seated directly behind the agent it made the business she was in so common.

During her hasty exit when tripping over Chris—she related to that as being 'sudden hysteria.' Such hysteria develops when an agent experiences a bad case of lost nerves.

She emphasized that she was 'a professional operative.' And that what had happened that day, rarely happens to individuals associated with her profession. She assured him that 'in the event that it did ever occur again' it could mean the end to her brilliant career.

Caring very deeply for her, Chris understood why she had chosen the profession that she was in. They bonded and ended their conversation. Chris declared that he wouldn't ever divulge information to anyone concerning Klara's past. Nor her present elapsing occupation.

CHAPTER TEN

The crookedness that Stephen and Klara are presently working on is a large shipment of clothing goods. And as they restudied it, at break, they conspired with Patricia Newmar and Hausan Sabb in New York, on a dope stacked prospectus to rid Zina Ali Khan—the daughter of a wealthy Iranian oil dealer—of her fat American bank account.

After work Klara leaves the De La Bourbon clothing factory. It is head-quartered in an unpopulated area north of Marsailles.

7:00p.m. All-the-while engaging heavily in drugs and drinks, the group of five whom had gathered at Stephen's apartment sat discussing the final details as to how they were going to pull off their caper.

8:20p.m. Moments before leaving for the robbery site Klara had to speak in a quiet murderous tone of voice to Ingras who had kindly spoken to her about going to bed with him.

"Fuck no, man. What do I appear to be, some kind of whore?"

Acting out his fantasy to seduce her, Ingras disregarded her warning and spanked her on the rear.

Slightly embarrassed, Klara turned to confront him.

Ingras pounced again, this time grasping her breast.

Instantaneously, he experienced a major surprise. Before he could let go, Klara pierced his face with a razor. It was a weapon that she always kept hidden over in her brassiere.

Ingras yelled, then perched holding his face.

Klara beamed with satisfaction. For it now seemed as though she had gotten her sharp and painful message across to him.

The steel wire fence that surrounded the De La Bourbon clothing factory was an easy task for Ingras. Within a few moments, he had a hole cut that was large enough for a person to enter.

The group moved very cautious out of fear of arousing the guard's suspicion who stood about ten yards in front of them.

All-the-while carrying a hand held chain that had an iron ball attached to the end of it, Ingras—the quiet executioner—crept slowly up behind the victim and before he could react—with tremendous force—Ingras bashed his brains in.

On the east end of the yard Pompinelli momentarily sensed danger.

Over his walkie-talkie he called out to Nichol.

It seemed that Nichol's walkie-talkie was on moments ago? They had just talked.

A tremulous bolt of fear overcame Pompinelli.

After making a second attempt to get in touch with Nichol just as Pompinelli was about to call the guard in charge, suddenly everything went black on him.

Klara had grabbed him from behind and with a tight grip glued to his mouth, she quickly cut his throat.

Quiet fright was now upon Corot.

There were beads of perspiration standing on his forehead as he stood shivering in horror, waiting for the monster whom was stalking victims 'out there in the darkness' to come and violently prey upon him.

As Ingras crept up behind Corot—he stood—as if he was frozen to his tracks.

While death loomed in the background, he remained still, with his head inclined; looking up peacefully toward the sky.

For a few seconds, Ingras' vengeance to murder seemed to have come to a halt. He acted momentarily as though he might have had sacred thoughts about killing such a weird individual.

After their job had been completed, Ingras and his friends headed for the ocean border. There a boat would be waiting for them to take them by watercourse to a dock where they would stash the goods and when given the word, they would deliver them to the address that they had been told to free them near Paris.

Stephen and Klara headed to his apartment where throughout the night they made passionate love.

West of Montpellier—en route to an associate of theirs private pier— Ingras had to raise his British arms rifle in fear as search lights from a helicopter flown by agents of de police scanned the area around them. That Monday at work, Klara observed with ultra caution whether or not she was a suspect in connection to the De La Bourbon plant robbery.

Once sensing that she was not under any suspicion a few weeks later she and Stephen drove to Paris.

While visiting Chris' lavish home they dined, played cards, and gossiped over a few joints and hard liquor.

Within a short while, Chris counted out to his friends a hundred and five thousand dollars. Of which their share each was twenty-seven thousand, five. Ingras would be paid fifteen thousand. And the rest would be shared by his three partners.

Immediately Chris gave a toast to their recent success and afterwards he hastily directed Stephen to his bedroom with the romantic thought in mind of having Klara share his.

While finding herself hopelessly trapped inside Chris' bedroom, Klara responded to Chris with mutual affection and for the remainder of the night the duo competed with each other in many forbidden areas of sex.

The ensuing day Chris had his machinists start preparing for the hum-drum task of making clothing from the stolen garments.

He would give new life to his current wardrobe collection when he added costly leather purses and boots.

Catering to mostly a female clientele he would turnabout a full line of fashions that had the long lean look; resplendent form fitting low cut full skirted gowns; and satin evening coats.

Ordered from 'he lied to his customers' a silk weaving concern in Lyons he stocked upscale head and body wear. And the simple look for evening. Black deep purple wool coats with leather cuffs.

High performance silver sequined dresses. And pin-striped, double breasted, gangster look business suits. He simply had happening garb that had a syntax of miniature jewel plots that would bring passion to the eyes of—even—the not so faddish shopper.

He was riant and socially a kook shouting instructions to his designers and diamond cutters.

He was their persevering reminder that 'If the de la Camille—de Masi—exploit—is—to—survive—'each organism' is—going—to—have—to—carry—his—own—load...."

CHAPTER ELEVEN

In the meanwhile through informal mail Marcus has been contacting the singer whose name he found out—was Rachel. He had been sending her offers to replace the dress that he threw up on. Also enclosed in his letters were recent photos of himself showing off at the estate—along with flowers and credit card offers.

Upon realizing that Rachel wasn't interested in his gifts he would now try desperately to win her love.

Immediately he took a flight to New York.

For three nights while Rachel performed Marcus would sit alone at his table obsessed with the thought in mind of Rachel becoming his lover.

On the final night of her gig just as Marcus was about to write her off his list surprisingly Rachel walked over to his table and made friends with him.

With a strangely destitute smile on her face she squeezed her way down into the seat next to him.

"Hi. Did I invade on your privacy," she stared at Marcus with mysterious eyes. "If so, I'll sit elsewhere."

Marcus shook his head, "No. No—o. Not at all. For it is indeed a pleasure to finally get a chance to talk to you."

"Talk, how nice," Rachel said terribly arrogant. "What subject could I converse upon that would be appealing to a cum freak?"

Instantly blood raced towards Marcus' brain, "What—the—fuck—did—you—just—call—me?"

"Sh-h-h," wiping perspiration from his forehead she calmed him down, "be—cool. Try not to take me serious love. I'm not a very serious person." She winked her eye at him.

Marcus appeared vengeful. He now sat painting dark pictures of the lady whom he would have enjoyed the opportunity of having a fling with.

"What a fool I've been," he said uneasily. "One can never judge a book by its cover."

"Why not," Rachel smiled. "Don't I resemble your dream girl to ya?"

Not really. Marcus thought boldly to himself. But, I still have this obsession to make love to you.

"You're more beautiful than I'd imagined," he lied gracefully.

Added to her disappointing personality she also seemed to have freshly aged a bit. That mug momentary, wasn't all that. Wow. Soberness made him take a close glance. Seeing her while she performed on stage she appeared to have been a portrait of beauty. But while viewing her up close he observed that she was knocking the hell out of twenty-five. To Marcus this was a big let down. He at present, was off into the habit of falling in love with women no older than twenty-one.

What the hell. He thought emphatically. You can't always have prime rib. There are occasions when a person will just have to settle for beef jerky.

Momentarily Rachel's gutter grammar was hushed. "Through informal channels we've already been introduced," she said skeptically promoting herself. "So—s there's no need to bother with names. I'm twenty five years old. Born and reared in New York. I have a tenth grade education. Comes from an impoverished family of eight. Been married and divorced. And at present—I live in a three room apartment with my son. Whom my grandmother baby sits while I'm doing shows. I've been singing with Blade for two years. And I have no other source of income. Now that you know my life's history; whew," she exhaled a deep breath, "let's—get—hitched."

"Wait—hold on; a, minute," Marcus reared back in his seat with both hands extended up in front of his face.

"Gee—e; what reluctant enthusiasm. I thought that my autobiography would frighten you. But I never imagined it would cause you to have a heart attack." While sitting smacking chewing gum Rachel hinted to Marcus that maybe she at one time worked as a theatrical performer.

"For a moment your lips were sealed—and suddenly they went zoom. Gee whiz—Rachel—I thought you'd met all of the weird ones.

Damn. What do I get; another Casanova. Another—sanctimonious— sex friend; that's what your are. A beast, who's out here roaming the streets each night hoping to find that ultimate piece of ass. And don't you try to convince me otherwise. I know your type. You'll screw any piece. Just as long as it doesn't have any strings attached to the end of it."

"Miss—" Marcus tried in vain to interrupt her.

"It's typical of your kind," Rachel wouldn't let him speak, "you don't like obligations. And as far as spending some cash on a broad; forget it. Don't you men realize that if a woman is going to be used—and most men use us—she should at least get paid. After all, the mental anguish of it is worth something. Sh-h-h. There goes that sound of thunder again. We've just lost another heart patient. Sh-h-h. Be quiet," she paused.

"Listen to the shock waves. They're being made by the sound of your footsteps.

Listen.

He's running to find refuge. Boom. He crashes into another wall of fire."

Marcus looked at her strangely. I wonder what kind of trip she's on? He asked himself. "Rachel, I'm—"

"Shut up—and listen. Would ya?" she cut him off. "Where have you been? Don't you know that when arguing with a woman we're always entitled to have the final say?"

All-the-while fighting an impulse to leave Marcus listened a bit longer in hope of becoming her friend.

"Now; where was I?" A strange and remote loneliness crept on her face as she now sat frantically thumping her fingers down onto the table.

It appeared as though she had lost her trend of thought.

"Is it possible that I could say something to defend myself," Marcus asked hastily. "I—assure—you—that it will be brief."

"Sure. Go right ahead. You seemed to have done a great job of interrupting what I had to say."

"Thank you. Engine lips," Marcus whispered low.

"Pardon me," Rachel stared defiantly at him.

"How can a person with such a beautiful smile have such a bizarre personality? It also seems that your ability to evaluate ones good character is involuntarily rude. You have intentionally vibrated a flow of bad vibes which you hope will cause an inter—reaction involving my emotions toward you. Your whole program is geared toward disrupting any conceivable thought I might've had concerning our sharing an intimate relationship together."

Rachel reacted now as though it was Marcus whom had suddenly flipped his lid.

"Sure; you—right," she said looking at him strangely. "Anything you say fellow."

"Now—since your scheme has been exposed, how about a compromise?"

"A compromise, why not."

"When was the last time you thought about changing your scenery?"

"Aw—shucks, the thought never entered my mind."

"Why don't you come out and visit California for a while? And let us West Coast people show you how to live. Maybe then we'll be allowed a chance to get to know each other better.

And who knows. Such an arrangement just might eliminate all of the static and feedback that we're now getting between our channels of communication. How does that sound to ya? Of course I'll pay for the trip. And if you want, you can even bring along your kid."

Momentarily Rachel sat as though she was pondering the outcome of his offer.

"The club's manager, Mr. Hausan knows me very well. He'll assure you that you'll be in the safety of good company."

Rachel spoke tensely, "Sounds like it could be interesting. And with people like Mr. Hausan vouching for you, I'm sure that I would enjoy my visit—there. I tell you what, I'll think about it. Okay?" She now looked at Marcus as if she somehow sought his guidance.

"That's it. I've had it," Marcus shouted frantically. "I wonder now, was it really worth me wasting my energy trying to relate to someone whose as distant as you. My number is on the back of the last photo I sent you. If you want to—call me. If I'm not there, leave a message on my answering service. I've communicated with you enough. I feel that my presence here—serves no further purpose. Chow—darling."

Of course Marcus would take the credit for Kanin Enterprise's continued success, but most insiders knew that it was Pitney's input behind the scenes that helped the company to grow. But strangely while finding herself abundantly rich, plop—she became a materialistic person who was spoiled by the luxuries that wealth had to offer one. One time, an unhostile home-girl, now occasionally creating anarchism, she became an eager partygoer and a heavy abuser of drugs. She also seemed to have adopted Marcus' grim way of thinking when relating to the welfare of their exiled brother Chris. "I honestly doubt that there will ever be any news connecting Chris' name to that of wealth," she commented rather boldly on several occasions.

CHAPTER TWELVE

6:30p.m. Wednesday. A month later. Newport Beach California. Inside an elegant beach house that had been designed by Chris,

Marcus is laboriously engaged in sexual intercourse with his current mortgage tutor; a brunette, named Terressa.

A knock sounded on the front door—and after no one answered— whomever the person was they moved to the plate glass window.

While fumbling to wrap a beach towel around himself, Marcus cussed—and in aggravation he went to see whom was so desperately trying to get his attention.

When he greeted the intruder quickly he became speechless.

Surprisingly before his eyes there stood his dream girl; the singer, Rachel.

"Hello—" she spoke with a gleeful smile while trying to look past him off into the house.

"Why don't you invite our company in," Terressa asked in a curious high pitched tone of voice.

"Sure—" Marcus replied ponderingly. I wonder how this little sticky mess that I've gotten myself into will turn out?

Rachel took a seat beside Terressa on the sofa while Marcus headed over to the bar.

As everyone sat still suddenly Terressa felt that it was her duty to disrupt the quietness there in the room.

"Oh, well; what the hell," she said in a subdued voice. "A party— is— a—party. Let's drink a toast, shall we say, to the rich economical gains that America has recently made." And then she whispered, "And to— three's a crowd."

And regardless—if our conversations seem to bore the other—we promise—not to be rude. We'll begin by being friendly—outgoing— and keeping our personal insults—mute. If we do succeed at such an almost impossible task, it should make it a fun-filled evening for—we few—whom are gathered here in this little secluded place. What's your brand miss," she walked seductively over toward the bar.

"I'll have a double scotch on the rocks please."

"Scotch it is. By the way, my name is Terressa honey. What's yours?"

"It's Ra—Rachel," Rachel replied nervously.

"You must forgive Marcus, he never was any good at introductions. Marcus, darling, could you please turn up the stereo; and set out the smokes? While I make our guest here a little something to get her in the mood."

Marcus now spoke in a more relieved tone of voice, "You've got it babes," he said then moved quickly to change tapes on the stereo all- the-while winking his eye at Rachel who relaxed back onto the sofa.

Momentarily a heavy downpour of rain splashed against the roof of the beach shelter.

The music flowed superbly from the stereo acoustical speakers in a good clear your nature kind of listening tone.

The trio sat swigging sizable intakes of smoke from the bowl of cocaine that Marcus had fired up. Far too quick Terressa experienced a rush.

Space and continuity became revised as she saw sparkles radiating in her mind.

For more than a sustained half-hour they sat mesmerized listening to the jazz—classics that were being played on the stereo.

Oddly while engrossed in her mood for the music suddenly Terressa's passion for songs changed to a wanton desire to make love.

She now moved uncomfortably as if an invisible alien had taken control of her physical being.

Spontaneously the stimulant possessed authority and commanded her to pursue erotic pleasure.

Now sitting highly aroused she appeared as though her sex preference had become female.

Gently she began to massage in and around Rachel's knee.

An undercurrent of excitement raced through Rachel's body.

How terribly odd she thought quietly. A female; fondling me. I'm going wacky with a frenzied desire to screw.

Terressa's hand began roving upward.

Now using the palm of her hand she caressed Rachel's mound.

Rachel let out a compelling whimper as Terressa softly massaged the opening of her vagina.

Standing with his penis fast becoming erect, Marcus could no longer resist the wretchedness of wanting to screw either of the females, so quickly, he joined in and began massaging Rachel's breasts.

By now Terressa had a finger probing inside Rachel.

Rachel's mind was tormented with sweet ecstasy as she resigned herself to Terressa's expert erotic probing.

As Rachel became almost totally humble, anticipating to be sexually devoured Terressa took a momentary pause to fire up another bowl of coke.

After hitting it several times she then walked poised over to the bar to pour herself another drink.

For a long light-year that ended up being two minutes—she stood mixing her drink.

Subsequently as she searched the room for the other party affiliates, she observed that they had departed then vanished into thin air.

Dressed as they were there was no doubt they'd disappeared into the bedroom.

Over on the bed she stood looking down at Marcus gently teasing Rachel with his tongue.

Intense wildfires of passion soared through Terressa's body.

Now wanting desperately to be sexually exploited Rachel began to remove all that she was wearing.

Frenzied, Marcus began to undress.

Admiring the rush Terressa—before Marcus could undo all that he was wearing—tore away her robing and hastily moved over to the bed to secure herself a role in what now happily seemed like it would result in a thrill of a lifetime.

While hovering over Rachel holding her buttocks steady— Terressa toyed with her vagina all-the-while kissing her passionately on her clitoris.

Rapidly Rachel's body temperature increased. Her eyes glittered— then she began to make a hissing noise as she squirmed back onto the bed.

As Terressa probed her tongue slowly and fervently inside Rachel she began to breathe hard and let out erotic groans. Then real fast she reacted like a supercharged nymphet writhing and wildly grinding her buttocks.

While—Terressa lit up a flame of passion inside Rachel Marcus added to her delight—kissing her breast; then gradually he worked his way descending toward her navel.

Quickly Marcus moved to where he could position himself downward around Terressa's bottom.

Terressa kept teasing Rachel's vagina with her tongue.

Marcus concentrated on the raw rondure opening of Terressa's anus.

While holding her buttocks steady he began gently shoving— then wiggling his penis inward—toward the meager hole.

Terressa shrink on each of his attempts while wanting him so desperately inside her she finally settled back and waited for the evolvable technique.

After a couple all out efforts trying to penetrate her—Bingo. He finally succeeded.

Slowly he contended through tightening flesh.

Rachel threw her legs wide apart as Terressa had now began eating away fierously at her vagina.

Marcus continued rotating gently and deeper; and deeper almost to the inner most depths of Terressa's anus.

Rachel laid squirming. By now as her mind had entered into a higher plane of passion she yearned for an object. An object that would penetrate deep enough to quench the burning fire that Terressa had created inside her.

With great intensity, Marcus pounded away.

Both females writhed and sobed while possessing second after second of pleasure.

In the midst of their pleasure Marcus tormented the duo as he abruptly positioned himself to screw Terressa the proper way.

Rachel quickly moved to where Marcus could taste her fruit.

Terressa grasped Marcus back all-the-while begging for him to screw deeper all the way down—deep down—inside her.

Soon Terressa screamed as she experienced a rushing orgasm that sent exertion then debility through her body.

Subsequently Rachel almost choked Marcus as she began grasping his head against her vagina. Her body convulged rapidly then she screamed while enjoying her most powerful orgasm.

Thinking that the party had ended Terressa quietly rolled over into the corner of the bedroom and passed out.

Before long Marcus was hard again and had Rachel in a state of mental deficiency as he was trying to screw her to death.

A few weeks went past with Rachel and Marcus confirming that they were profoundly compatible.

Because of his assets and particular lovemaking skills he induced her to sign a contract with him on a fifty-fifty—basis, that involved him building her a recording studio; complete—with equipment and personnel, if she in return for the favor would devote her voice to the music listening public—and her life to him.

Rachel agreed to become his singer; nonetheless, when effectuating the last part of their compact she explained to Marcus that 'getting to know one—could take a lifetime.' In conclusion, she insisted that they should wait at least a year before even considering his proposal of marriage.

Since the day that the weapons caper had taken place at Armsted Nuclear Base, things around the law compounds in D.C. were in total disorder. Working meticulous with the Pentagon the case had been assigned to the department of agent Daniel S. Throbs. An American patriot whom had always been known to solve crimes that proved to be too defeating for other agents in his field to solve.

While attempting to unravel the contemptuous murder secret Dan's search—for the implicated participators at large—would eventually lead him to several foreign countries before he could elicit enough positive information that would steer him in the direction of shackling the main suspects whom had conceived such an intriguing offense.

Organized with the information that he had gathered from the military men and also from the branch agents it had given Dan vital clues that inexplicably connected Gregory Steward and his wife Pamela's murder to the misdeed.

CHAPTER THIRTEEN

The doorbell rang at the home of the parents of Army Captain Gregory Steward.

A few cuss words echoed loudly outside then after Mrs. Steward found out who the strangers were her guest were allowed to enter the premises.

Glancing with a jaundiced eye around the living room Dan spoke, "We didn't mean to barge in on you folks so unannounced; Mr. Steward. And I do apologize for speaking so rude to your misses. However, in the future, I hope she's been informed; that federal law, is above—all—law. She must clearly understand, that depending on the criminal act, we can issue warrants—without the courts approval. We can issue them in any state—in America. And during any hour of the day. It really was unnecessary for her to ask us so many questions. Now," a note of command crept into his voice, "let's get down to business."

The Steward's were very quiet at the moment. They felt that it was in their best interest to not say anything that might additionally ruffle the huge secret service agent.

"Unessential, life can be like a jigsaw puzzle," he said abruptly reverberating like Peter Falk reciting dialogue taken from one of his "Colombo" movie scripts. "On numerous occasions individuals have had a hard time trying to make pieces of the puzzle fit in their lives. Now don't get me wrong, I'm no expert on misdeeds. However, an offense was recently committed and I'm the one that they gave the job to of piecing the damn antagonizing puzzle together. And I honestly admit, the puzzle that I'm currently working on might be distressful to solve. That's where you people can help me out. Please help me to try to piece this puzzle together?"

The Steward's again were quiet. They wondered now if the agent had all his marbles.

"Now that we're settled," Dan stared at them, "my first question: Do you know anything about your deceased son being involved in the robbery that took place at the military base where he was stationed?"

"I don't understand," Mr. Steward appeared amazed that his son might've been a participant in such a prohibited activism, "how could our son have been involved in that robbery? A crime which he gave his life protecting the things that were taken. It just doesn't make sense."

"Whether it makes sense or not," Dan said firmly, "we still have reason to believe that the murder of your son somehow—is connected to that crime. We believe also that whoever Greg's accomplices were, they murdered your son's wife so there would be no witnesses left to tell whom plotted the slick robbery of Uncle Sam's cargo."

"That's absurd," Mrs. Steward shouted. "Our son would've never conspired with anyone in a scheme like that. I defend him. Simply because he's a patriot."

Suddenly the phone range interrupting their conversation.

Upon answering it Mrs. Steward impertinently related to the caller that she was being detained by the F. B. I. then she hung up.

Dan continued, "Has your son ever had a friendship in relations to an alias Ben Harris? Whose real name is Perry White?" Dan had been informed that maybe a radical organization was involved in the annoying criminal misdeed.

"He, at one time, introduced us to an associate of his; whose name was Perry," replied Mrs. Steward. "And later on he mentioned that this guy had at one time worked as a mercenary soldier. Then, a few months later, he said that he'd quit being a soldier and began leading a group of people in a cause speaking out for their human rights. But that's about all we know about his friend."

"Hum—" Dan thought out loud. "I wonder if this Perry and Ben Harris are the same person?"

Quick perceiving that the Steward's weren't going to interact with him, Dan gave up on his preceding querying and changed the subject to how they could be forwarding in pleading their sons innocence.

After Dan had preached a sermon to the Steward's pertaining to their 'out law' son's involvement with the caper he then warned that if they'd withheld any major information that could be used as a hint leading to the arrest of the felons at lodge, they both would be placed in contempt of obstruction of justice. And would be fined accordingly: A ten thousand dollar fine: Two to five years in prison: Or, both.

As Dan was leaving he spoke to his partners, "That should give them something to worry about than trying to pretend that their son is not a holdup man."

Outside the house as Dan and his men walked toward their vehicle, a woman approached them. "Pardon me please," the lady's voice quavered.

Each agent stared at the other but neither replied.

Her eyes squinted. She was agitated by their actions.

Typical honky, she thought silently to herself. Upset because we share the same planet with them.

But even though they responded to her presence as if she was shit standing on the sidewalk, she'd still inquire about the reason why they'd visited the Steward's.

"You guys are from the F. B. I. right," she now looked Dan straight in the eye as if to say, I think that you're shit too.

Dan stood momentary scuffing his heels in the pavement.

After staring past the woman then exhaling a large puff of smoke from his cigar he then replied, "We might be. Who's asking?"

"You're investigating what happened to Greg and Maria Steward right?"

Dan's face now exuded a twisted smile, "You have the right people miss. What can we do for ya?"

"Is the reward money still available? That you were offering for information concerning the robbery?"

"It's as good as money in the bank," Dan replied.

"Well, if you're interested, I just might have some information that will help you out. Excuse me sir," she paused, "do you have any identification? I've watched television; and in most cases, when a person asks an officer to show them their credentials they quickly comply. Your badge would be just fine."

Dan stared at her as if she was pea brained.

"I'm just trying to be cautious. It's a habit. I'm always cautious when greeting strangers. Can you blame me for that?"

"How often do you see men dressed like us in your neighborhood?" Dan was sarcastic.

The woman grew quiet.

"Just give me the time; and the place; where it will be convenient for us to talk," Dan's voice sounded menacing.

"I have to work until four. At my place; 11763 South Farr. Around eight p.m. Is that okay with you?"

"We'll be at your place at eight p.m. sharp. Oh miss, if you don't mind me asking, what's your name?"

"Gordan. Angela Gordan," Angela lied about her maiden name.

At eight p.m. sharp the following evening the agents were sounding on Angela's door-bell.

While moving about half undressed she let them in then rushed off into the bedroom.

Through spreading mists that carried the smell of marijuana agent Hunt foul-mouthed his way to the bar while Dan fetched himself a seat and threw a milk case box over in the corner for the other agent to sit on.

While waiting for Angela to return Dan observed that on the table in front of him there was a thin piece of cardboard that had the remains of a white powdered substance on it.

"I wonder what kind of oppressed trip she's on?" he asked his fellow agents.

They pretended that they didn't hear him. Simply because it was normal that Dan was always babbling about something.

Having on a very dainty see-through evening gown and smelling like a French perfume parlor Angela emerged into the room and stood momentarily lighting her cigarette.

"Do you have the reward money," she asked slurring slightly.

"Yes. We have it," Dan disclosed a briefcase allowing enough latitude for Angela to get a slight knowledge of the tidy stacks of dead presidents. "But I must caution you Ms. Gordan," he said, "before we can make any monetary transactions, we'll need facts. Documented facts. Facts that can be used as evidence against those individuals involved in this crime. You also must supply us with new information.

Information that we don't already have compiled in our files. And—we could—summon you to be called as a material witness for us."

"Sure—e. Anything you say." Angela nodded then intruded, "Excuse me. Howard, darling, could you please come in here for a moment?"

A man entered the room carrying a briefcase.

"This is Howard," she introduced him to the agents. "He's a friend of mine. I asked him to supply us with a tape recorder. To record the information that I'm going to give to you. In the event that it's ever used for anything, I wouldn't want it to appear distorted; nor changed. And nor would I want anything to jeopardize my position at the post office. Now—" she switched on the recorder. "You can swear me in if you like?"

Being a gentleman Dan swore her in.

"Let's see," Angela sat exact on the couch, "Perry was my man."

While meticulously awaiting clues Dan quickly interrupted, "Pardon me Ms. Gordan, why should we want to know anything about him?"

Angela became frantic. "Could you just be cool for a minute," her words flowed as if she'd abruptly gotten insulted. "You fucking people don't know your ass—from a hole in the ground," such words distinctively were uttered in distress.

"How was that Ms. Gordan," immediately the redness began to creep into Dan's face.

Angela threw both hands up. Grasped at her hair. Blew out a large gush of air. Then sat staring malignantly at the agent.

"Quite theatrical," Dan seemed amused that she was acting so weird.

There was a brief pause.

"Have you finished your performance?" he asked.

"Perry and Greg were the best of pals. Inseparable," Angela continued. "Anyway, one night about a month ago, I overheard them talking about setting up the robbery of an army base. Or, nuclear base."

"You mean, an army convoy; whose destination was Armsted Nuclear Base. Right?"

"Yeah. That sounds more like what they said. Wait a minute," Angela seemed to have remembered something. "They also mentioned that some man—his name sounded like he was a white man—was going to buy the weapons from them—at top price."

Dan interjected quickly, "Hunt, take down this impressive information. Did they mention the white gentleman by name?"

"Not really," Angela couldn't answer the latter question simply because she was expanding on information that Perry had confidentially told her about how Chris looked.

"Some help," Dan said grimly.

"Please—let me finish; okay," she chatted further. "Once Greg had talked Perry into the deal, the next day he brought the guy over," Angela lied.

Immediately Dan's eyes lit up. "Now—w, we're getting some place. First try to detail to us what you think that the white male looked like. Then describe your boyfriend to us."

"Could I please hold the money?"

"Sure ya can babes," Dan passed her the briefcase.

Angela had an incandescence presence as she viewed the stacks of dead presidents who lay dressed in green—staring up at her.

"This guy, stood about six foot two," she now talked penetrating in a frequent voice. "He weighed about two hundred and twenty pounds. He had a full face. The kind of face one gets when he's been well fed. His eyes were blue. And he had reddish brown hair. Like that actor— what's his name? I can't think of it at the moment. It's right on the tip of my tongue," she paused momentarily.

"Um—m—it's coming. It's coming—g. I know his name. Bruce Willis."

"I see that you're very good at remembering names Ms. Gordan. Do you have any idea where this white male might reside?"

"Huh? I'm sorry," she apologized. "My mind must've wandered off."

"This white male, where does he live?" Dan asked her very raucous.

"That, I couldn't tell you. But he wasn't just a mere individual. Everything about the dude—his demeanor—detailed to us— that his ass was rich."

"You actually saw him," Dan appeared shocked.

"He was really at this meeting with Perry's group. We knew, that even though he wasn't dressed like a rich white, he was rich. And ones instinct never fools them when seeing someone carry them-self like he did.

There was something else about this man's character—you know— the type I'm referring to. The kind of person that goes out and does things just for kicks.

I remember when they were discussing the job, he had this certain luster in his eyes. It appeared as though he was totally obsessed with the idea." Sitting, thinking, Angela quickly sneaked a low toned subtle joke in her conversation, "Maybe even, climaxing—while they were talking."

"Yes. Uh huh," Dan listened to her staggered in deep thought.

"Ms. Gordan, could you please describe your boyfriend Mr. Perry White to us?" agent Hunt seemed like her conversation was torture to him.

"He's about six foot even. Weighs about two hundred pounds. Light brown skinned complexion. A slim full face. He wears a beard— and a curly low cut haircut. Oh, I forgot. He has brown eyes."

"Does he have any birthmarks? Tattoos? Some kind of scar, etc.

That we might be able to identify him by?"

"No."

"Did the white male have any scars?"

"No."

"Could you give us an address where we might be able to locate your boyfriend? Or, a relatives' address where he might be staying?"

"I'm sorry. I don't know."

"What do you mean you don't know." Dan asked angered.

"I don't know."

"How can we get at factual information, Ms. Gordan, if we don't know where to start looking for these men with these aliases?"

"That's your job; Mr. Throbs."

"What—" Dan got pissed off. "Look, you fucking, spook," he yelled madden. "Don't you go getting smart with me. I very well— know how—to do my job."

Angela now sat with her nerves tingling, "Mr. Throbs, the reason why I'm giving any information, to you, at all, is—" she hesitated.

"Yes—"

"Is because, I believe that Perry is dead. Normally, he stops by my place. But, lately I haven't seen him. And it's been quite a while since anyone else—has seen him. That's what worries me. He has never stayed away this long," Angela now began to sound grizzly. "Everything seems so eerie."

"Eerie; that's how you feel huh," Dan said with the overtone of sarcasm in his voice.

"It's weird, the kind of agonizing torture—and distress signals— that I'm getting. A desolate—empty—consuming feeling; that tells me, that something horrible has happened to him. It's quite possible, that the people that he was working with, has double crossed him; and dumped him out to sea—somewhere."

"Why should you think of such tragic things," Dan asked while playing an inaccessible psychiatrist over-scrupulously grading that Angela should receive a constant zero when it came to her having any brains. (brainpower?)

All of a sudden Angela's empathy seemed to have disappeared, "Look man," she appeared irritated, "I've slept with this guy off— and on—for more than nine years. If he was going to be away for a while— he would let me know. You must understand, we two were, very close. When he didn't have things, I went out, and got them for him. He done the same for me. We were sort of in each other's corner—ya know what I mean? There's no way that he would pull up without letting me know where he was headed. Or him, stopping by, to tell me goodbye.

I haven't heard from him in over a month. That's a long while for him not to call," she unexpectedly broke down in tears. "There's no way, that I'd rat on him—unless—I felt that he was dead. I feel that he's dead. And nothing that I can say—will hurt him now."

"I'm sorry that you're feeling so downcast Ms. Gordan," Dan tried to appear sympathetic.

"Your friend, does he have any immediate family in the city— that we can talk to? To see if maybe they've heard anything from him?"

"I know the street where his sister resides. I can give you directions there."

"How kind," Dan said. "Oh by the way Ms. Gordan; there's something that I almost forgot."

"What's that?"

"Of the fifty thousand dollar reward money, your share will only come to five thousand dollars."

"What—" Angela's temperature rose. "I thought that I'd be getting the whole amount?"

"Now please—e, don't get upset. Not yet; anyway. Because that's not the final blow. You see Ms. Gordan, of the total fifty thousand dollars in reward money, it will be divided and shared by many persons with information involving this case. Unless an individual gives us all the information that we'll need to solve this matter.

Now—w, I saved the cheerful part for last. When one gets paid, the Internal Revenue Service will withhold approximately thirty three percent of each individual's share to be retained for income tax purposes. And after tax, me and my partners get ten percent—for hazardous duty pay. So, if I were you, of the estimated fifty percent that you'll have left, I'd stash it someplace. Like in a bank's vault. Sort of save it for my old age retirement," he winked his eye at her.

The following day Dan visited the home of Perry White's sister.

It was after Dan's men had yelled a hypersensitive command for her to open the door that we find her committing herself in a protected fuss blurting out tough excessive cuss words at them,

"Whatta ya want—you—dumb—ass—cops? You pig mutha fuckers always want to come and lurk around in the black neighborhood— looking for criminals. Why don't you go out to white suburbia and spy on them. The commit more damn unstable crimes than we could ever dream of...."

Mrs. Taylor was so busy flipping her lips that she hadn't heard Dan disperse her a second warning telling her that they were from the Pentagon with a federal warrant to search her place.

Mr. Taylor tried desperately to reason with his wife who acted deaf and continued yelling at the law enforcement officers.

Louise had been suffering from a long past history of mental illness and had attacked the branch authorities on several occasions when they'd visited her home. She uniformly thought that 'they' were invariably spying on her and her brother.

Mr. Taylor reacted out of hidden fear that she might attempt the same demeanor with the agents currently at their door.

Scared faint during the crisis in the midst of him trying to explain to his wife that it wasn't 'the local pigs' that she was howling at—but 'the pigs' from the nations state-house was when the agents thrust upon and broke down their door.

As the men entered the house, Louise, distracted, and riveting in fright, ran quickly to hide in the bedroom.

Inferior Dan Throbs, stood holding a forty five caliber pistol while his partners flaunted heavy automatic weapons.

"I warn you; Mrs. Taylor," he yelled, "if you do not return to this room in five seconds, we'll smoke your ass out—with bullets.

Your home is surrounded.

All exits are being watched.

Now. When I count to five, is when the shooting starts. 1. 2. 3. 4." Dan had now began counting.

"Don't shoot. Don't shoot." Louise was frightened out of her wits. She quickly fast forwarded herself in the living room with her hands extended over her head.

Dan smiled to his friends then shoved her over onto the sofa. "What's with you; you fucking fool," he asked contemptuously.

"I'm crazy," Louise added a bit of theatrics to her insane role.

Slap. Dan smacked her to the face. "Now—w; are you still crazy?"

With tears spilling down her face and a leakage of blood exuding from her lips, Mrs. Taylor now seemed to've gotten her activism in order. "Now look, Mr.; I'm not really crazy; but I warn you, I— am—a— Christian." Quickly with the look of agitation pasted to her face she at one swoop relaxed her two hundred fifty pound frame back onto the couch. "And if you hit me again, I ain't gonna worry about it. I'm gonna tell God about it."

By now Dan had calmed down a bit. Wholesale and casual he said, "I'd like to make my job here as easy as possible. So out of the kindness of your heart—and your strange love for justice, please—e, Mrs. Taylor, be helpful. If you cooperate with us, I promise you—no harm will come to you. But if you do not, we'll have no other choice but to twist your arm to get at the truth. Is that understood?"

Louise stared at him with her mouth squeezed shut.

Dan sat noiseless for a moment waiting for her to respond.

Unfriendly seconds passed then unanticipated Louise decided to give in.

Dan learned from her that Perry often lived with his commune members at their church. But before he went missing he'd lived there at her house. She hadn't seen him since hearing about the weapons job. She too, like Angela, had a suspicion that something hideous had occurred.

Louise gave Dan a more affirmative characterization of the white male meticulously detailing information that her brother had unmask to her about his looks; habits; and the kind of automobile he has driving. 'Perry was always cautious when it came to dealing with strangers.' She briefly had a hindsight.

With what concessions the agents offered, Louise disembroiled Maria's name of any activity that tied her to any criminal misdeeds. She served one good purpose, however, she stub her husband Greg as being 'a greedy swine' who didn't know when Enough was Enough. "Oh—no, him bringing home all that dope from overseas—and selling it—wasn't enough. He had to go out and rob the store that was feeding him...."

After assuring the agents that she'd told them all the information she knew on Greg, Louise then passed sentence on her brother: "My, brother, Perry, he's the scum of the earth. He wasn't satisfied until he went out and dragged our good Christian name through the mud. May his sinful soul—grow maggots—and rust in hell...."

With all the recent info mobilized Dan had now collected enough slant for belief to legalize a case against the people involved in the robbery conspiracy.

With industrious effort he'd—like a brute—savagely pursue the individual—or man—who resembled a likeness to the persons face taken from the positive drawing by the artist at their headquarters.

Dan endured months of active extensive investigation and when winter came he'd narrowed the number of suspects down to three humans fitting the description of the man who was behind the weapons gamble.

The first suspect was an army Lieutenant whom was stationed at Fort Ord.

The other two whom were under suspicion was Fred Owens—a scrap yard owner who lived in San Francisco and Christopher Kanin son of the late business tycoon, Gerald Kanin.

Lieutenant Kerns had a reliable alibi as to where he was during the early morning robbery—and so did Fred Owens. So with only one suspect left to question Dan was left with little anxiety. He was secured that Christopher Kanin was the key person whom would tell him who—besides himself—had pulled off the wild ass frolic against The Government of The United States.

CHAPTER FOURTEEN

At this juncture Marcus had his hands full. He was up to his neck in occupation ventures. He was employed part time as director of technology and research at two of Kanin Enterprises subsidy firms. He was a partner in a law firm. An accountant. And executive vice president at Premier recording company.

In body and reliant on the field genius of alone tutors within six months he'd learned enough about the recording industry to deliver as an arranger: sound engineer: promotional advertiser: and a producer.

It was after he and Rachel had wed that he began to pursue his business interest with great self esteem. Inside a very short span he'd achieved establishing three highly successful acts. Enterprising entertainers that helped him publicize and plug two gold—and one platinum album.

Of course Rachel was his superstar. She also was empowered co- producing the trust's first gold album and was a lead vocalist on the platinum record.

Tonight as one drove past the neighborhood of upper class homes west of the bay bridge one couldn't but notice that there was some great assembly taking place at the Kanin Estate.

Inside the mansion closed ballroom Marcus spoke from a small platform: "We're gathered here tonight to honor our company's most consummate recording artist, Ms. Rachel B. Saxon."

When determining that callous statement chafed annoyance was revealed on the face of other Premier recording artist(s). First, etiologically it had been promulgated by two wanna be record producers that there were several other mortals about who had triple the capability that Rachel had, but they'd never been given the fortuity to prove themselves as she'd done. A standardized conservatism trailed. And Premier should've been on watch. Because years later such an action would make the business ail. But even though—at the moment—they were disapproving, before the event would end through sad expressions and twisted smiles they'd all take off their hats to Rachel on her recent success.

"Being the person who helped set up Premier and built it into what it is today, we honor this contestant in the fields of management, arranging, promotion, distribution, and working as a producer. She has galvanized artists of all ages and has shared with record listening audiences around the world her enterprising vocal abilities. It is the music listening public that has chosen her as being this years top entertainer. An honor she truly deserves. She has given them songs that they will continue to buy out of respect and commendation for her music. This lady of margin and popularity—I believe that where ever music migrates she would've ameliorated her talent to accompany it. To Rachel, I present to you, your first platinum album; and along with it, this plaque. From all of us here at Premier, we love ya."

With tears trickling down her face through garish applause Rachel beamed with joy as she accepted her award.

An hour or so had passed at the convivial entertainment social when in walked C.I.A. agent Daniel S. Throbs.

After he'd spoken to the servantry imparting his bunch identity she led them through the crowd to where Marcus might be found.

Chaired inside one of their closed guest rooms, Rachel, Marcus, and several of their friends were rabidly participating in activities involving getting high.

A gentle knock was persistent on the door. "Whose—the—fucks—there?" Marcus asked in a huff.

"Whoever you are, I bet you can't piss in a swinging jar turned upside down," Rachel exuded cheerfully.

"We're Law Officials," Dan's voice rang with vicarious supremacy.

"The Law? I don't remember anyone inviting them," Terressa said in fun adding a sense of humor. "Man—you have real radicals outside your door."

"I'm coming; I'm coming—Uncle Sam," Marcus grumbled then asked the party-goers to hush.

It took Marcus an extended fifty seconds to reach the door and before he could get it completely open Dan shoved him aside and entered the room.

Fidgety people inside the room were trying to gather up their hard drugs and at the same time trying to get themselves together.

"Hold on—n, just one damn minute," Marcus said ranting. "First, you jack-asses better identify your-selves. And—you better have a damn good reason for invading on my privacy this way."

Dan reached inside his coat pocked and pulled out his identification.

"Now—your search warrant please?" Marcus wanted to become belligerent.

Quickly Dan slapped out the search warrant.

Everywhere in his career Dan had always been a laconic agent, but tonight, he seemed more constrained. Why was he standing there concise, accepting Marcus' squawking with such patient tolerance.

For the first time Dan reacted in such a manner simply because the person he was now pursuing was the son of the man whom had backed many government political occasions while he was living. Dan's supervisor had warned him before visiting The Kanin Estate that due process of the law would have to be cleverly initiated when dealing with such influential people as the Kanin Family.

At which time realizing that Dan and his men were real Feds Marcus' friends were stricken with a sudden case of fright and in a slow scamper, they began quietly excusing themselves from the room.

Dan demanded that Rachel and Marcus remain there.

Earnestly peeved off regarding the narcotics and equipment left on the table in front of them he said sturdy, "You rich people sure can get away with a lot of things, can't ya?"

"Whatta ya mean," Marcus asked pretending that he didn't know what Dan was expressing.

Dan pointed to the coffee table and a couple ottomans, "Those—large quantities of drugs you have lying around?"

"Drugs—" Marcus acted innocent. "I wonder how they got there?"

"For the life of me—I will never understand—this law—that I uphold.

If we'd entered the home of a poor person and we observed them doing drugs, regardless of our reason for being on their grounds, it would be legal to arrest them for such a crime. But as always, the law seems to cater to the wishes of the influential."

"Such a statement could be true," Marcus said deliberately evading Dan. "But drugs—are not the issue here. So what legal excuse—do you have for invading my private party like this?"

Dan appeared annoyed, "You saw our warrant. But obviously you didn't read it. It gives us the authority to search your grounds for a Mr. Christopher Kanin. I believe he's your brother—right?"

"Yes. He's my brother," Marcus replied stunned. You'd think that he'd know that much. He thought to himself.

Dan remarked casually, "And concerning your private party, we find it in the limit of the law—and we find it to be formal—to invade upon the privacy of any individual—whom we believe—is connected to a crime such as the one we believe your brother has committed. And by you being an attorney, Mr. Kanin, you anyway should know, that Federal law—is above all law. So if our names didn't appear on your guest list this evening, it's not at all important.

Federal law also states; "that we are an invited guest where ever there are land harbors that are in the territorial boundaries belonging to the government of These United State of America. Now that you understand why, we're here—and Whom—might've sent us—maybe you'll be kind enough to give us a little information about your brother?"

"Sure—e. Sure," The tone of Marcus' voice now appeared as though he'd compromised with the agents.

Dan showed him a photo of Chris, "Is this your brother?"

"Yes. That's him."

"Fine. Where does he reside?"

"I'm not for sure; the last word I heard from him he was on a walk-a- thon touring the U.S.," Marcus giggled.

"Who organized this—Well I'll just be damn, Mr. Kanin," abruptly Dan was pissed off, "you almost had me going there—for a moment. You—smart—ass." Slap. He smacked Marcus in the mouth.

"Now—w, do you think that your memory is a little clearer?"

Quiet anger rose inside Marcus as he stood wiping away the blood that dribbled from his lip.

"Your brother, does he still work for your father's firm?"

"No. He does not," Marcus said hesitant then went on to elaborate.

"Chris is sort of a strange breed. An unconventional type you might say. The kind that keeps to himself. He split town immediately after dad died. No one has heard from him since. God knows where he's at. This crime that he's accused of—did someone get killed?"

"We won't know until all of the facts are brought out."

"Go, on."

"We have reason to believe that your brother was involved in the robbery that took place at Armsted Nuclear Base."

"You mean the robbery that took place a while back? The one that was so aired over the news?"

"Yes. That's the one."

"You're crazy. Chris would never involve himself in a work of evil like that."

"The persons face taken from our positive drawing shows a parity to your brother. And from the latest communication that we've gathered there's all sorts of grounds for belief pointing towards him. To be honest, he's the prime suspect whose involved in this case. Is your brother a very vandal person Mr. Kanin?"

"Chris wouldn't harm a fly."

"That remains to be seen. So you have no idea where your brother can be found right?"

"No. I do not."

"A family so small, you must keep in touch with each other? Your story appears rather shaky don't you think?"

"Just because there's only three of us it doesn't mean that we never quarrel. And quarreling—we've been really going at it lately. My sister and I. We've been discussing the hopeful business that we might receive in the coming years. However, instead of becoming malcontent and drawing knives against the other, we try to find cooperation by taking a fleeting leave of absence from each other."

"It seems—Mr. Kanin—that you are not willing to cooperate with us. Or—you staidly do not know of your brother's whereabouts. But whatever the truth may be, we have no election but to place you and your family under the suspicion of robbery and murder."

"Wait a minute," Marcus' shock spread. "Let me get this right. Besides Chris, me and my sister too, are under suspicion?"

"That's correct," Dan replied.

"No—way—man," Marcus roared vulgar. "You must be out of your fucking mind."

Quickly inner voices coached him to calm down. Why are you standing there arguing with that dipshit. You've studied almost every aspect of criminal law. Use what you've mastered to get him off your back.

"I don't think that you realize the total size of your brother's crime, Mr. Kanin?"

Momentarily Marcus' cocaine high apparently faded away. Urgently he now felt a sense of duty to protect his brother's precious name.

Standing brazen faced quickly he assumed the position of a pungent defense attorney. "What crime?" he interrupted the churlish agent whom acted so in control of himself. "I wasn't aware that Chris had been convicted of one yet."

"Can I and my partners here, borrow a couple joints from ya," Dan asked evading what he'd just overheard.

"Help yourself," Marcus said.

"Thanks. It gets awful boog out there again and again chasing thousandaire thugs with nothing to get excessive strength from. And that stuff is too high to buy on the streets. It's even higher with this panic going on up here in northern California. By the way Mr. Kanin, how do you get your hands on such a large supply? Never mind. You don't have to answer that. Because as you attorneys say—on the grounds that it might incriminate you. You don't have to see us to the front door either. Enjoy your party."

Quite relieved knowing that the authorities had departed for the night Marcus phoned Pitney and related the hot paltry information to her.

Two days later Pitney contacted Chris overseas and gave him an account of what Marcus had told her.

CHAPTER FIFTEEN

Occasionally Chris (alias Jean de Masi) found protection in dating. But because of whom he was dating he found it in his best interest to keep his current affair a secret. However discreet he'd been in the past with the private fling that he was having with UN Ambassador Harvey Bristol's wife, such a romantic band would soon be caste in the public eye.

On this selective Saturday night there was a revel being thrown for the Ambassador's wife's extraterritorial notable friends. Added to the guest list of the VIP's whom was to attend, Ambassador Bristol had reserved the presence of Monsieur de Masi: 'The homosexual' retail store owner. An unverified whisper that had been spread around town by curious peers of Jean's.

On the move as the servant girl directed Jean to the host of the party Jean marveled at the expensive décor of the Bristol tower.

Wow. A castle. Fit only for a king. Jean simultaneously recollected the amorous moment that he and the Ambassador's wife had shared—a week ago—in bed together.

"Well, well," the Ambassador exuded a grin to his friends, "if it isn't Paris' most prominent businessman in the area of 'female' fashions; Monsieur de Masi."

It became quite obvious to Jean as they examined him from head to toe that maybe the Ambassador had briefed them—before the party— about him being gay.

For a stuffed ten minutes or more Jean had to be cool restraining himself from vexation as he listened to the Ambassador converse about a homosexual corps Captain whom he knew that committed suicide when his boyfriend went straight.

Once the party had begin to swing Mrs. Bristol decided to borrow her shifty lover and show him off to a few of her girlfriends.

When meeting Margerie—simultaneously Jean sparked a warm conversation with her.

They chatted and after Jean had strayed a few feet away Margerie remarked to her friend, "I wonder if the rumors really true girl, that he has pudding in his pants?"

"Marg—" Dorian appeared embarrassed.

"Excuse me for a moment honey," Jean said to Mrs. Bristol then he switched his tail up close to Margerie. "My dear, dear, Margerie," he said in a feminine tone, "I had no idea that you were so interested in my sex. But to ease your curiosity, I'll let you in—on the real untold story. There—'is'—pudding—in—my—pants. It comes in a round container. A container that resembles the shape of a silver dollar in diameter. And it extends beyond the length of a foot ruler. How'd you like to spread your legs and let me drive about twelve inches—of—it— inside your old weakened body. I convince you, once you sample a good pivot from this top choice D_A prime beef, you'd know exactly 'what kind' of pudding—I have in my pants."

"Gee whiz," Margerie said drooling. "He's a classic. A real genuine classic. Now that my panties are steamed, cue me in Dorian; how many ways does he go?"

"Envy, darling. That's what I call real envy." Dorian blushed luckily then breathed to Jean as she led him away, "You really jolted her honey. Now she's standing there looking like shit melting on a stick. Oh Cindy," she sprightly attracted the attention of another friend." I would like for you to meet this gentleman here; he's the designer of most of my apparel. Monsieur de Masi—this charming lady—is Madame Cindy Langston."

"Bonsoir Madame Langston," Jean kissed her hand.

"Bonsoir Madame de Masi. Oops. I'm sorry. It's Monsieur de Masi. Right?"

"Only my bathtub knows for sure," Jean replied sheepishly. "And if that doesn't satisfy your curiosity maybe you can visit my boutique one evening—be sure it's after closing hours—and who knows—you just might experience the ultimate thrill. But I warn you, not many 'old farts—your age—' have ever survived such a pipe fitting sensation."

"Thank you for your kind invitation Monsieur de Masi," Cindy said. "However, I'm not a gimmicks person. I desire the real thing. A steel pipe would fit me fine; you know what I mean?"

Jean started to walk away then reversed his decision. "Please forgive me Madame Langston, if I'm being too nosey;" he said in a soft voice, "but while you're speaking of the real thing, your face lift darling, the person who dispatched surgery on it, must've been an alcoholic whom was suffering from a bad case of nervous hands."

"Well, I never," quickly friends had to restrain Madame Langston as she attempted to brutally assault Monsieur de Masi.

While standing over in an adjacent crowd suddenly Ambassador Bristol seemed stunned. He'd overheard part of the conversation that'd caused the brief disturbance and he now pondered quietly to himself was it true, those rumors that had been spread around town 'that Monsieur de Masi was queer?'

Could such idle gossip possibly be some sort of a diversion?

Behind his feminine gestures there was also a hidden intrigue that led the Ambassador to wonder what truly was Monsieur de Masi's sex preference.

As Jean and Mrs. Bristol went over to greet another couple the Ambassador spoke to one of his private guards, "Benson, my friend Monsieur de Masi there has me baffled. For some strange reason—I feel that he's playing a con game on us. So just to play it safe—in the near future—employ someone to keep a close watch on him. There could be a long list of spicy secrets hidden—that the glamour boy there with queer habits—does not want us to uncover."

"Leave it to me Ambassador," Benson said. "I'll keep a surveillant watch over him."

CHAPTER SIXTEEN

1986

Monsieur Philippe de Broglie was a person who was rather renowned for having a mordacious animation to seduce many women. Philippe also believed in free love. And without reservations he enthusiastically promoted his philosophy 'that variety was the spice of life.'

Often as a reminder that he still was a Casanova he'd quietly create a stir by trying to party in the panties of any female whom would cater to his silly little propositions.

With calculating mannerism Klara had found it to be very easy to win his trust. But in private she'd labeled him a chauvinist weakling.

However, unmoved by the fact that she was manipulating him, Philippe was totally influenced whenever she was in his presence. And because of his industrious desire to possess her she'd eventually be the reason why he'd go bankrupt.

A newsy report had briefly surfaced and then halted in the community where Philippe subsisted—and held a title to a business— that there might imminently be a commitment by hoodlums to rob— possibly a bank—financial—preserve—or an unknown money storehouse that kept huge tempting amounts of cash on its premises.

Since there 'd been one apparel plant robbery in Beilla that had been efficiently realized by unknown thugs, particular interweaving plant owners had taken the providence of protecting their goods. They were in hushed suspense that someone again might attempt to pull a heist of the sort on one of their businesses. One or two garment makers had purveyed themselves with some of the most neoteric devices that were usually used to protect property.

Not only had some of them had set in plain sight around their work site electrical wire fences, but they'd also intensified their number of security forces.

And dissimilar to the irregular vault system that'd been purchased by Monsieur de Broglie, Monsieur Mascarin had set at his concern a planned premeinheimer model no.—7-635-4 vault.

Once developed it'd been styled with non-penetrable steel and a cybernated interlocking door. And in the particular case that an outsider would try to meddle with it, it had a friction alarm that would decisively communicate signals by mum radio waves to the company's protection unit that was stationed on the plant grounds.

Next if one shunned those deterrents, surround the plant, before catching sight of the vault, one would come up against the seemingly unhostile faces of four well-trained Doberman attack dogs.

Consolidated with these minor obstacles, station just for the thugs, nearby, on the flank of the plant, there would be set up a decoy attack—guard unit. The decoy guard unit would be a radar alert unit that had a programmed robot handling the command of it. Its purpose would be to perceive any alien oncoming traffic—that it had not been programmed to let pass—and consequentially transmit signals to the real attack unit. Four plant owners leased the services of such defense units in the towns near Aix and Beilla, France.

Klara had assembled most of the info just stated from Monsieur de Broglie. He'd gotten ripped over at her house a few months prior to her web of intrigue and brought to light personal data when comparing his vaults model to Monsieur Mascarin's newly set up much highly proficient model vault.

Even though he was tremendously poppied Philippe showed a sullen attitude about his model not being as elaborate as his friend Monsieur Mascarin.

By now Klara had prospered working her way into (as some employees had labeled her) a self appointed imperial king there at the de Broglie clothing factory.

She'd fulfilled such an initiative simply by being magnetically glamorous—and awe so intimately chatty whenever Monsieur de Broglie was near.

Beyond the achievement she'd began thinking about the decisive details on a stratagem that would yield her and her mate enough medium of exchange that probably the two could retire off of?

Exclusively gaining access to Monsieur de Broglie's shipment orders, she ran across the outlet that he'd contact whenever he wanted to purchase his greatest number of dress material.

It was a costume plant—warehouse that was located about two hundred and fifty miles south of them. There also were two other cloth distributors in that same local.

Being the cheaply sales outlet that distributed goods to most of the apparel concerns in southern France, 'this would be the perfect spot to hit.' Klara beamed with excitement over the idea.

In the interim she contacted Chris to confirm whether or not he was still interested in the deal.

Chris agreed to it, that upon delivery of the goods, he'd pay her five hundred thousand dollars for a million and a half dollars worth of wearing apparel.

Quickly Klara made out the orders for a king-size shipment of the freight that was to be shipped from the commercial outlet to their company.

That night at Stephen's apartment she detailed to her general partners in crime the place—the calculable time of arrival—and pickup—by their house careerism vehicles; the trucks color description, and their intended return route.

Embodied in such an intrigue, unconscious to the other criminals Klara and Stephen had supplementary information about the Mascarin compound.

Stored inside the vault where he kept his patterns for garment making, there was also blueprints for semiconductor chips that were to be marketed by a French concern, for advance use in the telecommunication industry.

The Russians had gathered this information earlier targeting Philippe to siphon such info from. And in the meanwhile they'd commission Klara to see to it that such a well guarded secret, remain secret.

Since he'd been advised on how each factory district was safeguarded, and how their warning systems worked, Stephen had conscientiously familiarized himself with the many different aspects involved with such well tried methods used for protection—and he'd presumed how he'd get past that kind of defended material stuff.

Accordingly, for the pretext, he'd bring along with him the provisions he'd need to gain an unlawful entry to such a compound.

Also meticulously calculated in their plan they'd taken the preventive foresight in diagraming every little detail concerning their escape route from the plant once the job was finished.

Such being the case they'd ruled out any sudden staggering reversals that could be caused by inimical individuals who'd probably be protecting the plant owner's goods. The wicked duo had taken into account that if a problem did arise, it could result in their possible capture. Henceforth putting an end to either of their witty homicide careers.

Klara had also rigorously planned that the shipment of garments would reach her confederations intended target area around 7:30 p.m. that same evening.

Because it would be nightfall she'd calculated that such a conceal would make it much easier for her friends to pull off the robbery.

4:00 p.m. two days later the de Broglie company vehicles began loading up their shipment of garments.

Hot from one of his booze-hound friends who was in the defense forces in Montpellier, Ingras had the authorized sanction to pursue their caper in a military vehicle.

Around 5:40 p.m. the trucks began their onward course.

Outside Aix city limits Ingras affiliated safely into the traffic behind the de Broglie guard.

Once the network had traveled about seventy five miles the driver of the rear vehicle experienced a feeling of morbid excitability.

It was after he'd gazed a few times into his ridge mirror that he observed that out of all the ongoing traffic not once had the military vehicle traveling behind him had tried to pass.

The guard kept forwarding driving to a scarcely traveled highway that led to the de Broglie factory, and made their turn.

Precipitously as Maner was about to warn the vehicle driver in front of him Ingras blasted the engine speeding then colliding into the startled young man.

With a thunderous clunk he again rammed Maner's rear bumper.

Hastily while traveling in a state of fright accident prone Maner had straddled the lanes.

In retaliation Ingras maliciously ensued the vehicle.

Driving with their engines roaring up to high speeds again Ingras thumped Maner's vehicle this time forcing him off the road.

Hot tempered Ingras winged up beside Maner's vehicle allowing Michel enough time to blast the left window out.

Assuming that his friend's brains got splotched outside with pieces of the flying glass from the impact of such a blast the driver of the vehicle whom viewed the act now assured himself that if he wanted to live he pertinaciously must become serious in making a run for cover wherever cover might be found.

As he'd originally began picking up speed there was revealed in front of him a truck blocking the roadway.

In a phase of dread he kept going first whacking broadside into the parked vehicle then he jack-knifed off the side of it and was crippled to a standstill about ten yards off the road.

The driver sat soundless for a moment then when realizing that he wasn't traumatized, slit or slashed he sprang out of the truck and made a run for it.

In a second Stephen loosened a flame thrower.

On the dot Hupert's body was ignited with flames.

Immediately—scorching hot—and screaming—with nerves he jetted about seventy yards and abruptly collapsed.

Hastily Ingras' group began unloading the clothing merchandise onto their vehicles.

When the trucks were loaded Michel and Marcello headed for Montpellier with the heisted load of goods. The highway plunderers then sped off in the direction of the other plant they'd targeted to rob.

10:30 p.m. that same night.

Once they'd turned onto the highway leading to the Mascarin establishment, with an infra red scanner, Stephen searched to the left—then slowly moved his lenses focusing them in front of him.

About a thousand yards up ahead of the group and about a hundred feet off the road there sat an armored vehicle.

That has to be the decoy unit? He thought to himself.

Not taking any chances Stephen triggered his hand carried silencer laser missile.

Upon collision the vehicle became engulfed in flames.

When passing up the ablaze pile the group delayed their movement momentarily to let Ingras shoot his M.I.G. 7 Point 45 water propellant gun. It was a hand carried projectile that had been pointedly designed to shoot shells made up of chemical foam that would extinguish fires at close range.

The immediate action which took place next was simply a routine. The armored guard unit which was paid to patrol the plants was now only a half mile away.

They jetted down the road, made a hasty turn, and moved on to the premises.

Quickly Stephen enacted his radio wave distorter.

As Stephen and the band of thieves stopped to try to gain entry to the middle complex, the guard unit was reverberating their sudden radical counter-revolutionary attack.

Aerobic trained, using a trampoline, Stephen navigated himself across the fence.

Before the defense unit would perform their assault he had only moments to disarm the electrical flow of current in the fence.

Exhilarated and aggressively ready for combat the guard unit sped up behind them zeroing in on one of their vehicles.

Before Braun could shoot his miniature model 20 point 6 laser howitzer the protect unit let off numerous rounds of ammunition into the back of his truck.

Screwed up sitting viewing the remains of Braun's brains that had spattered onto his jacket, quickly panting, Ingras became an ugly destroyer.

Hoping to even the score, he aimed in sweet revenge squeezing off a round from his hand carried M-72 Law.

Amazingly the guard's armored vehicle was not damaged.

Momentarily Ingras was terrified; then, rapidly, he started firing his automatic weapon until its barrel caught fire and exploded.

The defense unit's vehicle had been planned with a diagrammed bullet proof shield protection that had been tested numerous times and proven striking against attacks by small scale bazooka model weapons.

While Ingras had momentarily slowed the protect unit down Stephen had been allowed enough time to position himself at his weapon.

Precipitantly—Smack. Like a thunderclap the vehicle went up in flames. But before the hideous clash had occurred, sensing that his vehicles was already doomed, Ingras had desperately made his escape.

According to the range of a target Stephen's weapon had been planned to penetrate up to ten tons of steel. Also depending upon the fabrication of an armored vehicle there were times when its ultimate effects would be delayed.

Setting the gage on high velocity he let go with a round.

Within a quick thirty seconds the weapon had recharged itself.

He observed momentarily that he had not damaged the vehicle.

He fired another round.

The defense unit's modified model DC-50 armored vehicle suddenly became a burning incinerator.

Exasperating, chilling, moans and screams of help, resounded in the darkness—coming from the group whom were bottled up inside the burning incinerator.

Once inside the factory the dogs became the robber's targets.

Scattered in front of them they dined on steaks that had been treated with a potent tranquilizer.

Within moments, with both eyes closed, they allowed the primed thieves to proceed, unharmed, while they committed the robbery at Mr. Mascarin's garment factory warehouse.

Using a soundless explosive Stephen quickly broke loose the vaults spin-wheel, then with a miniature computer, he recorded its combination digits.

The lawbreakers hadn't persevered the safe's resistance but a quick five minutes and the felons had taken the cash and began loading up the garments.

While finishing the job the clique was again council on how to preserve their freight until it was a safe time for them to have it delivered to their buyer. The group had been told to keep their heist stashed on a pier in an abandoned hold owned by a friend of theirs that lived outside Montpellier.

The felons survived down under a period keeping a keen awareness as to when it would be safe for them to advance with their business endeavor.

Soon realizing that the heat had cooled and the job was a success, Klara and Stephen headed in the direction of Paris.

Meantime, while en route, coming in proximation of the city of Lyons, the duo flowed toward a roadblock blocking their access to the city.

As they neared the group of officers their hearts thrashed in fear.

Once idled, directing his eyes in suspicion the short stubby policeman asked them for their I.D.s, "Could I see your passports please; Madame? Monsieur?"

In combination to her disguise Klara had brought along a photo to match her description. Stephen used his unvaried passport.

"How long have you been staying in southern France," the officer asked curiously staring a straight face at Stephen.

"About a year," Stephen replied.

"And, you miss. I see that you are a native of northern France. What brings you this far south?"

"I grew tired of the congested city life in Paris. So I decided to search for a smaller community; one, which I could find less happening around me all the time."

"And in which of our little provinces did you find this freedom in, Madame? That's if you don't mind my asking?"

"Oh—no. Not at all. Marsailles. Presently that's where I reside. And I hope to make it my home."

"And you, monsieur, I presume that you too have found freedom in Marsailles?"

Speaking with a Mississippi drawl Stephen pinched Klara on the cheek then replied, "The smile on my face says it all; I love your country; France is the place to be. And I'm also madly in love with this here little beautiful French woman." Klara respectively consented taking on the role of his lover by unassertively laying her head over on his shoulder.

"You can go. Next—" The officer let them pass then ordered his partner to copy down their vehicle plate numbers.

Automatically Stephen felt that they should abandon their auto which had drawn the composed officer's attention.

Touring around the city of Lyons imminently they found a prey.

As the dean gentleman sat squeezing the last sip from a bottle of liquor Klara approached him, "Hey pops; how about sharing your drink with a lady huh?"

Through a formless vision the old man saw what appeared to have been a female then quickly everything went faint on him.

The felon's ride to Paris now should be fine sailing all the way.

The following morning after arriving in Paris they found Monsieur de Masi at his home detaining a guest for breakfast.

Appearing to be a snuggle zestful tenant Klara sat at the table.

"What's for breakfast," she encroached while snatching up a piece of bacon off the tray. "I'm starved."

"Food—slut," Jean's lady friend said riled up then she whispered incensed, "she didn't even wash up."

"What did you say," Klara gritted her teeth. Dorian sat quiet.

"Whose this old worn out battle ax," she asked Stephen in a low voice.

"Calm yourself Klara," Jean began to act as an arbitrator. "She just asked were you going to wash up before joining us here at breakfast," he gave her the fish eye suggesting that it was the comprising thing to do.

"Who invited this—piece—of leftovers—to—breakfast," In a stew Klara continued to be even more insulting scrutinizing Mrs. Bristol.

"Well, I never," Mrs. Bristol scowled unsavory.

"Ladies please—s. Calm yourselves; for a moment," Stephen ventured in the role of being a referee. "Klara you're entirely out of order. This lady is a guest in Monsieur de Masi's home. You could show her a little human decency, if nothing else. I feel that you owe her an apology."

Favorably impressed a euphoric smile quickly appeared on Mrs. Bristol's face.

Painfully harassed Klara sat uneasy momentarily.

About the time that Mrs. Bristol's overweening pride was back to normal, Klara had recharged. "You're right, Mr. Boyd," she said peppery. "I do owe an apology; but not to this—wig—wearing—false— teethed—jackass—sitting—there—at the end of the table." She now held Jean's chin, "I'm sorry darling; please forgive me?"

Feeling that she was under attack Mrs. Bristol tore away from the table and charged upstairs.

"Why'd you have to make a scene like that?" sitting with veins twitching in his forehead Jean spoke as if he'd become a great deal offended by Klara's actions.

"Fuck off man," Klara roared in homicidal mania. "We're the ones whose out there getting blood on our hands;" her speech faltered, "making your pocket book fat; not that bitch." she hesitated.

Jean stared at her virulently.

"Man you've really got some nerves," Klara endured, "sitting there looking like a well groomed pervert—wining and dining that— old— dilapidated—broad. And you're such a sweetheart—who wants me to apologize to her—for sitting at the table and didn't wash up. Well if that's what you want, you are as insane as she is."

Fast Jean sensed how down in the pits she seemed therefore he immediately digressed from the subject, "I didn't mean to sound so insensitive Klara. Obviously you're under a lot of pressure. Tempers can occasionally flare, when living under such stress. You agree?"

Klara stared at him contemptuously.

"Let's be sociable; and forget about the little scene that was created here this morning. Okay?"

Around 1:00 a.m. that night as Jean was attempting to seduce Klara suddenly she became slumberless. She'd become quietly jumpy because her command had ordered her to enact another unreliable mission for them. This time her target would be an American agent whom was posing as a French Ambassador. With the information and infra red film that he was carrying the Ambassador could've been considered enormously explosive and a perilous threat to Russian secrets. The Body wanted him hit; and hit bad.

"Jean—" Klara laid her head distressingly on Jean's shoulder. "Do you love me?" she probed in earnest uncertainty that she would receive the reply she wanted to hear.

"We have a special kind of relationship," Jean answered involuntarily feeling she was coercing him.

"I guess what I really want to ask you is, do I really mean anything to you? Are we really close?"

"You're very close to me," somewhat restrained, he encouraged her. "You are as dear to me, as; as, my sister."

"I'm glad to hear that," Klara straightway relaxed on the bed.

She grew quiet for a moment aspiring to soften the tension that was riveting at the back of her mind.

"Since we are such good friends, why don't you do a good friend a favor?"

"Go ahead, shoot," Jean was cool.

"Why don't you lay with the Ambassador's wife the weekend and try to gather a little information for me? Do you think that you could handle that?"

"What kind of information are you talking about?"

"Info about an Ambassador staying at the American Embassy here in France. He goes under the name of Ambassador George Yukner."

"Klara there were very few risks involved in keeping your line of work a secret. But when it comes to me—"

"I'm glad that I could confide my secrets in you," Klara interrupted fast. "But there you go yacking again. How many favors do you owe me?"

Jean didn't respond.

"Was there any thing that you ever requested of me that I did not see to it that it was done?

"No—o. But how can you ask me to involve myself in a line of work that I've never had any training for?"

"I'm not asking you to become a hired killer. I'm asking you to do me a favor? When I stood guard over the jewels, and robbed garment factories for you, I was really doing you a favor. I did so by guarding your interest—with my life."

"You were also getting paid."

"That dough you gave me, ha, ha—a; it was peanuts. Especially in my line of work. I helped you, because—e; you're, you're, not just a lover to me, you're also a friend. Someone I care for very deeply. Can you understand what I'm trying to say?"

"Since you sound so convincing, I guess I can."

"Will you help me then?"

Affected warm hearted Jean smiled while biting her on the breast, "I'll—get—on—it—as—soon—as—possible."

A few days passed.

During Mrs. Bristol's next visit to Monsieur de Masi's home Jean became a liaison discussing the politics of how one might become an Ambassador.

Unaware that she was being employed to tell all Mrs. Bristol would spill her guts about the French Ambassador whom was 'sharing quarters' at The American Embassy where 'her husband' had tremendous clout. She boasted to Jean and had expressed such words to others numerous times.

In the meanwhile Monsieur de Masi was delivered the garments.

Stephen possessed his legal tender for services conveyed and boarded a plane where his destination was unknown.

Klara stayed behind. "I have to get my passport in order," she said good-bye to Stephen remotely aloof.

During Ambassador Yukner's boorish stay at the Embassy his typical behavior covered everything from political meetings; banquets; social gatherings, to a night out on the town.

Assuredly he was accompanied by an armed guard. Whom coincidentally happened to be a female. She deceptively posed as his wife during his general public and sequestered appearances.

Cast as a double agent Yukner had lay open to the C.I.A. the names of a certain number of Russian operatives whom were working in the U.S.

He'd also spread to the U.S. information concerning how Russia's military programs were progressing electing to transmit to officials inner plant and aerial view photos of their most influential nuclear development plants.

The Embassy was Yukner's lid during his stay in Paris until the photos were developed then smuggled by American officials to The Department of Atomic Energy in Washington, D.C.

For two days Klara watched the social contact going to and from the Embassy.

The next day, feeling a darn bit frustrated, she'd almost withdrew her conviction then about two thirty p.m. there appeared a jobholder leaving the Foreign Commission who resembled her.

With supplement touches of eye shadow, a splash of makeup— here—and there—I could easily pass for her. Hushed she considered such a veil.

The unsuspicious easy mark continued walking in the direction of her apartment.

Fast constrained about five blocks down the street, criminally poised, poking the nozzle of her automatic handgun softly to the scared stiff maid-servant's back; Klara introduced herself to the young lady.

"Hi. My name is Imlay. Don't even think about screaming. If you do, you'll be featured in tomorrow's headline news."

They walked cautiously up a step—up a flight of stairs to the moiler's apartment. Once inside within a while the young woman seemed to have become a bit more calm.

En route Klara had promised her that she wouldn't harm her if she gave her the information that she needed to get her job done. This info covered the helot's employment around the Embassy; entry procedures, also where the Ambassador slept.

A few hours passed and with the help of the maid Klara sat with frayed nerves while diligently learning the proper dialect she'd need when portraying her role as the villein.

In the interim they had a bite to eat and Klara tied the peon up.

The following morning Klara allowed her hostage to relax for a moment and during such a period of solace she permitted the young woman to prepare them both breakfast.

After feasting on ham, boiled eggs, toast, cereal and milk, she again tied the maid up and upon leaving she assured her that someone would come around soon and rescue her.

While pursuing her mission no obstacles would prevent Klara from entering and safely exiting the commission.

Portraying the maid Klara labored competently doing her chores.

In the intervening time she kept to herself clearly letting her coworkers know that she was in a bad mood; and didn't want to be bothered.

7:30 a.m. Without being noticed Klara must now move fast.

Phobic yet hedging forward, she inserted her key, then creeping, she turned the knob on the door that led to the Ambassador's room.

Once through the living room, while stationed in a small archway she intercepted an amplitude of arduous whines coming from the room where the Ambassador and his escort lay engaged in sexual misconduct.

Fear seemingly emerged out of nowhere. Like a thunderbolt, incalcuable, an unfamiliar feeling of terror crept over the Ambassador.

As he was about to leaven himself—to catch a breath of fresh air, within those split few seconds, an obscure fate startled him.

With repeated outbursts of firing from Klara's silencer revolver— inside a few moments—the Ambassador and his bodyguard lay dead.

More than an hour faded when the bond-woman's co-workers detected foul play and admonished the duty officer asking him to look into her mysterious presence.

Time was significant during the officers inquiry as to whom might have murdered the Russian secret agent there at the commission.

Time was equally important to Klara. During the hour or so that had hurried past she'd packed her belongings and was almost ready to kiss France farewell.

Before leaving for the air terminal she walked into Jean's bedroom— where he and Mrs. Bristol lay undressed.

"Well, my love, since this will be our last day together, we might as well make it a fun filled one. You—know—the—kind— of—action—I'm —talking—about—bedroom scenes filled with— forbidden games— and triple excitement...."

Peeping from behind a sheet that she'd now covered herself with Mrs. Bristol developed a sudden case of fright.

As Klara persisted quickly she began gathering her things together. Klara cheered her on, "Why don't you stay and enjoy the fun moms...?"

"No, thank you," Mrs. Bristol said feeling jilted then hurried past Klara down the stairs.

"What old fashion ideas," Klara said. "And she didn't even say goodbye."

On her succeeding visit to Jean's variety shop the Ambassador's wife wore secret shades where, behind them, an individual could visibly detect that her eyes were bulged all red and blue from what might've burst forth from a fight.

When Jean got a peaceful moment alone with her he found out that the Ambassador had battered out of her as much information relative to the affair she was involved in. And pertinent to Jean receiving stolen property, the Ambassador's operative had seen an eyeful on the sunset that the last load of merchandise was dropped off at the warehouse Jean and his business partner owned. The private eye had also sighted Klara and Stephen being a guest at his home a week or two before the property had arrived.

That jealous bastard has been spying on me. Jean was confused momentarily.

Implausibly, now while finding himself entangled in secret illegal activities, Jean pondered: Whom could I turn to for help, if the authorities came to arrest me? No one. He faced the grim reality of his situation with tremendous shock.

With a deathly look on his face he saw visions of himself interned in a prison someplace—him growing old—and consequently dying there.

I cannot believe that this is happening to me. He argued silently to himself. This—is—madness.

He saw himself as a fleer risking and giving up a normal lifestyle— hasty retreating each time a law enforcement official looked his way. And with each point of time that went past he'd live in habitual fear, that one day he might be captured.

Time now meant everything.

The Premiere was agitated by the ongoing issues.

On the expiring day Ambassador Bristol stopped by Jean's home.

Moderately minded, he'd "come to work out a compromise;" this is what Jean was told. But truthfully the momentarily polite Ambassador was simply trying to cover his ass.

During such an important meeting he meant to save his job at the Embassy and at the same time he was trying to avoid an awful scandal pinned onto him that involved his wife's infidelity.

In the course of their brief chat he expounded to Jean that he would shroud the information he, at present knew about, pertaining to Jean's passing fancy with his wife, if Jean would embrace the idea of leaving behind all the legal tender that he had stored in a French bank; his half proprietorship in the apparel push button plant; and his ware room.

Whereupon it struck the Ambassador that Jean was going to dissent, the constant decent Ambassador quickly threatened him with widening arraignment. Communication that he'd gathered about his blind and barred misconduct there in Paris.

Harvey talked more, fast, lying, telling Jean about how he'd had him under surveillance for several months. And that he'd gathered inside information from a secret service friend of his that Jean was linked to a left wing radical group of French militants whom, in their personal theory, "was the opportunists that devised the robbery of those two clothing concerns in Southern France."

Hence Harvey really shocked Jean when he let him behold photos taken of Stephen and Klara in the course of their stay over at his home.

". . . But since the French authorities have no real evidence linking you to the crimes," Harvey stared him in the face, "it would be in your best interest—and mine—that I dispose of these important bits of information I have in my possession.

If you do things my way, you would be free to depart the country without anyone ever knowing that you played a part in these crimes.

And as an additional favor, I will also provide amnesty for you, in one of our neighboring countries."

Jean quickly interjected questioning the Ambassador about how he'd be able to secure amnesty for him in another country.

Tensely pursuing the matter Harvey emphasized that he was influential and powerful enough abroad, "to pull off such a small task."

Retreating intentionally, Monsieur de Masi accepted the Ambassador's offer and pledged to him that he'd never involve himself in such a hazardous vocation; 'not ever again.'

Concisely Harvey told Jean what a determined bad boy he was, all- the-while maintaining such a splendid camouflaged act during his stay there in Paris.

He concluded his chat by cautioning Jean in a grump tone of utterance, "... Your present stay in this city, is—one—week. A week only," he terminated extremely.

After the Ambassador left Chris sat inaudible momentarily.

Swept up in deep concentration he was trying to make sense of his current predicament.

He mentally did brainwork—thinking of his father—bodying forth how sadistic and brutal he was toward him.

His spirit, obviously, is still subsisting? He wondered. That evil predator who keeps building unbearable obstacle courses—courses that hinder me from moving forward. These brick walls—that I have to always try to tear down. I—know—you're—here. You're constantly ravaging my life with inconveniences. Leave me alone. End these plagues—right now.

My brothers getting killed wasn't the problem either. He calmed down a bit. Evidence of your hatred toward me was present, long before then.

Maybe I should have tried to please you by going to college? Even if I would have succeeded—at—becoming—a—failure—it would have been better than being an outcast....

After recollecting on the past and studying the reasons why he believed that his dad disliked him Chris reconciled that the answer was that to a great extent his father was no different than any other human whom had horns deep set besides his ears.

Maybe I'll change my image. He thought noiseless to himself. Yes, that might be the answer.

That night Chris established a connection with an unsanctioned plastic surgeon, who for a tainted fee, would direct plastic surgery work on an individual if that person took the blame for anything that went wrong during surgery.

During the manipulation of performing the dilatory incisional operation there was a passport being made up in Chris' name.

After the one week time frame that the Ambassador had allowed Chris to remain in Paris had faded he spread the news about Chris' unauthorized activities and they immediately put an A.P.B. out on him.

Chris stayed in hiding for more than three months and at the crucial moment he was smuggled out of the country.

Once again settling on foreign soil, sitting hushed, Chris now Mr. Morio 'Geno' Lorenzetti, concentrated on where he'd arrived—at this point—and time—in his life. I wonder, Mother Mary, was I born under a dark sign? My guardian angel's name—must—have—been—named—doom. Yeah, that has to be her name. Because every time I pursue a goal, trouble arises. And like a tumbling pyramid, suddenly everything seems to crumble and fall apart. How in the hell can one man be plagued with so many dark fates? He now inclined his head toward the sky, "If there's anyway possible—please—s, please; try to find someone else to torment with your cruelties."

CHAPTER SEVENTEEN

August 1989

While Chris chilled underground for a moment for over a year Klara, Stephen, Patricia Newmar, and her accomplice Anwar Sabb, had been subdued admirers of Ms. Zina Ali Khan. They now were in the departing stages of thoroughly finishing their intention to liberate her of her enormous bank reserves.

Connective and reverentially rubbing elbows with the gem the duad had transiently met Ms. Khan in 1987 at a London restaurant.

She befriended them and every since she rendered a conversation they'd plotted against her in their current scheme.

Aided by a friend of hers named Randy—Patricia had succeeded at keeping Zina under surveillance.

Distinguishly a person with faggot habits Randy a twenty six year old electronics engineer could've also been suspected of being a goofus priss.

Being a journeyman thief and locksmith it was perspicaciously a fantasy come true when Pat asked him to tag along with Ms. Khan to observe what her daily activities were like.

Within a short while he'd get a chance to pick her locks.

"Wow. Super—" he seemed elated over the idea.

"What an idea. Rocket—jockey." The task of photocopying her passport etc. and passing them on to Pat was exciting. While duplicating those items he knew his moment of ecstasy would arrive.

He would carry the scent of hers for days pending he'd get the chance to sniff her undergarments; cologne; letters, and douche powder. Oh how such a liberal eroticizing act of thinking set fire to his blood.

A blistering Monday, Randy's first day on the job. He inquired about an apartment in the building where Zina lived. Available the same weekend there would be a fancy six and a half room condo adjacent to hers.

After offering the landlord a larger amount than he was asking for as a down payment on the lease Randy secured the studio living and quickly put his plan in motion.

Immediately after moving into the room next to Zina's he bugged her apartment and began listening in on her phone conversations.

After hours of listening then jacking off several times he managed to get her voice down on tape.

Pat's gonna be so proud of me. He said to himself with a pleasant smile.

The reason why Randy and Pat got along so well was that Pat would do awful freaky things with him.

Give you an example? Sure—why not.

Pat would call him up and say to him that she had another dangerous assignment for him to undertake. And as usual, if he took the job, there was a special treat lined up in store for him.

Before taking the Zina Ali Khan case Randy had requested such a treat.

Upon arriving at Patricia's apartment with some info, she didn't hesitate to offer him his gift. In the bedroom anticipating—she'd pasted to her pubic area, six one hundred dollar bills; this would be a down payment for him to start work.

Randy wasn't shaken at all when she told him that she was on her period. He quickly spread her legs apart, sprayed her body with whipped cream, then went searching to find her strawberry fillings.

Going about using ultra precautions Randy watched Zina's every move.

It took only two months and he had gathered the information that his friend needed to complete her scheme.

10:30 a.m. a week later. At First International Bank and Trust Company Patricia Newmar was tyrannically engaged in repair of the computer system in section B-5 on the fifth floor of the bank. She was an employee of Barlowe's Systems Incorporated—hired by the bank to work as a computer technician and programmer.

Side carried in her bag she'd brought along to work with her that morning an evolving micro-miniaturized laser computer circuit unit that was discovered with the hint in mind of tapping into banking terminals and safely re-routing perspective bank account holders assets.

Once Patricia's Mars 4 unit had fast immobilized First International's system, it wasn't sixty seconds before an attached unit had copyedited the information it needed from the master files—quickly clarifying that Zina was still an account holder.

Immediately Patricia's unit disarmed First International's systems alert decoder.

After visually verifying how much assets was in the account the unit then checked all—in deposits—withdrawals—and last it audited the account. Then on a final scan the Mars 4 unit photocopied all information and quickly sent the results back to Patricia.

After she'd read the results she speedily re-entered the systems flowchart locating the master files and filed a false amount increasing the cash reserve that was supposed to be in the account.

12:30 p.m. the trailing afternoon. Escorted by a celebrant friend of hers named Shaun, Klara character dressed as Zina, leisurely trudged up to the teller window at First International.

Within a short while they left smiling to each other with over two million dollars in legal tender on them.

Evidenced the same day at work Pat had a childish innocent look pasted to her face. Her coworkers pondered: What event is she privately celebrating?

En route to take her vertical coffee break she was quite merry with her assistant helpers—constantly feeling a sense of liberation—walking with her heart pounding—slowly toward the elevator that led to the company parking lot.

Anwar greeted her inside—the two rode the elevator to the third level—exited and went to engage themselves in devilish activities around the wide world.

Even though she regretted abandoning her work mates she was highly exultant gloating cock a hoop affirming to Anwar that she'd never have to return to Barlowe's Systems Incorporated to work as a computer programmer again.

The thieve's adrenaline flow heightened.

They divided the loot and immediately dispersed.

On the adjacent sundown the couplet—Patricia and Anwar—boarded a flight and went flying high above the Atlantic. Their destination, England.

CHAPTER EIGHTEEN

December 12, 1989

Throughout the course of his first three months in London Chris worked as a common laborer. He worked long hours at odd jobs with the constant thought in mind that he'd soon become a resident of such a prosperous working community.

One day as he was browsing around an art museum he became interested in a beautiful Italian female.

While marveling at an expensive Van Gogh painting he deliberately hit against her.

A bit bashful and obviously afraid he managed to speak hoping that she wasn't going to embarrass him or make him look like an idiot.

"I'm sorry Madame. I—didn't—mean—to—snag—your—stocking."

The young woman became his personal mentor. Speaking with a linguistic comprehension of the French language and noticing his American diction, she spoke, "Such a come on might've swayed a person during the forties; but not now. Would you care for a brief lecture on how to approach an Italian—British woman."

"Go right ahead," Chris replied.

"Most ladies of the near twenty first century have to be impressed by your present image. First show a little bit of class. If you don't have any, borrow some from someone. Understood?"

"On the contrary," Chris began to perspire, "teach me the principals.

How should one begin his approach?"

"Your colliding into me was no accident. You did it on purpose," she paused.

"Please continue," Chris looked at her with an idiotic stare clamped to his face.

"I'm finished," she said abruptly then stared at him with the snobbishness of a highly arrogant egotistical shit ball.

Chris stood speechless momentarily.

"Gee'z; the little tot—has a stone in his mouth. Want mommy to remove it for ya?"

"Please forgive me;" right away Chris appeared macho, "hi, I'm Chris. I, I mean, Mr. Lorenzetti. Geno Lorenzetti."

"You're not a very good spy you know."

"A spy. What gave you the impression that I was a spy?"

"For two weeks, on each of my visits here, you've been following me; why?"

"I admit—I've frequented this gallery—regularly—within the past two weeks, but in no way was I spying on you," Chris confessed that he was innocent.

"My bodyguard says that you've been watching part of my daily activities. He also says that he caught you one evening straying around our property. What—if you don't mind me asking—do you—be eyeballing in the dark?"

Bodyguard. Hum—m? Chris pondered the reason why she should need the protection of a guard.

"Pardon me Ms." he said, "I can see that you know plenty about my daily routine; so before I get myself into an awful heap of trouble, have you ever considered the possibility that maybe I'm attracted to you?"

"That's normal. Stand in line behind the long list of aristocrat men, here in London, whom also find themselves attracted to me. And since I'm so alluring to those whom have plenty to offer me, what great riches—I'm dying to ask, do you have to offer me? Riches that such an elite group might not possess?"

"Plenty."

"Plenty of what?"

"Plenty of nothing."

"You're in."

"In what?" Chris now looked at her as if she was an oddball.

"My search has finally ended. For years—I've been looking for a gentleman that has your unique qualifications. Your prestige. A man that has 'a position among the peons'. You have nothing; and—plenty—of—it. So plenty of nothing is enough for me. Do you have a pen? Oop—p—s. I forgot. I have one down in here someplace." Stirring up the young woman began searching inside her purse.

What a twist. Chris stared at her momentarily with reluctant admiration. Now she seems like an overdosed lunatic.

It was inconceivable. He never imagined that once he'd made her acquaintance she'd be so—out—to—lunch.

"Here; take this card," she said all-the-while smiling happily. "Call me this evening. We'll have dinner together. It's—on—me."

"Maybe father was right," Chris commented out loud. "About me being weird. Somehow we oddballs always seem to attract one another...."

Geno kept the dinner allurement in mind. And as things turned out he was glad that he followed up on it.

Wrapping up the couple's friendly harmonious evening of getting acquainted Chenelle became an outwitted victim whom allowed herself to be seduced by the graceful guy whom had quickly swept her off her feet.

It was just as mother nature had blue printed it: that these two congenial adults enjoy an indelible night of romance together.

A week vanished. Even though the two had become involved in sexual commerce Chennelle would act chilly towards Geno. Simply because he was precious to her and she had a fixed purpose of marrying the man.

She wrapped herself in a cloak allowing him to only see her occasionally. She was cautious also because she was the only daughter of the formidable boss of the European crime syndicate.

She'd pictured the embarrassment that she'd meet squarely with if ever her father found out that Geno worked as a down scale laborer. For sure, it would cause him to incite prompting him to maybe have Geno thrown out of their house head first.

Yet, faced with her total situation, Chenelle positively had a game plan.

She'd convince Geno that they should go together for awhile and build on their relationship. Such a move would allow her enough time to see to it that Geno would be better established. If he had such a status, she knew it would definitely be a plus when introducing him to her influential father.

. . . However, my timing would have to be perfect. She tried to picture how her father would react when first hailing the activist Mr. Lorenzetti.

A month faded. Chenelle approached Geno congenially agreeing with his plan of setting up a boutique. A workplace like the one he'd mentioned that he owned while living in Paris.

For a brief period Geno embraced the idea then refused her offer. Although when realizing that Chenelle for whatever the reason, believed in him, he felt quite composed, afterwards, asking her to help him get his own modeling agency started.

After intelligently debating whether Geno seemed capable of running such an operation Chenelle decided to go along with his plan.

Geno was persistent getting his business established in less than two months.

Regardless of how ambitious they were to get going, compared to the soft agency that Chenelle ran the two fledging businesses— one that was public—the other one invested in secrecy—would only have in common the use of the name—modeling.

Geno's agency would be operated in a manner to cater to the elite of London; whenever a party needed the services of a call girl; gay partner, or they just wanted to freak out in some chambering untraditional sex manner.

At the first opportunity Geno hired a freelance photographer.

Directly the photographer introduced him to a house full of eye catching ungullible ladies whom would sell their souls to the devil if the price was right.

Plump the ball was rolling in Geno's life.

Through Chenelle's bodyguard he joined one of his friends who made movies who set him up with this underground movie connection based there in London.

Once the momentary snapshots for their cyclical local and international magazines were finished Geno would commit himself behind locked doors to shoot his nude modeling scenes.

Tonight a role player and a favorable inclined female actress would unbuckle their most secret sex fantasies.

The succeeding month the acts that they would have performed would be shown to his movie viewing audiences on nationwide X-Rated screens.

Geno's acts soon became fiendish. He'd now employed several teenage girls whom would debut their bodies managing all kinds of incestious, sodomy, and sadistic acts.

Provoking his desire to become an overnight millionaire Geno's purpose grew. His urban market also grew.

He became so pathetically moved by the number of felonious film distributions he was selling that suddenly there were no acts too rotten for his band to dramatize.

He wanted to acquire big bucks in a hurry. He directed his energies at producing top billing shining pornography films. For it now was a possession to keep flowing with the kind of rubbish that his lustful minded clientele wanted.

It wasn't until he'd employed two thirteen year old girls and presented on screen them having sex with their sick gang that he impulsively realized how much of a fiend from hell he'd become in pursuit of him becoming a success story.

He soon turned to drugs trying to find a way of smudging out the actual reality of the sickness that today existed in his life.

"What have I done? Can someone please answer me?" he shouted struggling with his conscience. "Why should I have such strife and misery cast upon me...?"

His clamoring plea for help rang out with a sense of urgency.

Instantaneously he admitted to himself that what he quickly needed was divine consolement.

He went into seclusion at a church.

For two days he came and sat noiseless straining his mind pondering where he might eventually wind up on the road that he was currently traveling.

The archbishop comforted him.

Inspired by endless despair he appealed verbally for someone to coax him.

While examining the wide world an intense illuminating energy filled his frame and vital force.

He felt momentarily absolute; like maybe he possessed influential qualities.

It was a forceful power—unlike any power he'd been trained to accept.

Something that increased his moral and communicative skills which fast led him to believe that such a present force that was holding residence inside of him was incontestable—The creator?

With decidedly acceptance, from deep within his vital spirit he sought future guidance—advice—and bearing from such a force.

"Authority of the outer limits—and earth: I speak not, seeking mercy, however, I do ask why is there so much chaos in my life? Why can I not stay within the confines of what is considered moral behavior—in the eye-sights—of my fellowman?

I've stooped so low—that I've lost what little respect that I had for myself. And I'm also unable to show any toward my sisters and brothers on this planet. What awful crime—have I committed—that I should deserve such alarming cruel punishment?

Show me evidence of my wrong deed so I might be able to live with this powerful sentence that has been handed down upon me. Have I committed such a humongous sin—by just wanting to become such a small creator? Building structures. Using the natural inborn qualities that I possess as a builder.

My spirit of sanity is fighting against the wicked demon of despair. Awaiting in a hallow corridor of my mind lurks the constant thought of suicide. My emotions have reached a boiling point. I hate all that life has to offer me. Help me to rid myself of the many evils that my father and his ancestry before him evidently were cursed with. Help me to prevent the horrible tragedy that might occur providing that I continue to wander blindlessly in my sickness.

Help me. I'm walking close to suicide. Voices keep ringing out loud. They're telling me to get off the bus—right now. I feel that you'll grant me my wish and that you have put into effect the initial forces to help me combat my problems.

At the second, proof against dialecticism, it was close. Chris had made contact with a powerful irreligious something.

Whereat living on impiternal appercipient as a defective prototype— his petition for relief landed clearly hearable on the ears of a deleterious force whose been bringing forth menticide to individuals for many centuries.

To balk or continue walking, as far as providing therapy and protection for Chris his gist—the aspect of such—and his pulverized matrix was thrown to seemly sound contrarious—eristical thug spirits.

Special entrancer's, who left him wimpled whereby he could persist being ablative—troubled and a jinxed aesthetic cut.

CHAPTER NINETEEN

January 1990

"That's it. Move in a little closer," Geno instructed a male actor who should've paid attention to his script.

"Keep it up," he insisted.

With faltering steps he maneuvered the camera lens to where there was a retake panoramic shot of a blonde's vagina.

"Action," he shouted.

The camera at one swoop began showing the over excited couple present passionately making out.

Plaintively shrieking tearful whines of pleasure she began clawing her nails into his back.

Coming to the end of the filming session unexpectedly Chenelle drifted in.

Thinking little or nothing of his surroundings she beaked Geno daintily on the cheek with a kiss. "How's work today darling?" she asked.

"It's our everyday normal routine sweetheart," he said resentful of his surroundings. "Someone bursting their balls over there. Someone crying out pains of joy over here. Nothing new and exciting going on. How about you? How's your day coming?"

"It's the same old monotonous grind with me. Shopping around town. Visiting my aunt Cecelia in the hospital. Etc. But maybe it won't be such bad news in your life—when I tell you about this brilliant offer that you're about to receive."

"Out with it girl." Obviously he was anxiously waiting to hear what she had to say.

Chenelle hesitated.

"Come on; woman. What—is—it?"

"I talked to dad briefly telling him about your background as a builder."

Geno gazed at her adrift.

"I didn't go as far as to mention your corrupt past; believe me," she tried to put him at ease.

"What—Well, I'll be damned," Geno looked as if a ton of bricks had just been lifted off of him.

"When do I get the chance to meet him?" He was single minded alert to her conversation now. "How about tonight?"

"No way," Chenelle vocalized double quick. "Father will be resting by now. He normally relaxes when he's not busy. You know, go to bed around 9:00 p.m. each night."

"We'll make sure that we catch him first thing in the morning then, huh?"

"In the morning—it—is—" Chenelle terminated.

Quickly Geno closed out the filming session and retired for the night. Once relaxing in bed in his mind he began scheming on a master plan when corresponding with Mr. Diangelo…. What can I show him as proof that I'm a builder? If I expose my background as being the son of building tycoon Gerald Kanin, the authorities would be on my case with the quickness. Man, I have to get on the ball….

The pursuing morning as Geno was about to leave for the Diangelo's someone rapped on his door.

Upon answering it he angle catching a glimpse of the British authorities whom fast acquainted him with who they were then instructed him that they had a search warrant.

During their concentrated search of his premises they unclosed a large quantity of narcotics. And after catching sight of the unallowed contraband they then hooked on to him five counts of felonious fishy conduct.

They would use as evidence at his trial a roll of film projecting from start to finish teenagers tackling sizable unvirtuous procreative acts.

Combined with the weighty charges of white slavery he also would have pinned on to him the charge of sodomy. Even though he was not picturized in the acts that were consistently performed by the actors, consequentially crystal clear, under British law he was responsible for their character actions.

Two months later he was found guilty of his crimes; fined twenty five thousand dollars; interned, and started serving a ten year sentence in captivity.

After Geno had been in custody for nearly five months chiefly pulling a few strings here and there Mr. Diangelo—with a cash incentive— kept wheedling on the cadre until he induced them to let him go.

After being released Geno was to serve a three year period of probation; and Mr. Diangelo was to be totally responsible for his person.

For them having so much faith in him Geno in a hurry felt deeply indebted to the Diangelo's.

Mr. Diangelo kept his promise to the authorities by setting Geno up with the capital to acquire his own building firm.

CHAPTER TWENTY

Mid September 1990

For the former two months Geno has been committed to choosing a qualified group of employees to work for his firm. During the time- binding process he was introduced to fifty or more promising diverse and thrown out of work applicants to fill the job positions he had open.

Up to the minute faced with ever changing advance techniques in the building trade industry he'd be faced with the belabored task of selecting individuals with almost master talent to produce the in-demand products.

Singly when a fit group of cortege had been formed Geno's weight would be to find out of three promising architect prospects, one good one.

Rear to the conscientious screening of Patroni, and then Mangelli, it was then decided that their price was too high leaving him with no other alternative but to choose another prepared individual.

Before leaving France while having a conversation with Klara she had told him about Patricia Newmar's background as a computer whiz and how she'd better advanced and finished their daring scheme against Zina Ali Khan. Since she was at this instant exiled in England and had come to him seeking to fill the position, Geno saw no reason why he shouldn't grant her the chance.

Once Geno had informed Patricia that the job was hers she accepted however demanding that as an extra perk Geno would have to hire her friend Anwar.

Giving her request his undivided attention all-the-while considering at the moment that Anwar would not be paid for his employment, Geno fast decided, why not? Really he was impressed that she'd recommended him. In that case he took on two employees for the price of one.

Patricia would work in the work drawing office where she'd be in charge of scale modules; blueprints; layouts, and system and components design. Anwar's office space was set up adjacent to hers. There'd also been an unqualified person added to Geno's list of employees; Stephen Blass. He'd been in exile in the country for nearly a year and had contacted Chris for work after he'd seen the job advertisement in the paper.

Being tutored by Geno his position would cover the areas of research and project management. Of course, Geno and Chenelle's duties would comprise of existing as the business executives.

Christopher Kanin, a man with such inevitable ambition, his moment of repute and glowing, had finally loom in sight. He knew that once he'd been given the chance to create on his own the rest would be easy.

While sitting alone in his living room he was calm and felt whole. Swept up—a warm sense of accomplishment surfaced in his heart.

For a complete hour, he would lay buried in an awless, meditative, slumber, really swaddle; enjoying the most fabulous kind of a mighty charge.

Ready and willing Chenelle had set fire to an all out campaign on sales planning; publicity, and sales promotion.

After contacting fresh client after prospective client Geno endured very many bids and put pen and ink on numerous deals.

When he initially started the business secretly unknown to their close friends, Chenelle and Geno were also working as estate agents and leasing brokers. Such negotiations would be a huge part of their business that resulted in them having a stable cash flow. That additional loot increased the band's profits. The prosperity allowed

Mr. Diangelo to have the resources to quickly pay back the interest he owed to his underworld friends.

The cost of some properties they'd lease was on the market priced from $450,000 to upwards of $940,000; and occasionally, four of five million dollars.

A prosperous rewarding adventure quickly was ahead of the beginning firm.

Since Chenelle's hands were full in the management branch it now was suggested that Ms. Newmar be given a farther workload. She would be asked to employ her skills in the areas of marketing; public relations; forecasting; financial control; work study; engineering; component testing; inspection; beam fabrication and assembly.

Annexed to Stephen Blass' workload he'd be privately lectured in the areas of purchasing; building control; inspection; building maintenance; land acquisition; and bureaucratic services.

At the existing time, in charge of more than thirty work personnel, each managing director had their hands full with chores.

Two weeks hadn't moved forward before Patricia had introduced her new methods for designing buildings. Using her Saturn 3 building design innovator computer graphics design set she quickly designed chutes for concrete access that would carry maximum loads in a speedier process than the latest model designed.

Nevertheless after completing such a task she discontinued her experiment until their commercial enterprise had constructed two factories and three housing complexes in Liverpool.

And in the cities of Shefield and Portsmouth Geno's concern built two schools; a factory; and a towering office building. Within one year these projects would've been completed and Mr. Diangelo and Mr. Lorenzetti would start to mature with the sum of two million dollars in their joint bank account.

Leaping into 1992, 93, through 94 after the real estate market had recovered from a slumping economy the immature trailblazers would've had constructed on 90 acres of empty development land a one million sq. ft. mall that cost $173 million dollars; and a 700,000 sq. ft. mall; its cost $140 million. They built a single level festival marketplace with a three story retail store development complex. Adjacent to that there were two 33,000 sq. ft. professional buildings which had installed in them modern energy saving devices. Each building had landscaped grounds with accommodating private roads and freeway access.

They built an affluent subdivision in Kingston Hills.

They leased Victorian farmhouses—country houses—19th century gentlemen residences in Peninsula Heights; Hampsted; Cheshire; Manchester, and The Isle of Man.

There were leasing opportunities and property developments happening near The River Thames and a couple projects in Scotland and Wales.

They built and rehabilitated luxury condominiums and townhouses.

Constructed a quadruple tower center in London.

Built a concern that had a wellness center—child care school establishment, a rehab drug clinic and bill paying center all under one roof.

They rehabilitated properties at St. Katherines Dock. The Docklands. Worked at Jacob's Island Berkeley Homes Development and Canary Wharf.

Mr. Diangelo was highly affected by the productive effort that his future son-in-law had made; and so were the British authorities. They were so seized with this recent superior success that they swiftly referred that his probationary period end. Such an expeditious reprieve was mentioned after it had been forecasted that Geno would soon become a billionaire Realtor developer.

CHAPTER TWENTY-ONE

Currently existing as executives both Marcus' and Pitney's motion towards enacting and transacting business in the building trade industry had dealt a devastating blow to the financial stability of Kanin Enterprises.

And in amplification to the troubles that he was having at the concern Marcus had to square up with yet other financial woes. Because of his permanent whoring around Rachel had filed a writ for divorce and during the ensuing process she'd joined forces with a clique whom were attempting a hostile take-over of Marcus' recording interest.

Since being plagued with such problems the corporation's executive board demanded that Pitney and Marcus work out a solution to their problem of mismanagement, or face the consequences of being ousted from the board.

Pitney would pay Marcus a visit and try to discuss alternatives that might help them to solve their restraining problem.

On this chilly Saturday night as usual there was fun and action happening at the Kanin estate.

As the whoopee and hoopla progressed around 12:30 a.m. Pitney showed up.

She used her key to enter and as she emerged through the doorway she snuffled oozing through the breeze the strong odor of drugs.

As she ventured further inside the left-wing living room there she witnessed a group sitting around engaging heavily in alcohol.

Subsequently while finding her way to the area where Marcus was impound detaining his visitants she had to act snooty with a band of females whom were abusing addictive drugs and made smart remarks about how she was dressed and sought to find out "Whose The Smart Peg that invited her to the party...?"

Then just when she thought that she'd encountered the greater number of obstacles that were in her way, before seeing Marcus on the dance floor, she had to ruthlessly shove a young man whom had forced his way on her and was turned on wrestling and seductively pulling her body up close to his.

Embarrassed and wilt from struggling with the paranoid brute quickly she interfered with Marcus' dance, "Could I see you for a moment? Please—If you don't mind?" Pitney combated hard to keep a stiff upper lip.

Momentarily Marcus tried to snub his sister. Continuing to dance he chatted more frivolously yakkety yak with the blonde he was coming on to, "If it's not important sis', I'll be with you in a moment."

"It's important. Very important," Pitney moved about impatiently. "Lake Tahoe—could be fun..." The blonde said ignoring Pitney. "Could you please take a hike?" Pitney yelled fighting an impulse to swear.

The young lady whom was conversing with Marcus suddenly grew quiet and stared at Pitney dwelling on should she smack her to the floor.

"Now that we have a moment of silence, I insist Marc, that we go some place where we can have a talk."

"It's a rare occasion that my sister insists on anything Ms. Posoda. You can lay odds on it, that whatever she has to say, warrants attention. Please excuse me," he kissed his friend sprightly on the cheek. "Enjoy the party. Father Divine will return in a jiffy."

"Marc, how long has this kind of public gathering been going on here at the house?" Pitney stared Marcus in the eyes.

"This is the first party that's been thrown here in over three months sis," Marcus lied on purpose.

Notwithstanding Pitney wasn't impressed. She spoke even tempered all-the-while exerting much of her energy to try to control the anger that was inside her. "En route to finding you, I passed my old bedroom—and I just couldn't believe my ears. It sounded like there were four or five lovemaking animals in there. What are you running here, a bordello?"

"Just some of my friends in the entertainment business," Marcus replied cool as if he didn't give a hoot about what his associates were doing. "They like their privacy. So they can engage themselves in their kinky group activities. But they're all the way live. They never cause anybody any problems."

"From what I can see—it's quite lively all over the place tonight," again Pitney expressed how turned off she was with the scene. "Inside the dance hall area it appeared as if there'd been a drug invasion—in there. You're talking about an exhibition of odd looking characters: they were all bummed out. James Brown was singing, 'Get on the Good Foot' at the speed of 100 r.p.m.'s, and they were surfing to the speed of ten. Oh, how awful weird they looked. But forget them," she said quickly digressing from the subject. "The reason why I wanted to talk to you is—I wanted to know whether you've heard anything from Chris? On all of my attempts to reach him a message keeps coming back saying that he was deported. That's all the information that I can gather over the phone. I even contacted the French authorities and they said that when we find him—they too—would like to know of his whereabouts. Marc—" she took her brother by the arm.

"Come; let's sit down a moment."

They were seated facing each other.

"Do you love me?" she asked sincerely wanting to know what was her kindred's true feelings towards her.

"Why of course," Marcus responded as if she was putting him on.

"I'm serious Marc—do you really love me?"

"Pitney, I love you," struggling to utter such an unused word as "I love you" Marcus sounded convincing enough to his sister.

"Do you love Chris?" not wanting to know the real answer Pitney forced herself to interrogate him on such a subject.

"What provoked you to ask such a dumb question sis'?" By all appearances it was revealed that Marcus was irritated. "Chris is a blood relative. He's someone special."

"Someone special huh. You haven't heard from him since he left— and—and you can sit there—and honestly say, that he's someone special," she uttered riled up. "You certainly have a strange way of proving such a pretense. Why haven't you attempted to find him? And welcome him back home? Is it because you don't have the necessary funds to locate him? Is it because he had trust always confiding in you, and you did everything in your power—to discredit—him as being a man? By robbing him of his many contributions to the firm? Are you torn to shreds because father gave you everything—and gave him nothing…?" Pitney had now began yelling in defiance to how cool Marcus was as she related to their brother. "Have you too—like our mazed dad—labeled him as being incompetent? And a born loser?" As her deranged mimicking exploded out loud in his mind Marcus covered both ears.

"Or is it because you feel guilty about knowing how you cheated and manipulated him. And swindled your way into father's heart— leaving no room open for him to see the aspiring and genius qualities his vernocular son had?"

"Stop it. Stop it." Marcus screamed.

With tears trickling down her face Pitney now calmed her enraged screaming down to the tone of an emotional plea, "What is it Marc; tell me what's with you? How in the hell can you sit there and tell me that you love him—when you know it's not true? Oh, Marc; we're family. Chris is our brother. A person who shared the same bed with you. Played games with you. Ate at the same table with you."

"We slept in the same bed. Played games together. Lived under the same roof. What's so special about that?" Marcus interjected sarcastically.

"You're, you're, incomprehensible," Pitney yelled. "You seem to thrive off of people's emotional traumas. And, and you appear unshackled by your actions." Percipitantly Pitney grew shitty. As she tried to unpin the tension that gripped at her mind she uttered growling words that coursed very fast out of her jaw, "Fucker—You're in—hu— mane." Exempt from blame she then vocalized a final comment. "And vicious—and tough. For all you know—Chris could be dead. And I'm moved—thinking that you really don't even care."

Thrusting steam rapidly erupted all over Marcus' forehead.

Numb and trembling Pitney grasped both hands then the blood relatives grew hushed.

They sat momentarily with feelings of distant emotions being vibrated between the duo.

As the air cooled a bit Pitney began another conversation.

"Now that I've gotten all of that off my chest, what are your plans to bring the company out of the red ink it's submerged in?"

"Red ink. I never realized that the company was in the red," Marcus stared upwards toward the ceiling hoping momentarily that he could avoid the subject.

"Whether you show concern about the problem or not," Pitney stated seemingly tortured, "it still exists. Chairmen of large corporations normally excel in many fields before they're chosen to run a company. They're not chosen by a relative whom feels that one is capable— when—one's—not. Your inaccuracy to perform the duties of a chairman is forcing us into a bankruptcy situation."

"What about your role as a chairperson sis'? I know that the corporation is fully aware of your credibility as being a leader."

"I admit that I could show some improvement in certain areas," Pitney acknowledged. "But you're a complete failure. And you don't even have the guts to admit it."

Marcus' eyes flickered, piercing.

"To be honest," she said, "Chris is the only person whom can help us out of the predicament that we're in. But don't bother. As always, I'll take it upon myself to take the first initial steps toward contacting him. You don't have to worry your cute face about that. Also it will be my final effort to try and maintain what little spark of communication that this family has left to share between us."

There was a brief silence.

"You—are—a—strange—breed—man," Pitney burst out loud. "Even though you're clearly aware that our business interests are crumbling—you won't lend a hand—to see to it—that it doesn't happen. Such thinking, it's hard for me to understand. It seems that all you wish to succeed at is a good time. But don't despair my conning kindred, I believe in Chris. I believe in him as a human being that has sensitive feelings toward another person's plight. And I feel strongly that he'll come to my rescue. But why am I confiding all of this in you? You could care less." Dash—Pitney had a brainstorm. She'd in a second began scheming.

Her first goal would be to oust Marcus as chairman of the board.

She'd brilliantly insert a clause in her father's will that would give her complete control of Marcus' shares of the firm's Class D and E stocks. Aided by other close associates after her plan was in effect she'd contact Martin Goldstein III, 'the family lawyer' whom she'd slept with on occasion, and those parties together would create a scheme which would result in Marcus being demoted.

Marcus would be told that his demotion was because of his incompetency to handle corporate affairs.

He'd be left totally unaware that within awhile he'd be removed completely off the firm's payroll.

"I guess I'll be seeing you in the morning huh?" Pitney shammed.

Free slinging her coat across her shoulders and all-the-while escorting her toward the door, Marcus replied, "Bright and early sis'. I'll be there—bright and early."

CHAPTER TWENTY-TWO

May 1994

Patricia Newmar and Anwar Sabb had their special Science lab section there at the work site. Anwar was into far out avant-garde architecture. He'd managed to design a nine story office building with asymmetrical creations. He mapped out buildings that had loft type space with principal areas normally 40 by 30 with high ceilings.

As the months evolved Patricia would be toying with formulas that dealt with curing processes in concrete to prevent shrinkage and stress; different compound elements combined with steel; computation of advance sheer connectors that relaxed the building's concentrated load; inadequate bracing; studs, and fireproofing. Appearing hyper normal she'd now become theoretically obsessed with her research.

Geno's firm soon began getting newer contracts to build timber steel warehouses; hockey rinks; more schools; gymnasiums, and creek bridges. Thus added a few more million dollars to the Diangelo-Lorenzetti joint bank account.

It had taken Pitney three years and nine months but she'd finally prevailed in contacting Chris. When she told him of her adversity he willing heartedly listened.

In respect to the headache his sis' was experiencing, Chris anxiously set aside his plans, put on ice his express prosperity, and began lending his talent to benefit his family's cause.

With all of his acquired artistry he taught Pitney how to maneuver her skills to win bids from the competition. Also keeping it a secret from his co-workers he even helped her win bids that he could've gotten awarded to his firm.

Foremost he encouraged her to become a leasing broker and to possibly seek a management and financial firm to support their operation. Such an idea would be Pitney's first priority.

By phone and in person he allowed her to use his chief architects to support her with each venture.

By using Chris' top rank entourage and his innovative ideas Pitney would soon begin to bring Kanin Enterprise out of the red ink it was floating in.

During the adverse period of helping Pitney out of her predicament Chris had once again experienced a triumphal moment during his life span. For he was super overwhelmed at the fact that he was able to comfort her and serve her. And at the same time contribute greatly to the well being of his relative's influential name.

Chris' motives for doing what he did never ever mattered to his sis'. She singly had a different motive in mind. She was simply manipulating him. And she did so at his firm's expense. All-the-while knowing that her actions might one day cause trouble for Chris.

Even so without caring about her motive, Chris responded to her with love; respect, and brotherhood. And it was because of the love that he had for his kinsfolk that Kanin Enterprises would still be able to compete highly with the other prominent realty developers around the world.

Geno was going over a towering office plaza with Patricia when he was paged on the intercom: "Mr. Lorenzetti, there's a call on line three."

After having the call transferred he took it in his office down the hall. "Hello, my son," Mr. Diangelo spoke with a speech impediment from old age; his defective American English diction; and an added ailment, his recent laryngitis.

"How's you—getting along with the building projects?"

"Are you referring to the Quasarano towering Ren Cen Center?"

"Yeah. That one."

"Ms. Newmar is a little behind schedule with some new developments of hers. But as you know, she's only one person. And—one of your greatest assets."

"Do you have the right people for the job? You know what I mean Geno; people whose gonna take care of business? If not, we'll hire some new ones."

"It seems—that I've chose the right personnel, Mr. Diangelo. Our employees are the best. And for the first time in my life—I'm going to give thanks to my guardian angel. Her timing my success—couldn't have been more perfect. I feel so confident about everything."

"I'm glad you feel so happy my son," Mr. Diangelo communicated. "And, too I'm happy for you. But, Geno I need you to do something for me? As a little favor, you know."

"Anything to please the boss," Geno said not having the first idea of what Mr. Diangelo wanted.

"I'm—not—the—boss," Mr. Diangelo commented seemingly pissed off.

"I'm sorry, Mr. Diangelo. I didn't mean to upset you."

"Aw—w it's nothing—my son. We senile people become irritated over the smallest things. Forgive me if I roared at you?"

"It's forgotten. Please continue."

"I have this friend who works for me, and my friends back in New York. And they wants to stay here in England for awhile. Sort of break the monotony of their regular job." Temporarily he gripped the phone.

"I'm here," Geno said.

"Maybe, I should say something to keep them busy for awhile.

I know that you and my Chenelle, are the boss. And you don't want anyone coming in trying to take over. And that could never happen. But maybe you could use a little extra help around there. You know, sort of let my friend work as an assistant supervisor—or something. Anything—for a front.

Then too, maybe you could add a little work to go along with the job? Could you get this done for me my son?"

"Why certainly; Mr. Diangelo," Geno was pleased to do him such a favor. "I'll create a position for you immediately."

"My friend will be here at the house tonight for dinner. We eat at seven. Be sure to be on time. And Geno; wear a suit. And tie. And one more thing; please don't call me Mr. Diangelo, in front of my friends. They have so much respect for me. A name like Diangelo, sounds; sounds, like a person whose mob connected. You follow me?

My name should sound like the name of a priest. Father Diangelo. And never say Tony. Remember we break bread early."

7:30 p.m. that evening. The crystal golden chandelier was faintly lit.

As the servitor's moved about friendly around the executive posh prepared dining-room table, blending in and conducting business like chit chatter, were Mr. Diangelo and a female companion; two other males and their escorts, Chenelle and her fiancee Geno Lorenzetti.

Their animated laughter was suddenly hushed when in walked a woman dressed smart in a diamond studded evening gown. Also intriguing was the upper part of her face and head that was hidden behind a veil.

"Oh, how charming," The elderly lady who sat beside Mr. Diangelo was right away jealous. "Almost mystifying," she said. "I'll bet money 'It's' a Thelma Houston look-a-like.' Has she come here tonight darling, to be interviewed for an occult movie—or something?"

Ignoring what she'd said about his newest guest Mr. Diangelo smiled and vocalized, "Finally you join us." And at the same time Carmen with grace sat through the pain as he with an immovable grip assaulted her leg beneath the table.

The entrant took a seat in the vacant chair at the upper end of the table. She sat facing Mr. Lorenzetti.

Quickly everyone's suspicion grew.

"My friends," Mr. Diangelo began to ease their intrigue, "here's a person—whose a personal friend of mine; and for several years has been a good friend of the family; Ms. Susan Terranova. (The family that Mr. Diangelo had mentioned was concerning Ms. Terranova's ties with the rackets he was associated with there in England.)

At once the comer heaved up her veil.

Almost asphyxiating off of his cigarette Geno appeared as though he'd perceived a ghost. Or its equal. Maybe the revival of a heinous witch. For the awesomely spectacular lady there in the room was none other than Klara Vladimir.

"Please forgive me, my son does such beauty startle you?" Mr. Diangelo asked.

"Startled; no," Geno said catching his breath. "Beauty; yes, she's a striking beauty. Her beauty survived the last tango in Paris," he mentioned swallowing his words.

"Please speak up—my son. So's we can all hear you?" Mr. Diangelo was eager to know what he'd muttered.

"I said," Geno raised his voice a note, "that she looks unflawed. Like—a—fashion—model."

His supplementary compliment right away sparked a bit of jealousy in Chenelle. With obvious dislike, her eyes danced in the direction of Geno; then towards Ms. Terranova.

"Do you two know each other?" Universally a keen person fast Mr. Diangelo became inquisitive.

"I've—at—one—time had the pleasure of enjoying the lady's company," Mr. Lorenzetti said reluctantly. "We bumped into one another during a jolly affair in Paris."

"It was an event being held to honor an elite group of merchants," Klara vocalized immediately attempting to aid Geno with the right words to say.

"Oh. I see," Mr. Diangelo said with a stroke of wit. "You two then, should get along well—working together?" Overshadowing his strangely curious smile Mr. Diangelo expressed bewilderment.

Mr. Lorenzetti harbored virgin vibes.

Quietly exploring her own jealousy Chenelle appeared cool. She fought off the sudden impulse to question Geno about what kind of relationship—it was—that he'd shared with her father's lady friend.

While keeping her inflamed thoughts to herself Chenelle said, "We need more beautiful women with your technical skills—and background—in the building trade industry Ms. Terranova. Judging from your portfolio I'm afraid, or should I say, deeply worried that if I don't go and refresh myself with a little bit of research, you'll be the next person in line to take over my job."

"Chenelle, I'm shocked by your words. Do you feel that by my presence—your job position has been threatened?"

"Oh—no. Losing my job is one of my smallest concerns. It's just that I've grown so accustomed to being around those male chauvinists there at our work-site. You can imagine how they try to dominate we few females that help make up this industry.

Indeed I'm thrilled, to have another female working beside me. I'd welcome the cooperative efforts of anyone who could help me put those jocular wimps in their place."

"I assure you Chenelle, your personal cause will be highly defended."

"I'm glad to welcome you on as a partner," Chenelle continued. "And you're just in time to help me clear my desk of a very important workload that I have piled up...."

"Geno revolved over in his mind: What male at the corporation was Chenelle referring to as being a chauvinist? For he'd always thought that she was fond of the guys that worked along beside her? Also while listening to the women's conversation Geno found himself puzzled—and at the same time—impressed—by Chenelle's almost perfect American—English diction. How could a lady of Italian decent speak American English with such intellectual depth? Tonight maybe he would ask her?"

"... Of course you've heard of that ridiculous myth that men are supposed to be more intellectually prepared to be a realty developer. Believe me hon', it's just a myth. We women of the 21st century have proven them to be highly incapable in so many fields."

"I'm sure darling, that the two of you will become real good friends," Geno interrupted suddenly. It seemed that he'd become fed up with the innuendoes that Chenelle and Susan were personally directing toward him and his corporate staff. "And with our future wedding plans coming up, you two should be seeing quite a lot of each other. You know how excited women get—when it comes to planning a wedding."

Momentarily everyone grew quiet.

"Now that we've all been formally introduced, let's eat," Carmen interjected quickly and began gobbling down food.

Again Mr. Diangelo became embarrassed and squeezed her sending excruciating physical punishment to her knee. And fast he no longer was a mannerable person. He decisively grew angry and began shouting insulting profanity at her.

"You damn slut. Excuse yourself from my table. Showing off in front of my friends. Know—what; leave—my—house. Immediately. Tonight. Roselli will drive you. Go—" he pushed her as she moved slowly—with her dignity left in tact—from the table.

Struggling not to appear frazzled an eerie feeling crept over the guest who were assembled. Yet, they sat one by one, faking that they were comfortable.

"Now that we all are on one accord—let's give a toast," Mr. Diangelo said straightening his tie. "To the appointment of Ms. Terranova to the board of directors of the Diangelo-Lorenzetti firm. It' growth. And to your health. And mine, "while gulping down his drink he looked in the direction where Carmen had exited.

After they'd dined and chatted for a while as the company began leaving Chenelle came up with a brilliant excuse that would give her the opportunity to spend the night over to her father's house.

As they were heading towards the house lackey who was standing holding their coats she spoke to Geno, "Geno," she held his arm while mildly resting her head over on his shoulder, "darling, you wouldn't think it rude of me if I stayed the night here at dad's would you?"

"I wouldn't give it a second thought, my love," Geno said. "But I must admit, my jealous instincts sense foul play."

"You, jealous; darling? I'm flattered. But really dear, I have a splitting headache. And I wouldn't want you to label me a complete bore when it came to my spoiling a good lovemaking scene tonight. What I would really like to do is, to see if I could borrow a little of

Ms. Terranova's time. To see if maybe I can learn a little more about her."

"I doubt if you'll gather much information about her tonight. It's so late. But if it's important to you—suit yourself. Get hot on her trail. I'll see you in the morning."

"When coming back to the dining-room Chenelle perceived that her father and Ms. Terranova had faded away.

Confidentially there in the bedroom Chenelle couldn't sleep. She tossed and turned as if she couldn't control the type of tormenting dream that she maybe was experiencing.

She awoke and checked the alarm clock. It was now past 2:00 a.m.

In a second as she'd began to dose off a whack sounded on the door.

Upon answering it she stood face to face with Ms. Terranova.

While standing there a quiet forward excitement raced over Chenelle's body. Then quickly tears began pouring down her face as she and Susan held each other in a time consuming embrace.

"I thought that I would never see you again," Chenelle wept quietly. "I thought that you were gone forever?"

"Sh—h—" Susan delicately stroked her hair. "I was never far away my love," she whispered in her ear. "I was only as far away as your imagination." She now began exhaling intense surges of respiration around Chenelle's neck.

"You—you and my father, when?"

"You remember, after you and I attended art school briefly? And went vacationing in Sicily? And your father had come along with us— to sort of act as a chaperone?"

"Yes—"

"Later he approached me—in private—and asked me to perform a mission for the organization. In the process of performing that mission we became better acquainted. Afterwards we decided to become intimate friends."

"Did you two make love tonight?"

"He fooled around," Susan smiled. "Maybe tomorrow? We can talk over there." She nuzzled Chenelle's breast while leading her over toward the bed.

As Susan continued to explore Chenelle's forbidden fruits flames of biological urge tormented Chenelle's body.

Soon they became proactive in a highly explosive lovemaking scene.

Within a short while they both climaxed sending bolts of pain and pleasure, then finally fatigue, through their bodies.

During Ms. Terranova's first day on the job she and Chenelle stayed a business distance apart from each other. They disposed of their supervisory duties attending to chore after chore all-the-while acting as if there was great animosity between the two parties. But there were a few keen co-workers who had observed, that even if they seemingly weren't getting along, Chenelle's pretended hostility toward Ms. Terranova, yet was quite friendly.

Being the royal commander's there at the workplace the two set the rules and enforced them.

Both individuals worked extended hours constantly putting up a front of not communicating but before the day would end it turned out that it would be Chenelle's voluntary duty to teach Ms. Terranova different aspects about her job position. And yet what was even more odd was the fact that Chenelle had lied to Geno convincing him that a closer relationship with Ms. Terranova seemed absolutely unwise.

Their suspenseful exercise quietly bothered Geno. Combating the many work-loads that frequented her desk daily 'she—should have,' he rationalized empty, "without squabble welcomed Susan's help?" And an independent reason why she should've welcomed her help was that she didn't know very much about the building trade either?

And among other things how could she have gone against her father's wish by not wanting Ms. Terranova to be a board member of an installation that he had half ownership in? What was the shoving force behind her actions?" Geno couldn't control his sprinting thoughts. A matter of fact he was quietly flustered.

There has to be a missing link here? He was thither tormented. Yet I must be very cautious when thinking about quizzing two intelligent manipulative forces like Klara and Chenelle. Sure I will. But what's her cause for responding to Ms. Terranova's being here the way she has? Her role of a griping enemy of Susan just doesn't fit.

Like sand through an hour glass—flowed incidents from Chris' past were being observed and with unrelentless vigor it would be inevitable that one day soon he'd come in contact with the person whom was so vigilant in pursing to prove that he was indeed a criminal.

Agent Dan Throb's investigative search for the alleged robber and murder suspect, Christopher Kanin fractionally had led him to the city of Palermo, Italy. Working side by side with C.I.A. agents Duggan and Hunt, the period of such a search would've been put into full gear around October 18, 1981, and was ongoing.

In a mad rush with the Italian authorities assistance he'd scrutinized the international shipping documents of Kanin Enterprises and discovered that after the robbery had taken place at Armsted there was a shipment of prepared concrete slabs that was sent to Palermo by the firm. And when digging farther he learnt that the signature of the same person who'd signed the shipping orders in San Francisco had also signed for the slabs upon their arrival in Italy.

After buying information from buried sources it was revealed to Dan that a man fitting Chris' description had stayed temporarily at a hotel in Palermo.

While he was there at least two observers saw with their own eyes that he associated with one of Palermo's most prominent citizens whom many in that city believed that he was connected to the mob. Such a rumor had merit however, not only was the warehouse owner mob connected, he also was actively functioning as a Russian operative.

During their last day of communicating inside the warehouse that was owned by the prominent citizen the source confirmed that he overheard some exact strange noise 'like the unusual sound of an air hammer or jack used to break down concrete' going on inside.

After the noise had subsided trucks were seen leaving the warehouse and they believe it ended the stay of the seemingly wealthy shipping magnate from the U.S. who'd stayed in their city for awhile.

As Dan's association tried in vain to solve the mystery involving the noise, for the first time—since trying to piece together the crime—his eyes flew wide open. Intuitively he thought, Well, well, he's trying to become rich. And he'll go to any extreme to see that he succeeds....

From the person whom owned the warehouse—whom had the tenacity to act as an innocent party as to what had taken place on his premises—Dan was told that 'he remembered' during a chat he had with Chris that Chris mentioned to him that he'd be visiting Lebanon to take care of increased selling.

The most popular place to sell building materials in war stricken Lebanon would probably be Tel Aviv. Dan relied on his instincts.

In the meantime with keen interest Dan checked the dates of the prominent businessman's—in port—shipping documents.

Bingo. He finally hit a small jackpot. He found a note which stated that after Georgieo and Chris had agreed upon a price for the shipment of arms delivered to him, the rest of the goods that had been sent by The Kanin firm were to be transported on to Tel Aviv.

During the agent's first week in Lebanon they had headaches trying to get any person there to cooperate with them. Then as they were about to pursue their first lead swiftly the case took on a different twist. While initiating a conference with the authorities there they informed

Dan's clique that 'all the persons you seek are not amateurs alone, whom plotted and pulled off the daring robbery against your government....'

The authorities brought to their attention that a suspected bunch of professional soldiers might've been interconnected with Christopher Kanin's crimes.

CHAPTER TWENTY-THREE

Dan continued weariless in his effort at pursuing to track down Christopher Kanin. After paying a number of blind sources for information involving Chris' activities in America, Mexico, Lebanon and Italy, Dan began to unweave his first lead that would point him in the direction of his suspect in Paris, France.

In Paris he questioned the owner of the garb manufacturer that Chris had recently been a part owner of. In which time he confronted Monsieur de la Camille with Chris' whereabouts—he sealed his lips and didn't air any information pertaining to Chris.

And when Dan showed a photo of Chris to a few of the employees that worked at the garment factory they too shut up and wouldn't breathe any information to the agents: 'concerning Monsieur Jean de Masi's deportation from France….' You could hear them discussing the issue among themselves as Dan and his band moved on.

A quiet towering anger quickly spread through Dan's mind as he left the concern rack—reinstating his call independently, "Modern men— and women—always ass holes. You'd think that he would want to uphold the law. And help you catch a suspected criminal whose at large. Hell naw. Men like us who enforce the law are the first persons whose put on trial. You'll think that they were all fucking priests. While talking about law officers one time—a woman once said to me—" Most times they act like saviors of the darn planet. But they're nothing but beasts. Animals. Whose been known to commit murder just to prove that they can bring any man to justice…." But that lady hasn't been well briefed. What she didn't know is, that a civilian will hide a criminal. And when you bust their asses for aiding and abetting one, they'll try to convince you every time, that they were acting as a responsible citizen when doing so. And yet, I understand why one does it. That person who'd become worthless could've been a loved one; or a dear friend. That's all swell. But if most of the evidence points toward an individual whose suspected of a crime, in most cases, he's the one who committed it.

It's as simple as one—two—three—Christopher Kanin committed a crime. He's guilty. And he's gonna pay for it. If it takes collaborating with strangers. Scrubbing the floors of The White House. Or sucking the Prime Minister's penis. That smart ass—belongs—to—me. You get my drift?"

While sheathed in a stirring state of thwarting neutralization Dan fast realized how stray he was acting so he toned down his voice, "However, I must admit," he said more in sorrow than in anger, "he's really had my back up against a brick wall. I'd give a month's pay, just to get one glimpse of him. Just—one—glimpse."

All at once Hunt and Duggan burst out in laughter over the senseless feud that Dan was having with himself.

Touchy Dan propelled Duggan aside then ordered him to take a taxi back to their living quarters.

Dan tortured himself with years of expansional investigative arraignment and had almost scratched his head bald before he was able to get a whiff of the first lawful conveyance of news that would put him hot on Chris' tail. A trail which would eventually lead to Chris' capture.

Upon his appearance in Paris Dan was clued in by Monique who personally made him conscious 'of the real untold story.' He'd made a deal for the ware-room that Chris had left behind after being deported from France.

Monique indulged in extreme overkill when telling Dan about how Chris was connected to terrorists whom in darkness had pulled off two four months apart—and four—twice a year unallowed schemes while living there in their country.

How the tough guy revolutionaries had briefly changed their occupation and robbed garment factories to help support their activities there in France.

Why was Monique being so helpful? He stepped forward with such independence simply because he wanted to remain friends with Armoir his lover. Armoir was grasped for a second and ordered on the hour as being the glaring new prey of Mrs. Bristol.

Since Monsieur de Masi had been ordered deported—and Mrs. Bristol could no longer buy his services—she'd put forth a referendum to pay for the prowess of Monique's friend: a heroic bull male there in Paris who had an exterior reputation in both the American and foreign military community as being a predominant one in his vocation when it came to sexual attractiveness.

During Armoir's grievous titillative fling with Monique and Mrs. Bristol, whoso was dyspeptic, he also binded in an amorous dalliance with The Ambassador's maidservant. The Ambassador had hired his services for her when he himself could no longer perform the duties involved.

If he had to deal with his newest arrival—in the event of another scandal, I wonder how would the smart Ambassador handle getting rid of Armoir?

Would there be enough lid left over this melting pot to keep it covered?

Flash bang in the center of such controversy while trying to define what he was being subjected to momentarily Monique affirmed what a dooming impact such an affair would have on his life. If it ever caught the public's interest?

While suddenly finding himself being almost driven to an incurable state of insanity, cost what it may, he would go to 'any extreme' to break up that ludicrous affair that Armoir had recently involved himself in.

"How could he do this to me? Trade in a Rolls Royce for a Volkswagon?" Monique seemed shaken.

Prior to gleaning this last bit of information it was the only time that agent Throbs and his friends had left a snitch with an actual smile on their face. They could barely exit the door before bursting out in frenzied laughter.

Standing staring out the window when seeing them make fun of him Monique threw a fuck you sign at them and switched his tail back over to where one of his gay friends stood marveling at a gown.

Momentarily Dan would try to keep Mrs. Bristol's affair a secret from her husband. Since being plagued by the worldly news of corruption aimed at different politicians in Washington D.C. he was trying to avoid an awful scandal pinned on to one of America's powerful figures while he was yet currently in office. And he most certainly didn't want to have one pinned on to one of their dignitaries who was representing our country's interest abroad. So he decided that the proper thing to do was to put Mrs. Bristol under surveillance.

Dan kept her under surveillance for a short while then one evening after she'd visited her friend Margerie he decided to have a little chat with her.

While suddenly surprising her out of the dark Dan asked in a polite manner, "Can I offer you a ride home Mrs. Bristol?"

Seized by terror, uneasiness and mortal dread was noticeable on the senescent woman's face. "Oh, my goodness," with her heart pounding fast Mrs. Bristol began to tremble.

"I beg your pardon Madame. I didn't mean to frighten you," Dan said pulling out his identification card. "My name is agent Daniel Throbs; from F.B.I. headquarters back in Washington D.C. I'm here on business. And I would like to ask you a few questions?"

"Whew—" a sigh of relief fell over Mrs. Bristol. "You nearly scared the living daylights out of me. How can I be of some service to you, Mr. Throbs."

"Is there some place where we could converse in private? In an environment that would be comfortable for you?"

"Well—" she became hesitant to answer. "I'm thinking. Yes; I know of a spot. There's a place called Armoir's. It's an eatery that's located on the north end of town. I'd love to have dinner there this evening."

"Armoir's; it is. May I?"

7:30 p.m. Over dinner Dan questioned Mrs. Bristol about Christopher Kanin.

"Mrs. Bristol I don't mean to pry," he stared her straight in the eye," were you at one time—seeing a gentleman who uses the alias of Monsieur Jean de Masi? The garment factory and boutique owner Jean de Masi?"

A slight fear crept over Mrs. Bristol.

"Since my first question left you so mute, do you at present, know the stead where the guy might be kicking it around; with someone else?" Dan was in a repellent mood.

First nodding then shaking her head Mrs. Bristol mumbled out something and then she replied, "I'm sorry Mr. Throbs. Jean didn't leave a forwarding address. Not with me, anyway."

A bit of moisture built up in her eyes and at the same time she began to sweat.

"You mean he left without even saying goodbye? You'd think that if not you, at least your husband would've objected to such?"

"Objected; I don't understand?"

"From what we've gathered from the French authorities one would think that there was a private feud going on between the two. They say that he has often expressed his dislike for the man. He stated that 'if there's only one person present when Monsieur de Masi is deported from France, he'd like to be there to personally bid him farewell.'"

"That clearly expresses his feelings towards Jean," Mrs. Bristol said regrettably. "And if he also opposes anything, he objects to me keeping my sanity. It breaks his little heart to see me so calm, during the storm. Yes, if Jean was being deported, Harvey would've enjoyed being there to see such an event take place. But regardless of what anyone says, I believe that Jean's still here."

"You think he's still here in France?" Dan interrupted quickly.

"Yes. Still here. But, only in spirit."

"Spirit; that seems vague."

"Why vague? If he was still in the flesh, I feel that he would have contacted me by now. Even though our romance was short lived, when we were together, it was really true love. No, Mr. Throbs, I don't think that he's still in the country; I believe that he's dead."

"Christopher Kanin—dead—" Dan was shocked. "Now that, I seriously doubt."

Outrageously disgraceful. He thought hushed. There's nothing that one could say that could discourage an old fool who thinks that she's the jewel in that younger man's life.

"During the time that you two spent together did you ever observe what his daily activities were like?" Dan asked. "For example, did he take trips on the weekends? Or associate with strangers? Go on regular business trips? Things of that nature?"

"Not that I recall," Mrs. Bristol briefly reminisced. "Whenever I wanted to contact him he could easily be found."

Dan was sitting eating his food very cushioned like then while in the process of laying his silverware down he fast lost it, "We're not talking about your ill infatuation for this guy Mrs. Bristol," he violently rammed his fork into the table.

Then while caging his anger he abruptly lowered the tone of his voice, "What I'm trying to find out is, was he ever involved in any illegal activity? Or during anytime, did he arouse your suspicion of him being involved in such mischief?"

"Yes—" Mrs. Bristol's composure darkened. "He was involved in some illegal activity."

"Would you care to elaborate?"

Momentarily they both grew quiet.

"This German broad—" Dorian said trembling.

"German broad—" Dan contemplated that he had another lead.

"Yes—She was a friend of his."

"Pardon me; could you identify her from one of these photos?" Dan reached inside his pocket and pulled out a group of photos.

After looking briefly at them only the second one that Mrs. Bristol had looked at was concise enough for her to believe that it might've been Chris' friend.

"This face looks like hers. But the hair; it's not the same."

"Thank you. Please continue," Dan said.

"Anyway, one morning, she and a friend of hers stopped by the house. I will never forget her friend. He had such a broad smile. And that southern accent. Man—was—he—from—the—back—woods.

Jean made them welcome. But I considered their presence to be a personal intrusion. Simply because, Jean never told me that he'd invited anyone else to brunch with us. She came barging right in—and took over.

It was obvious that she wasn't dressed for the occasion. Smelling like an unbathed skunk she snatched up food off the table like she hadn't eaten in days. Maybe months. Jean and her cowboy friend tried to embarrass her. But she was determined to make an ass out of herself.

She never concerned herself with my being present. Totally, ignored me.

She had me so upset that I quickly departed their company.

Jean stayed and talked to them.

I'd already observed that they weren't from our elite crowd. So I contacted the house servant—we're very close—to sort of ease drop on them. And would you believe it, their whole gang were criminals."

"You're kidding me," Dan said bemused.

At this point Mrs. Bristol began to lie carefully. She was trying not to implicate Jean as being a criminal like she'd implied that his friends were. And thinking over the matter fast, she was also trying to keep her act clean.

"They discussed some goods that they'd stolen from a warehouse in southern France, and wanted Jean to buy them from them. They bickered on a price for awhile and Jean refused to purchase the goods—because their asking price was too high." "That's odd. Hum—m? Go on," Dan said.

"The following day I had one of our guards to tail and inform on this lady of mystique. She didn't leave the premises at all that day. But as it would turn out she'd become a person of another face. The next day she went out on the town wearing makeup—a new hairstyle—and had changed her walk.

My source said that a day later she put on another face and entered the Embassy; stayed there for maybe twenty minutes or more, then left.

A week passed. And it was discovered—after her quick departure from France—that a Russian who was posing as an Ambassador there and his armed defender were killed by an unknown assailant. Quite a lady huh?"

"Indeed she is," Dan replied seemingly aggravated.

The duo was quiet for a moment then after clearing up his throat Dan asked her in a polite manner, "Do you have anything else to add; to the information that you've already given us?"

"No—o, that's about all I know," Mrs. Bristol appeared as if she only had three and a half senses left.

"Tomorrow—we'll be interrogating your sweetie. Pitiful shit ball. Can't keep his poon tang corral. Say—it—ain't so: Today—there are too many politician's mates whom will drop their drawers at the drop of a hat. You think it will be easy to find your husband tomorrow?"

"Yes."

"Where?"

"At the Embassy. During the mornings. Why?" Mrs. Bristol became curious.

"The information that you confided in us gave us very little to go on. And I'm very sorry Mrs. Bristol. But at this point, we'll have to involve you and your husband in our investigation."

"Why should my husband be involved?"

"The lady on the picture?"

"Yes—"

"She's among our top ten most wanted list. She's a Russian operative wanted in connection to more than five murders in the U.S. and three in our ally countries. More than being a secret agent she's a deadly assassin. Who never leaves a job undone.

You know the standards that a man like your husband is supposed to abide by. They're the highest standards. Top secret information could have been easily—and unknowingly—siphoned out of you and passed on to our enemy.

So, as of this moment, I have no choice other than to place you under arrest. And if you take my advice—which might not be helpful to you in the future—it would be of utmost importance—that you stop searching for the fountain of youth. If you feel horny, pray. Ask for forgiveness for even thinking such a sinful thought. And after you've done that—then try resting your hot fanny at home.

'Love is a many splendored thing' Mrs. Bristol—it has been said. However, sometimes it's unattainable. Therefore, in my opinion, rational behavior such as yours, can be considered simply, immoral. Which leads me to conclude that it is impossible for you to try to seduce all of the eligible bachelors of this ever so small—but large—country you live in.

I'm curious—was the excitement of chasing that young buck worth losing it all? The life that you and your husband have built? How are you going to cope with the humiliation?"

Dorian was speechless.

9:00 a.m. the following morning at the Embassy. Ambassador Bristol is confronted with the issue.

Before the Ambassador could offer the men a seat, agent Hunt spoke, "First of all, my name is agent Yory Hunt. I work for the Pentagon. And this here gentlemen is F.B.I. agent Daniel Throbs. Ambassador Bristol you're under arrest. You have the right to remain silent. You have the right to an attorney...."

Quickly the Ambassador grew pale. "I was about to offer you gentlemen a seat," he exhaled heavily. "But instead. I think I'll have one myself."

All at once the Ambassador began grasping for breath.

Agent Duggan quickly rushed to his side and began nurturing a cardiovascular test on him.

After they were assured that the Ambassador would live Dan affronted him with his situation, "The way things stand Harvey, you're in some real deep trouble. It's okay if I call you Harvey?"

Mr. Bristol was mum.

"We've digested enough information on you—to expel you from office. The charges that will be brought forth against you concerns your wife's relationship with an alias, Monsieur Jean de Masi.

Now that you know what—this matter is all about—before you summon an attorney, or answer any questions, let me briefly enlighten you on Monsieur de Masi's background:

His real name is Christopher Kanin. He was born in The United States. The son of one of America's most prominent real estate developers; the late businessman, Gerald Kanin.

He's wanted on three counts of murder; that we know of. Illegal possession of stolen military weapons. Contraband. Interstate and international flight. Espionage. And additional counts that we do not care to discuss momentarily.

One of the murders took place right here under your nose. It was through your neglected wife that he amassed the information as to where agent Bitelan was staying. Simply because, it was much too easy for the killer to gain entry to the Embassy without anyone becoming alerted or suspicious. Man what a damn fool you've been played for."

Now the reason for him being arrested seemed clear to the Ambassador.

Seemingly enjoying tormenting the aging man Dan spoke contemptuously about his wife's adulterous behavior, "I cannot see how a man of your rank, would let your wife's lust for young men interfere with the sensitive position you hold? Faced with the threat of such a scandal, it would be like committing suicide. And to think that you'd want to give up thirty years of unblemished service, and let such an incident—as the one that has occurred—wash it all down the drain?

By all appearance how could you have been so dumb—as to let those lawbreakers siphon out of you two—info that led to the slaying of one of the best undercover double agents that our government has ever had. Regardless of how unimportant you thought that his visit here might've seemed. What kind of chump are you? A lame brained idiot. I would say.

And—your—hot—seated—wife—what she didn't know at the time, was that Monsieur de Masi's female special business mate was—and—still—is—one of the elect intelligence agents that the Russians have working for them.

With her and Monsieur de Masi still at large, we have in our files a long list of slain covert operatives and diplomats that she and him have managed to dispose of.

Monsieur de Masi can lead us to her. We want him; and we want his lady friend. Without compromise. They—are—ours. Dead—or—alive. So to end a wordy conversation Ambassador, in what country did you offer him refuge in?"

"A close contact of mine said that he was exiled in England," The Ambassador replied quickly. "He can be considered a very reliable source."

"I'm sorry Ambassador," Agent Hackett consoled the wryly faced gentleman while leading him toward the door," Helen of Troy fell a whole city. Don't be embarrassed by your wife's scampishness. She only fell one man."

The next day Dan communicated with the Ambassador's source and he was informed of the exact location in England where Chris could be found. That night Dan's crew was off to London.

CHAPTER TWENTY-FOUR

Within the meanwhile a recent downward spiral of hard luck had started plaguing Christopher Kanin's life all over again.

When questioning his financial stability there at the joint operation— it was a fact that he'd accomplished producing certain million dollar projects but added to his rapid success he'd also completed a few ventures which were failures.

Patricia Newmar the innovative scientist in the design department of the Diangelo-Lorenzetti firm somehow had screwed up on her latest developments.

Sure, she'd succeeded at developing a new kind of plastic form; marketed it, and had reaped—for the company—enormous profits. And added to her successes was her ability to decrease brick work size. She had computer graphics that showed grid coordination detailing smaller space and the use of larger components. She'd even created an advance metric system that was within limitations of building codes which showed diagrams—and gridlines that dealt with elevation, heights, and daylight factors. All of her latest attributes were well established to accommodate her theoretical designed Ren Cen— 3D and ultra high tech buildings.

Being intriguingly tantalized by the industry claims that new material schemer's were mass producing superb assembly plants; developing ingenious construction systems etc., with the quickness, as things were, it added venom to her connected efforts at being a leader whom others in their field would respect.

After hiring a group of uneducated architects, with Patricia pitching in they began experimenting on a new formula that dealt with beam fabrication.

During their tampering and testing process the young architects invented a process that dealt with fewer elements involving the chemistry of compound steel.

Immediately when deciding that they were ready to sell their ideas they became involved in a pact with the company that produced steel for Geno: Delmar and Associates.

These new steel beams would be flexible aim to suit the structure's weight by ton. Also included in their deal with Delmar there was indiscreet outlines that discussed less cost at pricing concrete and concrete masonry; cheaper studs; connectors; framing and rough carpentry; finish carpentry; roofing, and interior.

Green lights were flashing everywhere. Putting to use a sketch formula that conformed with all building legislation they ceased to use their experiments and marketed their latest radical change in steel beams.

After organizing a high rise suite and the Quasarano towering renaissance culture center was when the vandalizing blow came. After four months of full development it had a section of slab—that collapsed.

More than a hundred and fifty people died during the smash. Such a tragedy forced the Diangelo-Lorenzetti Company to try to renovate their business approach.

Quickly hit by enough lawsuits each day that flew by now Geno's group was on a turbulent ride to stay afloat in the building trade business.

It highly irritated many investors when it was broadcast more than once that what was—only days ago—a profitable company—thenceforward it would be one that was busted—conducting a hunt for a joint partner—and shuffled by a takeover bid all at the same fucking time.

With sudden failure yet again staring him in the face—the only glimmering goal in sight for Geno now—before seeing himself lying continuant on his face out in the field ice again—there was a bid that was to take place on a two hundred and fifty million dollar project in America.

Coincidentally there were two projects coming up. If only Geno could win the bid; mainly the most lucrative one—it might would help him overcome the situation that he was currently being plagued with.

It was a sure bet that the well established firm's would be bidding on the largest of the projects: The Buhl project. A construction project of an advance 21st century industrial design college campus that would operate beginning the new millennium concentrating its efforts on modern space age technology. Technology that also would include exploring military combat maneuvers etc. Included were two government tank plants and hockey rinks.

The other project was the Martinelli Villa deal.

The Martinelli Villa package offered construction on two hospitals—a thirty seven story town center—condo complex and a thirty two bedroom villa. A structure which would be built with twenty-six baths; six kitchens; three tennis courts; four pools, and two waterfalls.

If such a project would be completed by the scheduled date there was an optional clause that stated that one would be allowed to build a superb twenty first century university building. A complex which would house and teach intellectuals on how to build mechanical robot repairmen and aerospace equipment that would deal with servicing spaceships—and warships traveling to and from planets that have habitats and industrial complexes in outer space.

With two weeks leading up to the deadline for the bid to occur momentarily realizing that Mr. Diangelo was losing sleep over his organized crime family's investments, Geno suddenly found himself in a tough unmanageable situation.

As hours passed he was overcome by great stress wondering whether it was possible to win such a bid.

CHAPTER TWENTY-FIVE

Geno is at the home of Mr. Diangelo and they're engaged in conversation discussing their company's plight. Mr. Diangelo expressed himself in an even tone of voice, "... Please forgive me my son if I seem to be sticking my nose where it does not belong; but, as an investor I have to protect my interest. Therefore, I feel that we should take a serious look at what's causing our problems and find a way to solve them," he paused.

"Our company has the potential to become one of the worlds greatest builders, but with those recent tragedies being a menace to use, we will soon be forced to go out of business.

We need to secure a large contract. And we need to get one immediately." Momentarily a chilling creepy fearful silence popped up on Chris' face.

"As a final solution," Mr. Diangelo kept talking, "we simply need to win the bid that's taking place soon. If we lose it, that means that me and my investors will suffer a great loss. And, at that moment, we have lost enough money my son. Now, I'm talking to you plain and calmly; you deal with such a burden. Because the constituents that I'm connected to do not tolerate losses."

"I beg your pardon," Geno interrupted quickly.

"We simply allow a person to repay us," Mr. Diangelo ignored him. "And if he cannot pay us back, we use other means to collect our debts. If we cannot secure the Buhl deal, or the Martinelli contract, it will then be out of my hands. I will have no other choice but to turn you over to my friends. I don't want this for my little Chenelle. You know what I mean?

It's bad enough that she had to fall in love so young. But, to become a widow so young I don't see this."

Instantaneously Geno became petrified.

Quickly his mind traveled back to the rumor he'd overheard about Mr. Diangelo having mob ties.

But, even so he thought to himself, it's a little late to worry about that now. I must find an alternative to deal with the problem at hand.

"I have in mind a plan; that just might work," he said to Mr. Diangelo with a speech thrill. "Let's consider for the moment that we lose the bid to our competitors."

"Yes—" Mr. Diangelo found him to be distracting.

"I think that there's a chance I can persuade the firm that has the best chance of winning the bid to sell out."

"How can this be done my son? You've lost me."

"The tough as nails competition will probably be Kanin Enterprises; you agree?"

"Yes—"

"And you know also that politics plays an important role in how you go about securing contracts in this business; right? The company on average—with the most prestige normally obtains the best bids. When it comes to political persuasion I can be considered a professional sharpie in that field. Trust me. Mr. Diangelo. For I'll be willing to stake my life on it that we'll win the Buhl—maybe—even both contracts."

Sitting pretending that he knew nothing about Geno's background Mr. Diangelo said, "With such vigor and enthusiasm, I see no reason why not to trust you my son. Your instincts have certainly been beneficial to us thus far. But if your plan fails—I—warn—you. I'm going to have to act. And when a Diangelo becomes riled up—there's not enough water on this major planet that can put out the roasting flame one of us can soar."

Geno sat thinking through ponderous irony. Parching heat—that's probably what I'll have to go through in order to get the Buhl bid if Marcus has anything to do with it.

The next day environing conditions around The Diangelo-Lorenzetti firm were wandering at its right-angled pace. Business drill was still deplorably unharmonious.

With the bidding for the Buhl and Martinelli projects advancing Geno had the appearance that he was very jumpy and on edge.

What small business his company would acquire for those who were using his services now, to them he constantly seemed in a hostile mood and under a strain.

At his home when Chenelle could find the time to visit with him he would chew up the scenery with her, arguing over small things. Things that any wholesome minded person would've paid very much attention to.

Out in the field while surveying a new building site he riled the crew leaving many of the workers being sore at him.

When he returned the trailing day they would show their resentment by sneering at him, labeling him 'the one man holocaust.'

Geno's weariness grew.

Then undivulged, a week before he was to leave for the United States he began ailing. Such a swift indisposition befell him at a reception that his close clique and a few peers were throwing to honor him.

Sensing how deep in the pits he was Chenelle appropriately took pity on him; first by becoming involved; and communicating to him that she truly was a friend of his. Seriously telling him that she respected him; and appreciated having the opportunity of being his mate. And that she would be there to give support to—her—man, whom she realized at that moment, really needed someone to help him try to become a proud individual again.

Chenelle convinced Geno to stay home for a few days. And while he'd be convalescing she'd take 'however long it would take' to help nurse him back to being healthy again.

Fast she cared for him helping him to gain the twenty two or more pounds he'd recently shed.

She did everything practicable to help strengthen his mind.

And precisely did rumors fly.

AL WOODS

A few weeks afterwards it was circulated that during Geno's low quiet profile—while attending the revel—he'd persevered—to an extent—after having a mental breakdown and somewhat of a mild heart attack.

CHAPTER TWENTY-SIX

Dan's perennial effort at pursuing to solve the weapons caper was reaching a salient point. During his little stay in England aided by agents at Scotland Yard he'd pin down his suspect believing that Chris Kanin was either Stephen Blass or Mr. Lorenzetti.

The time had come finally that he was going to find out precisely what the man whom had outsmarted him for a long while indeed looked like.

New York City. Mobilized there were many executives jointly conversing in a meeting at The Waldorf Astoria. Subsequently that night those same attendees would assemble attending a feast being held there in honor of the popular builders of the world. Kanin Enterprises ranked number one amidst the group whom was convening.

The first day Geno could not meet such a grueling schedule. I brought along my good luck charm. Traveling up an escalator he examined a gold medallion he had around his neck. I hope it makes me a winner? He was trying to be in a good mood but his most urgent and dearest wish momentarily was that his brother Marcus had made up his mind to attend the affair.

But why should I worry? He thought in lifeless silence. Marc would die of heart failure if he could not participate in such a classy event as the one being held here these two weeks.

After getting himself a room Geno hastily searched his belongings to find something to wear out.

215

When packing he'd only brought along one suit to wear not knowing that his studied brief visit to New York would extend to almost a week.

With his clothing spread on the bed Geno noticed that he didn't have a shirt to match his tweed suit.

Well, it's not here. He held a conversation with himself. And I can't blame Chenelle. She's been quite helpful. But, I need a shirt.

Down the corridor to the escalator he went in search of an emporium.

On the second level of the building while talking to a security guard an aesthetically well formed female drew his eyes in her direction.

Hum—m. Such sophistication. Class all the way. He thought quietly to himself and momentarily charmed at her beauty. She's probably a native New Yorker too?

As she promenaded up near to him he indulged in wish fulfillment.

My. Oh my. Oh my. His eyes stared persistently frozen at the free slit that was cut in front of her dress. If it had been cut one inch further, it would have revealed to him part of nature's most beautiful gift.

An approach was quite necessary as Geno stood pondering how to come on to her.

Repeatedly shy Geno found that it was tough to make his advance. "Pardon me; miss," his heart hammered speedily.

"Yes—" she smiled at him with the kind of smile that stirs a man's imagination.

"Is there a garment mart located in this building?" his voice quavered. "A place where I might be able to buy a shirt? A freak incident occurred—and the one that I'd intended to wear—was ruined."

"Um—m; let's see," she thought momentarily. "If I'm not mistaken, I think that there's one in the west wing of the building. Near the ice cream parlor. You can't miss it. Take the escalator to the first level, turn left, and you should see it immediately down the corridor."

"Why thank you very much," Geno spoke with a British accent.

Feeling that he'd failed in his approach, and suddenly left wordless he turned to walk away.

Quickly she called out to him, "Are you here on business? Mr.—"

"Lorenzetti."

Mr. Lorenzetti are you a foreigner?"

"Yes. I am. And what might your name be Madame? That's if you don't mind my asking."

"I'm called Rachel."

"Are you here on business Rachel?"

"No. But my husband is. He's in the building and land development business."

"What a coincidence. So am I."

"Are you going to attend the banquet tomorrow evening?"

"Are you going to be there?"

"Why of course."

"To dine beside—or even near to—such stunning divine feminine beauty—I'd indeed be honored. Please fill me in on the time of such an event?"

"It starts at 7:30 p.m. See you later." Rachel said quickly then walked away with Geno's solid lifelike image delineating in her imagination.

As he wandered around enjoying the hotel sites he created a visual fantasy of what it would be like to dominate her mind; and possess her body? And fast, he viewed in his mind what it would be like to possess the body of simply any green, unused American woman again.

7:45 p.m. the next day. Before leaving to attend the ritual Geno bestow thought upon how he'd form a new alliance with his brother Marcus? After all such wouldn't be easy since the two hadn't seen each other for many years.

How would Marcus respond once they were alone and Chris had revealed his identity to him?

He washed down half from a bottle of Remy Martin then left the room.

The social convention was filled to its capacity with—by all appearances building tradesmen from all corners of the planet. Evidently the late 1980's and medial 90's were truly a jump in the right direction for any corporation that chose to be involved in the building trade.

The superior land development businessmen had their own private sectors which they requested that it be roped off.

They sat on an elevated balcony section above the crowd where they could be a table gaper at all of the activities that were to take place that evening.

Since Geno represented only a small business interest compared to The Kanin's; The Strassubaunn's; The Glazier's and the Featherstone's, it was going to be a problem for him to get a seat in the seating section where his brother was sitting.

After three unsuccessful attempts testing to see if he could bribe the man in charge of the reserve seating section Rachel came to his rescue and he finally secured himself a seat where the VIP's were sitting.

He'd only been seated momentarily when affirmed bellow rang out in the group seated approximately three tables from his.

It took only a few seconds for him to guess who all of the sturdily vigorous noise was coming from; simply because he'd been trounced upon by that person's voice long before others had ever been exposed to it.

Deplorably for many there it seemed that the only change that had taken place in Marcus' life was that he now was almost unbearable when making his sarcastic remarks and sorry absurd jokes to individuals.

As Marcus steadily praised himself and bragged out loud Chris sat refined on his seat all-the-while wishing that his brother would stop making a public idiot out of himself.

After listening to him for an hour filled five minutes or more through a pensive state of relaxing his thoughts Chris absorbed the disturbing voice by controlling its high pitched volume down to the tone of a prolonged nagging whisper. It was truly a miracle that he'd found a kind of confinement and explainable resolve that would let him enjoy the remainder of the activities that were going on there at the jamboree that night.

For a brief period Chris continued to relax his mind.

Like a clap of thunder while he was centrally focussing on the problem a noise shuddered his slumber.

The band shell appeared as if it exploded then quickly it became engulfed in a kind of fog.

Many bodies haul ass for cover and those who remained in their seats hearts throb in considerable fear wondering what had caused the substantial explosion.

When the blackness cleared a high energy rock band named Blade was making their debut live and on stage.

Radiant with excitement Rachel turned thumbs down on several clad bottom rock monsters as she searched the crowd for a lunar dance partner.

It was now a mystery to some of Rachel's friends as to why Marcus never wanted to participate anymore. You're talking about a person whom once was a party hound, when first meeting him he had notoriety as being one of the best dancers in their clique. But no more would this funky groove master's fancy leg work embrace the dance floor again. He had to live up to the name of being a top dog executive whom was going places.

Rachel's eyes while dancing searched the reserved seating area for Mr. Lorenzetti.

As she stared at him she began to imagine naughty—raging—affectionate—ecstatic biological thrills standing moving about feeling that they were engaged in a stinking love making scene.

After the flesh pounding quickie episode was over she struggled past the rhythm frenzied crowd to where he was seated.

Totally exhausted she fell over onto Geno's shoulder.

Sitting engrossed in a transcendental meditative state of mind Geno awoke suddenly to find ascending over him his dream come true.

"Would you like to dance?" she asked politely hoping not to be embarrassed.

"Dance; how does one go about learning to do that?" he said joshing.

"By building a dance floor that's elevated higher than the Empire State Building," Rachel responded. "That's about the only way one might be able to move about freely amidst all of those sophisticated drunks out there on the floor. They're so uncoordinated. No freedom of movement. No flaunting gestures."

"Sure—you're—right," Geno said. "Let's dance baby." He was terribly staggered by Rachel's tongue lashing words relative to the dance patrons present.

Rachel grinned rather sheepishly clinging onto Geno as they danced to the rhythm of three long playing ballads.

Once seated back at the table Rachel kept eyeballing Geno with a strangely curious smile.

As her elite friends continued their boring gossip she sat in a dream world viewing X-rated scenes of Mr. Lorenzetti performing as a macho lover in bed with her.

Marcus became upset. "You've already shared your most secret fantasies with the public darling," he said demurely staring off. "The most fitting thing to do now, would be to shed your gown. Don't you think? Then the world could see what you have to offer."

Rachel became furious but she restrained herself from public embarrassment by shouting out her counter insult in a low voice, "Gee whiz darling, tonight you have the manners of a Doberman. What's wrong? What's causing you to behave like this? Is it the new brand of coke you've been using? You're so edgy.

But, in the future when you get ready to go off the deep-end with your pretended jealousy—try shoving a tampon down your throat— until your period of anxiety has ceased." Then quietly—in a very lady like manner—she excused herself.

With stinging words like those it seemed like what once had been a permanent marriage, was now in serious trouble, and rapidly heading toward an annulment proceeding.

As the waiter rendered service to the social band assembled, Rachel who was now seated beside Geno, sucked down a huge double shot of liquor.

Again Geno was plagued with a problem that drove him into meditation.

Rachel had been seated for maybe twenty minutes when the band called her up to do a closing number.

Her first tune was an up-tempoed rock tune and her closing melody was a rhythm and blues rendition of "For The Good Times" that left the patrons spellbound—and some—in a horny mood.

Upon securing a chair, she quizzed Geno, "How'd you like my singing?"

"You have great vocal abilities," he commented all-the-while not trying to be critical.

Her handling of the stirring blues song seemed to have also left Geno spellbound. Or his mind had drifted off leaving him in deep thought momentarily.

"Your style," he continued, "It's hard to explain. The songs—or should I say—the last one—was the kind of gingerbread ballad that touches the heart of the listener. It reminded me of a past relationship."

"I'm glad you liked it."

"I'm one person who enjoys listening; sis'." he uttered oppressed.

"I beg your pardon?"

"Oh—I'm sorry," Geno thought hastily. "I forgot your name and called you Ms."

"Ms—" Rachel was delighted. "That's a choice one makes when they want to live life free—as—a—bird." Abruptly she then whispered, "I'm in a totally free mood tonight." She winked her eye at Geno. "One should also seize such an opportunity when one can."

Bearing the woe of the country on his conscious at once a substilate smile lit up Geno's usually joyless face.

221

Oh—h, he must have heard me. Rachel was a little ashamed. How embarrassing. "Since you're going to be here in the states for awhile," she quickly digressed from the subject, "why don't you come visit us out in California?"

Before Geno could reply she had him by the arm, "Come; let me introduce you to my husband."

Geno was immediately concerned that such a notion was out of order. Not to mention that he didn't know how her husband would react to his wife leading a total stranger over to his table and introducing him to such an elite band of individuals as those that were assembled at the festival that evening.

"I'd be honored to meet your husband, Rachel. However, it doesn't appear to be the proper time to make his acquaintance. Like most of the businessmen here tonight, primarily I believe he came to the event for the purpose of discussing business; and business only? Such being the case, I feel my intruding would be an invasion of your husband's privacy."

"Nonsense—" Rachel said to him and kept pulling him by the arm. "Mr. Lorenzetti, this is my husband, Marcus Kanin. Marc, meet Mr. Lorenzetti. He's a developer from England."

Thoroughly getting a rush of excitement seeing his brother up close—Chris greeted Marcus with distinct courtesy." It's an honor to make your acquaintance Mr. Kanin," he said. "I've heard so much about you where I come from. And I've been dying to meet you."

"The feeling is mutual; I'm sure," Marcus greeted him in a snobbish manner.

Astonishingly fresh out of the blue an idle moment of stillness fell between the pair.

"The building trade—what—a—business," Marcus said. "What organization do you work for fellow?"

"I represent Diangelo-Lorenzetti Builders," Chris responded. "We're based in London England."

"Diangelo-Lorenzetti; hum—m. Never heard of them."

"I find it to be very odd that you've never heard of us before now Mr. Kanin?"

"I'm sorry that I haven't been briefed about you or your business operation Mr. Lorenzetti. I simply haven't been keeping abreast with concurrent events. Also, it's very hard to keep track of every small enterprise that pursues our line of work on a daily basis."

"Small enterprise—we're number one in England," Geno said with a high pitched temperament.

"Number one, huh?" Marcus only overheard bits and pieces of what Chris spoke. The rest of his words were garbled.

He quickly felt exceptionally peculiar. For whatever the reason was he was almost bonding with the foreigner standing there conversing with him. He had to make sense of what was taking place.

As Mr. Lorenzetti kept rambling episodes of Marcus' early youth trek in his mind.

Wandering back into time Marcus was troubled over the matter. Could he have total recall and remember? Where had he overheard THAT VOICE that had all the earmarks of someone he knew before? Currently coming from the puzzling unidentified face of the gent whom was calling himself Mr. Geno Lorenzetti?

Rachel enthusiastically promoted her interest in the handsome foreigner.

"Darling why don't we show Mr. Lorenzetti our great American hospitality by inviting him to stay the weekend at our house?"

"American hospitality;" Marcus riveted his eyes on one of the waitresses. "Yes; he'd probably be overwhelmed with what Newport Beach has to offer around this time of the year. You are single; aren't you Mr. Lorenzetti?" He asked smiling while staring twice at the waitress' revealing outfit.

"Me single? Why of course." Geno's mind had roved off momentarily.

Rachel ogled at him, dream stricken. "So it's settled. You agree to spend a few days with us," she encouraged.

"Sure. Why not." Geno replied.

"Geno accepted our invitation darling. I'm so thrilled."

"Huh—" Marcus said trouble-plagued. The thought of the man's voice was on his conscience. "Sure, my love. I'd be honored to have Mr. Lorenzetti as a guest at home. Thank you for accepting our kind invitation."

"I'm delighted," Geno shook Marcus' hand.

Marcus pulled out one of his business cards. "I'll put my hotel room number on back of this. We leave for California at 12 noon Saturday. Call me."

Business had picked up tremendously at Kanin Enterprises. Every since Pitney had set in motion Sparling Management Company—and A.B.I. financial firm—their cash flow was far beyond stable.

To coincide with this reported prosperity their nationwide contracting and new construction had improved their bank account from $1.1 billion the year prior, to their current stage, now averaging approximately $1.4 billion.

The resultant day all of America's adult building firms bid on The Buhl and Martinelli Villa projects. It was intelligible that most of the firms were making a fruitless effort in their pursuits. Simply because they were unable to compete with the recent technological discoveries that had been made by Kanin Enterprises and their new rival, The Diangelo-Lorenzetti firm of England.

It'd been predicted that when the strong bids were all in—these would be the two companies whom would be competing against each other trying to win such a bid.

When The Lorenzetti firm was confronted with the issue of smallest space—largest components—series of enclosure of space that would be functional—economical—and aesthetically pleasing—plus complete building structure flexibility and durability, it was insidiously stomped by The Kanin firm.

They'd judiciously matched wits in this area of interest by storing data they'd bundled pertaining to The Diangelo-Lorenzetti firm's recent flattening.

They proofread and summed up a one hundred and ninety eight page report on the tragedy of the collapsing sections of slabs. A reversal of fortune that kept Geno awake many nights. Grievously these were research concrete slabs that Patricia Newmar's unskilled group of workers had tested and evidently produced the formulas for.

Unrevealed to individuals around them, while sitting facing each other the Kanin brothers experienced something that was staggeringly paranormal.

As Chris sat momentarily tormented in his mind and spirit over the possibility that he could lose The Buhl or Martinelli Villa deal his brother Marcus sat lock on and unscrambling his thoughts.

Through the channels of mental telepathy he listened in: "Chris, you simply cannot afford to be a three time loser. It seems like every time you pursue something—things just don't turn out like you'd expected them to. Every time you try, failure always stares you in the face. But Marc's venture's seem to always be a success. Why is he so successful? The forces of the inner limits of the universe willed it to him. Not only did they bequeath to him our father's fortune, he also inherited his cruelness. And with a vile mind similar to that of Gerald's manifesting itself in the form of Marc, only God Himself has the power to combat the arrant attitude he has when getting into normal scraps or aggressive conflicts with people. He can be consciously brutal."

Chris at once gazed at Marcus out of the corner of his eye and when their eyes met Marcus quickly dropped his head and stared down at the floor.

Momentarily he marveled at what he was experiencing. A sensorial moment lapsed and during that conscious period he'd right away became aware that Marcus had heard his inner thoughts.

Marcus was still. Beads of perspiration built up on his forehead. His mind almost exploded as he confronted it with open questions about the gentleman there bidding against him.

He concentrated puzzled. Thinking whether or not he was going insane.

Geno Lorenzetti; was he his exiled brother Christopher Kanin?

No—He tried to convince himself that he wasn't. He's not Chris. His thoughts continued tormenting him.

Seemly the pushing tactics that Kanin Enterprises used to approach winning the bid on The Buhl and Martinelli projects were lawful and in order.

Chris accepted defeat with a bit of hope left. And time moved forward.

Marcus, Rachel, and Geno together headed to southern California to have a fun filled evening at Newport Beach.

Routinely obedient, Marcus and a few corporate heads had paid bribes to the ranking subordinates who oversaw the handling of the bids taking place there in New York. En route on the flight he was giddish laughing at almost anything not humorous and gloating over how he'd outsmarted and cheated the competition again.

After swimming the ternary engaged in an early evening fish fry then topped off their day smoking marijuana and dancing to the rhythm of country and western—and rhythm and blues tunes.

They left their secluded hideaway around midnight and caught a flight to San Francisco.

Over in the mid afternoon that Sunday Geno stood at a dead stop in the huge living-room of the Kanin palatial residence with his eyes deep seated looking at a portrait of a golden good honest woman hanging over the fireplace.

"She reminds me of a person I once knew."

"What-t?" Geno wasn't aware that Rachel stood near. She at once stalked him gulping down a bloody mary.

"That's my husband's mother; Mrs. Elmira Kanin. By looking at her portrait one might think of her as being very evil. But I sense that hidden behind that grim face of hers, she was at one time a very lovable person. How do I know this," she paused, "her eyes depict the beauty that was in her character.

It was rumored that she was boozer. But it doesn't show. She seemed like a virtuous lady during the moment the camera captured her in that photo. It also seemed like she wanted her picture to be a cherished item for someone in her family to remember her by; after maybe she was gone?

I believe that she wanted them to see beyond her sated expression, and remember her, for the kind person that she really was?"

With external secretion building up in his eyes Chris gave a slip of the tongue, "I remember," he said plunging momentarily in sorrow.

"I beg your pardon?" Suddenly Rachel stared at him with mental inquisitiveness; thinking that maybe he didn't have it all up there. It could have been a mistake—bringing this weirdo to our house? She thought hushed.

And what is even more odd, is the reality that he's almost as touched—and foolish—as my husband. The two certainly have some similarities.

"I'm sorry Mrs. Kanin if it sounded like I was talking to myself," Geno started to explain. "That portrait just reminded me very much of my Aunt Cecelia. God rest her soul. A sweet lady she was indeed." Chris' manner of speaking sounded like he could've had a bit of Irish background in his blood.

"You don't have to be so uncomfortable around here Mr. Lorenzetti. And since it's personal, I can understand your sudden reminiscing. Your aunt must have been awful pretty? And a very warm—and loving person? How warm can you be when it comes to loving a person Geno?"

"Mrs. Kanin—" Geno was shocked that she was so consciously intimate with him.

"You can call me Rachel." She moved closer to him then whispered, "Consider me a lamb. Very gentle. I'm not at all like those other women animals that broke your heart."

"You're so amazing," Geno didn't know how to respond. "Maybe even unbalanced. No one ever broke my heart."

"Unwilling to step off on the edge?" she was a pro at such a come on. "You certainly do act like it. You're so edgy. And almost reduced to jelly around me. Come here." she forced her way on him.

Reaching forward then pulling his body up close to hers she began to tease him.

Terminally frightened Geno's temperature began to rise.

Holding on to him with a wedge like grip she kissed him grinding her body next to his.

While appropriately occupied in exotic utopia, at the height of such hanky panky, with sweat rolling down his face, Geno lost control.

"Take it easy hon'," he remained a gentleman and while posing as one he tried to convince Rachel that what she was doing was radically inappropriate at the time. Also that she was precociously forward.

"I can't believe this madness," he yelled down low. "Your husband is right upstairs. We three arrived here together this morning; remember? If you don't have any respect for him, respect yourself.

Me, I realize that I'm a guest at his home.

How would it look—me taking advantage of his generous hospitality—first—by lodging free at his home—eating his food—then screwing his wife? Did you know that a man's home is his castle?

He'd just as soon shoot me—for disrespecting his home—than the latter.

So be nice; and control yourself."

Rachel stared at him with lust in her eyes and dared him to advocate the same. "Your conversation is hauntingly out in the ozone man."

"Why don't you show me around this stately home you and your husband have here?" he continued to destroy her interest in him eluding to mere small conversation. "Maybe by the time that I see all that It has to offer you'll be too poofed out to want to play around."

At 7:00 p.m. dinner was served.

After learning numerous tricks of his trade, now inactively considered a procurer, Marcus momentarily had evolved.

He was in a league with the type of call girls who serviced high paid athletes; politicians, and top ranking motion picture industry type figures.

He placed at Geno's disposal that evening an attractive highly intelligent mouthy dinner date. She was the kind of broad any man would flip head over hills just to have a fantasy one night stand with. A well proportioned spitfire dynamo redhead who came in the shape of a buxom 38-24-36. A woman of action.

All-the-while during their dinner engagement and afterwards—at the movie set—she bored Mr. Lorenzetti to death.

During their informal association the most quietest and communicative moment that was shared between the deuce was when it became apparently urgent that Laura should use the bathroom: 'before she dripped in her seat….'

Geno's soft colored moment had arrived after he'd realized that she'd vacated the seat prompting him to inconspicuously leave the premises. No longer would he have to be irritated by her endless gossip and knowledge of W. Somerset Maugham, Guy de Maupassant and Henri Rene Albert.

Around 12:00 a.m. Marcus and Geno sat having a drink in the living room.

". . . Kanin Enterprises and Associates is the largest building firm in the U.S."

"Excuse me for butting in Marc on your conversation," Chris said. "I have something very important that I have to talk to you about. There's so little time left."

Nearly simultaneously there was silence.

Precipitously Marcus had an increase in temperature. Beads of perspiration appeared on his forehead as the heat spread quickly all over his body. There was an annoying amount of steam that nibbled at his nerve ends with the threat of severe panic.

"Marc, are you listening?'

Marcus sat motionless. The only sound that could be heard coming from him momentarily was a fast pounding heartbeat that was registering inside his body.

"I'm sorry that I couldn't reveal my identity to you before now," Chris explained to him. "Please understand, I decided to keep my visit here a secret for only one reason—I—was—afraid. As your already know, the F.B.I. is still pursuing me. My second reason is—that I wanted to protect you and Pitney from being embarrassed."

"Embarrassment," Marcus said, "we're more—"

"Please let me finish," Chris interrupted him. "My face has been changed. I had plastic surgery done. But my voice, it's almost the same. With the exception that I speak the British—language and a little French in broken diction. Before I continue, how's Pitney getting along? Have you communicated with her lately?"

"She's getting along fine," Marcus replied abruptly staring straight forwardly at his brother with a look of ponderous fear on his face. Then precipitously his voice rose angrily, "You're dumb for taking such a risk? Or out of sync with reality. Why disguise yourself from your own flesh and blood? What you've done is totally out of order Chris. How could you let me be misled in such a manner?"

"I'm sorry Marc," Chris responded. "I was desperate. Quite desperate I'd say."

Marcus fussed, "Did you realize that if you get busted, you're going to have to do life in prison?"

Chris was thunderstruck suddenly; his hope dissipating.

"I'm glad to hear that Pitney's doing fine," he said. "How's she doing financially? I would imagine that what she began with, and has accomplished thus far, she must be worth maybe three hundred million—or more?

"I imagine she's well off," Marcus remarked acrid. Set over against any of his sister's career achievements his outspoken words were simply not his true feelings.

"She burnt a lot of midnight oil getting there—too—buddy."

Precipitously it impinged on his consciousness the many counter productive moments when he and Pitney had arguments over his impolitic spending and the misuse of money that the firm had accused him of stealing out of their corporate cash supply.

Because of their many arguments involving his unwise waste she'd recently humiliated and brought shame upon him exposing his unsavory reputation to the media who had him constantly headlined in the news.

Then she paid a professional book keeper to calculate his private shares; paid him what he was owed, and fired him as the head of their facility.

Again, however, probation was harmoniously constituted for Marcus. But for certain this time, his job was on the line if by chance he didn't adhere to all of the conditions of his probationary period.

Consequently Pitney could not grasp—not even at this juncture in life—that Marcus was quietly suffering serious despair; consciously wrestling with an inner demon; himself. A force that would simply not let him determine where he fit in society. Or for what it mattered, he wondered occasionally, why was he ever born?

He'd managed to keep his expensive drug habit a secret from key players there at Kanin Enterprises. They'd never discover—that of the more than forty million dollars that he and a senior book keeper had funneled from the corporate fund, of Marcus' twenty nine million dollar share, twenty two million dollars was spent on his lavish lifestyle and buying narcotics for him and his friends.

An evil thought came to Marcus suddenly. She's an ominous force to deal with. Corrupt as any individual can be. If I have to have her disposed of—to put an end to her wicked female activism—that's what I'll do. Remove her from the face of the earth.

Chris had now began to feel uncomfortable. After being in exile for far too many years he could tell that his brother was not interested in embracing him nor making him feel welcome at what was once considered to be his home too.

Flustered, Chris said with non endurance, "Marc, I'll come abruptly to the point. The reason why I'm here is—I need The Buhl project. Or at least The Martinelli deal. It could mean, that without such a commitment, my firm will not survive.

It will be like a second chance for me. If I lose out on such it would finish my working at the building trade.

You have enough money. You have the business—as a whole—in the palm of your hand. Whatta ya say, can I at least have The Martinelli deal?"

Momentarily plunged into deep sorrow Marcus burst out, "You want The Martinelli bid handed to you—just—like—that—huh? In that demanding tone of voice you just used?"

"It sounded more like—I—was—begging," Chris interjected. "I never intended to sound demanding."

"On the contrary my—dear—brother—I know all about The Diangelo-Lorenzetti firm," Marcus quickly digressed from the subject. "I was being cautious when you first asked me had I ever heard of your corporation. But what really is a shock to me—is to know that my brother is tied in with the mob."

"Whatta ya mean mob?" Chris had now began to feel peeved off. "All of the business that's handled through my facility is 100% legit. It's the best thing that's ever happened to me. It's my whole life man can't —you—see—that?"

"Yeah, we both can be found cremated at the stake," Marcus grumbled in a low voice.

"Please speak up?" Chris asked him to.

"Forget what I said," Marcus' face contorted with repressed anxiety.

"Marc I beg of you, if there's a tiny bit—of—kind—consideration—to—be—found—in that dark heart of yours—please-e—I beg of you, let me have one of the jobs?"

Unequivocally blunt Marcus conveyed to him. "I'm a little beat now. Give me some time to think on the matter." It was the end of their conversation.

Marcus momentarily thought about his wearing drug habit. His being fired as the top ranking boss of Kanin Enterprises. He felt that his sister had a cruel streak—in cahoots with the board—and that they went straight for his jugular vein when they discharged him offering him severance pay and in the meanwhile threatened that they probably would give him the boot from his high paying job position.

Winding down, he felt further vexation of the spirit when it impinged on his conscious that his marriage to Rachel was now fully over.

Drisk soul drenching despair was what he felt momentarily. His complicated past haunted him.

Staying at his home was his brother Christopher Kanin—a man whom he'd treated terribly inhumane and mephitically cruel hearted as long as anyone could remember.

He was now asking him for a final favor. A favor which in reality might not have been asked for if their dire family relationship had been reconciled from the starting point.

Tomorrow he was uncertain—what would his answer be?

The adjacent day Chris nurtured the domain of possibility that Marcus would come to the right decision and let him have one of the jobs he'd asked him for.

He also hoped that Marcus had contacted Pitney and informed her that he was visiting there at The Estate for a few days.

However, as his day would turn out, Chris would forget all about his immediate family. He'd spend the remainder of the afternoon fighting desperately trying to stop Rachel from sexually assaulting him.

7:00 p.m. All-the-while dinner was being served Chris sat in expectancy of Marcus' answer.

8:00 p.m. As the brothers quietly managed to shoot a game of pool Chris felt the urge for an interchange of speech.

"How did your day go at the office?" He asked his voice quavering.

"Everything went okay," Marcus replied. "A few new projects were on the agenda. But none that were too challenging."

"I'd hoped that Pitney would call today? Maybe she was too busy?"

"Maybe she'll call tonight," Marcus said all the while lying. "I informed her that you were here. However, I explained to her that my phone might still be tapped. We both agreed that she should be very cautious when trying to contact you."

"That was very thoughtful of you."

Marcus began pouring himself a drink.

Still anticipating good news Chris chat, "I don't mean to rush things—or seem imposing Marc; but I only have a few days left. To assure my investors whether I can—or cannot—secure The Buhl—

or Martinelli bid." he paused momentarily confident that he would receive a yes reply.

"Will you—" he started talking more.

"Here—have another drink," Marcus gave him the kiss off.

"Thank you. But I don't care for another drink," Chris said trying to keep a stiff upper lip. "Did you reach a decision on the jobs?"

"This liquor was imported from your part of the country," Marcus said evasively. "It's one of the finest brands on the market today. Naturally I assume that people over there have real good taste also? What about ambition; do individuals in your country have a lot of that? Taste and ambition go hand and hand."

"Myself," Marcus plowed on determinedly with his adverse statements about life, "I'm a man who has good taste and a heap of ambition to go along with it. Any man who possesses senior qualities—must know—that in order to succeed at any particular occupation— you have to work at it. Do you follow me?"

While bearing to listen to Marcus talk Chris sat immobile— quietly fretting.

Then precipitously he felt a venerable crippling sickening throbbing headache.

His entire body ached and seemly at the stem of his brain trickling down his back throughout his entire body there was a tremendous increase in temperature. A steamy torturous heat that vulnerable twisted inside his veins then shot itself upwards pouncing around his mandibles then winding itself through his forehead—and immediately it raced fast to his brain leaving him thinking that he might expire at any moment now.

With a visible mass of vapor in his eyes—through a clouded vision his mind went traveling back into time where he began to recapture episodes from his childhood.

Clearly he gave thought to the long continued freezing rainy days and nights of durable labor he had to get done out in the field.

He saw how he and Gerald had worked undrooping— continuing— plodding side by side at their trade in the building industry. Work he did rendering support toward Marcus' high cost tuition for college.

He saw the staggering smash up that had occurred bringing forth death to his kin leaving the family to suffer distressing emotion which would eventually cause Gerald to shut down any communication he had with his eldest child. Later such a fate would drive Chris to realize that seemingly after his mom had died none of his kin cared for him?

He saw his lovable—as good as they come—mother—Elmira—how his father had put tremendous pressure on her and as a result of such it forced her to become a problem drinker. Also because of her mothering support she gave to Chris he stopped having any feelings for her which prompted her to later succumb of a subdued heart.

It was revealed in his collective memory the reading of Gerald's last will: How his father showed his gratitude towards him by leaving behind a small cash pile; as a token of his appreciation for his many contributions to the business.

It surfaced in his conscious even during those years how Marcus capitalized—exploited and took advantage of his ideas and—in the future he was heading their father's firm which Gerald handed to him on a silver platter. Marcus a person who never did barely anything good in his whole life span; only Gerald would've caused such a badgered fate to fall upon their family and plunge them in further deep doo-doo.

Chris wondered about himself; how could one man's life be troubled with as many incredibly bad luck episodes as the family inflicted ones that he'd encountered during him lifetime?

Such an existence as his was—momentarily discontented—he felt that the predicament that he was in truly must've been pre-schemed by the angel of doom and slated on the calendar to occur on this date. "I'm sorry Chris… But I find that it's impossible for me to let you have either of the bids," Marcus said audaciously.

Precipitantly after Marcus had barked such insensate words, soft in the head, and asquint looking, Chris rushed toward his brother dead set on avenging his cause.

Consumed with extreme terrorizing rage before Marcus could react he whomp him with such a violent force that the impact of Marcus' body propelled the large bar aside sending him crashing wounded in atrocious pain up against a glass scene encased in the wall.

While persevering the deep felt pain from the cuts and bruises that he'd received from the shattered glass clinch to his body Marcus even though he was outmatched, wimpish self tried desperately to fight off his attacker.

Endowed with inferior punching power Chris punched him several times then kicked him in the stomach.

As pain ripped through his body Marcus rolled away stumbling trying to avoid catching a punch to his face.

Chris kicked at him again then he sent a storm of sharp blows to Marcus' side then he followed up with counter punches to his mid section.

Double quick blood began at flood pace coursing from Marcus' mouth.

As Marcus lay noiseless for a moment Chris sat geared for action. While sitting anticipating hearing a groan from his victim Chris sensed that he still had a breath of life still left in him, so he quickly decided to put out Marcus' flame.

With the distinct stupor of murder on his face while sitting straddle Marcus he began to pound tired on his face.

Marcus outer face quickly began to look like a crushed tomato.

Within a moment Marcus body went debilitated in Chris hands.

While moving slowly up off of him Chris tarried hoping to hear a hiss of discriminate noise from him.

A moment passed.

Stark staring insane Chris sat thumping his fist in his hand. "Don't you groan no more; you hear," he spoke to the open air. "Die. Die. You dehumanizing degenerate," he voiced fretfully. "Satan can't live forever. Die—" he shouted gripped with murderous insanity.

Minutes elapsed fast and by his own initiation he deserted his ruthless doing then in tears brooded over the matter. And coinstantaneously, currently tied to such grief he started crying uncontrollably.

Right away footsteps could be heard rushing toward the room where the brothers were.

Appearing like a heavy sedated alien Chris walked out into the hallway.

Curiously wanting to know what had caused all the commotion downstairs Rachel attempted to walk past him into the room.

Chris grasped her arm.

Life threatening fear engulfed Rachel momentarily.

Standing frozen in one spot she asked in a trembling voice, "What's going on? Where's my husband?" Then she tried to free herself from him.

"He's where a Judas is supposed to be," Chris said staring bluff at her. "He betrayed a loved one—he's now paid the price for his betrayal."

This guy has crossed over. She thought quietly.

While observing how strange Mr. Lorenzetti had began acting then realizing that he and her husband had went to the rec room to talk on a friendly base, she must now—as she tried to make sense of things—act or do something about the tense situation that she had become a part of.

Even though she'd become fast alarmed she arrived at enough self control to try to compromise with almost anything that their daffy acquaintance might've momentarily had in mind.

As they headed down the corridor she wrangled silently to herself considering what'd caused her to be in the predicament she was in. You're dumb; dumb; dumb, the urging roomer said, when it comes to choosing a man. Extrasensory perception; not you. You have no sense of evaluating one's character. Your crystal vision told you that Mr. Lorenzetti seemed like he wasn't playing with a full deck on his first day here at the house. No—You were being cool-l; you thought. You should've asked Marcus to ask him to leave—then. No—Your feminine intuition would have been put on trial. And— Rachel—don't— like—being wrong.

"Did my husband get drunk and pass out Mr., Mr. Lorenzetti?" she asked in a softened voice.

"Out—" Geno looked dazed. "Yes. He's out. We're rid of him."

Still clinging tightly to her arm he now opened the door that led into her bedroom.

Within a few tensely filled moments he'd undressed her and began making terrorizing love to her.

For more than a half hour canal horny and sexed up fleshly groans and painful labored sobs could be heard coming from the room.

When the uncivilized performance was over Chris apologized to Rachel.

Externalizing no sign of shock as Chris was leaving Rachel laid in a careless heap with a ecatasiating smile fondly on her face.

Once inside the rec room she caught a casual glance of her husband as he lay on the floor crying out in unmitigated pain.

Completely non serious she began screaming out loud for help.

Marcus mumbled something to her.

He managed to say enough to her for her to comprehend that he basically wanted her to keep what had happened there on that night hushed.

Then fast before Rachel could phone for the E.M.S. service he'd slipped off into a state of unconsciousness.

The adjacent day as Rachel, Pitney, and Salvo waited silently shrinking in fear by Marcus' bedside something—an unearthly force— seemly showcased itself in him; and phenomenally it revised him.

His condition which the doctors had stated would continue to touch bottom stunningly became upgraded.

Immediately after he was able to exchange communication he held a brunt conversation with his wife and sister getting it off of his system about the secret visit that Chris had paid him.

While hoping that his wife sympathized along with him over the matter he suavely suggested that it would be a polite act on her part if she would not seek charges against his brother for assaulting her; in the event also, that he should die.

Pitney was psyched out and in tears as Marcus verbally published how much friction was between the deuce; and talked about his hostility; estrangement; and warped rancorous malice that he held in his heart toward his brother. He then promised them that once The Buhl and Martinelli Villa deals were completed, all of the capital made from such would be sent to Chris to keep his firm from going defunct.

CHAPTER TWENTY-SEVEN

On the same day of Geno's arrival back in England Klara was summoned to Mr. Diangelo's home.

"Good afternoon," he rested her coat. "What would you like to drink?"

Klara quickly turned white as a sheet. Never in her lifetime was she ever more frightened.

Sensing that another hit was in the making she ordered a double martini.

"I hope that it suits your taste my dear." Mr. Diangelo took a seat beside her. "Before I give you your orders, maybe we should talk."

Klara nodded her head.

"In the ocean you have big fish; and you have small fish. For some reason, it always seems that the big fish want to eat the small fish. That's what Kanin Enterprises is trying to do our little company that we have here in England. We've even asked our enemy to consider merging. We wanted to—sort—of—act like a subsidy firm for them. They said to us that 'Kanin Enterprises and Associates—already have enough subsidy corporations.' Do you know what that means?"

"No. I'm sorry. What does it mean?" Klara asked fraught with danger.

"It means that they are a threat to our survival. We have a monopoly interest in mind. Such arrogance could mean an end to what we've been constantly trying to achieve. It has to be toppled."

"How do you topple a corporate giant?":

"You infiltrate their hierarchy. Get to those in top ranking positions. Corrupt their minds; or blow their brains out."

"How do you accomplish that? There are so many of them."

"You eliminate the most important ones."

"'Tis good."

"We want Marcus Kanin and his sister out of the way. When that's done we'll deal with the other V.I.P.'s in another manner."

"Please forgive me for interrupting, Mr. Diangelo." Klara stared at him with an explosive look on her face. "It seems that you have a—whole—lot—of—elimination—in store for yourself."

"The elimination must be performed by a capable source. I've heard that The French Riviera's beautiful—even—during springtime. Maybe you and I can take some karate lessons there—when I again—pay you a visit. Breaks—when one has avoided being harmed during a dangerous assignment—gets an assassin pumped up—before they kill their next victim, I should know I've disposed of enough of such corporate white trash since being tied to The Costra Nostra. Don't brood over the matter. Get—the—job—done."

"What about Geno?"

"First we make him an offer. If he bargains too hard with us, then we'll have no choice but to eliminate him—too."

"I see."

"I hope he returns with some good news. However, here's a plane ticket; in case he doesn't win the bid. You'll be leaving for the U.S. in four days." He held up his glass in a farewell toast.

Smiling grimly Klara toasted along with him.

After Mr. Diangelo went back upstairs Chenelle, whom had been listening from inside the study quietly dialed Geno's number.

She let the phone ring and ring but there was no answer.

Trembling nervously she then went over to his house to wait for him. During the time that Chenelle was en route to Geno's home he'd made it to London and dialed Mr. Diangelo's number informing him that they'd lost both bids.

Without further delay Mr. Diangelo ordered Klara 'to pull the hit' on The Kanin's.

Back at home hooked up with Chenelle that night Geno learnt some very shocking news.

While chilling—drinking wine and listening to the stereo Chenelle finally got up the nerves to tell her close acquaintance what was going down.

"Geno;" she stared at him stone faced, "well, first I better inform you that while you were away, some American agents came by here asking questions about you." She paused momentarily to see how he'd react.

Geno responded casually, "What did they want with me?"

"Primarily they wanted as much info as I could give them about you. Things like, what was your real name. How long had you been living in this country. Did I know where you came from before you became a native of England. And so forth."

"So they wanted my autobiography? Something describing my past history?"

"There's something else too Geno," she momentarily became hesitant to speak.

Geno mumbled, "Yes—" hoping not to be devastated by what she would tell him.

"It wouldn't be fair for me to keep something as important—as this from you," she said with morbid anxiety.

Almost in a state of cardiac arrest Geno raised his voice a note, "If it's of a serious nature—please—don't—keep—it—from—me."

"Your life may be in danger." Again Chenelle paused.

"My life in danger," Geno shouted shaking her up. "How do you know this?"

"I overheard papa and Klara talking this evening about your family."

"Klara. Is that what you said? All-the-while you knew Susan was faking. But you led me to believe that you two were strangers. I knew something was wrong. Now I know."

"Such a small issue isn't at all important; right now."

"Your father and her, they were discussing me?" Geno was obviously frightened now. "What did they say?"

"They were; they were—" Chenelle quickly became afraid.

"What did they talk about? Please tell me," dreading what he might hear, Geno begged suddenly with a calm countenance.

"She's—been—ordered—to—kill—your—brother—and—sister." Chenelle started crying.

"When?" he asked.

"She's leaving for the states as soon as papa hears about the bids."

"That's insane. Come on. Let's get to the air terminal; right away."

Wincing and tremendously pale Chenelle said, "A smart man sits and thinks over trouble."

Geno yanked away from her heading quickly toward the front door.

Kneeling beside the bed Chenelle thought about what would her papa do to her if he found out that she'd informed anyone of what he had planned. She embedded her face over into her hands and began crying uncontrollably.

The following day agent Throbs returned to Geno's home. He'd brought along with him this time, The British authorities and extradition papers.

Upon his arrival he found out from Chenelle that Geno had gone into exile in another foreign country. Consequently after The British cops had finished smacking her around they finally learnt the truth.

CHAPTER TWENTY-EIGHT

There was a bomb threat at Heathrow so Geno was stranded for two days at a hotel.

At a secluded airstrip outside San Francisco Kanin Enterprises top brass was preparing to take a trip to a small community outside Mexico City. They were going there to inspect the building site of their recently acquired project; The Martinelli Villa.

As Marcus exited the magnificent limo he'd been a passenger in his cell phone buzzed.

"It's me. Pitney—" the voice said. "Before we board let's have a chat?"

Marcus trudged the approximate twenty yards or more to the stretch vehicle his sis' was riding in.

"Hello Marc. How's your day going so far?" Pitney gave him a light kiss on the cheek.

"So far, it's going great sis'," he said lounging beside her. "But I think that things will go even better, now that you're here."

"Well," she blushed, "I'm the one who can indeed make your life better." Her words sounded like a joke. Or was she actually being smart? Marcus wondered.

"Can I assist you with anything? Business wise; or private?" she tried to be sincere.

"Gee; thanks sis'," he said showing all of his front ivory. "Business wise, I have everything under control. But the latter subject, I'm doomed. And up the creek without a paddle."

"Outside of your troubled love life how are you feeling mentally?"

"My life, Pitney, truly it's in ruins. For the first time ever, I feel so deep in a cave of despair. It's like I almost don't have a friend left; in this world."

He now reared back comfortably on the seat and began pouring out his feelings to his sis'. "Lately, Chris has constantly been on my mind.

My thinking of him has had me so deeply disturbed that for several nights, I've had to take sleeping pills in order to try and get some sleep. When thinking about my recent cruelty towards him, I somehow feel that this time I should have been more understanding towards him.

Since experiencing the agony of defeat, for a second time he's probably so bitter that he couldn't forgive me for all the pain and suffering I've caused him.

I've robbed him of his chances so many times. Why? Why did I have to turn my back on him this time?"

"I don't argue the fact that you've been cruel to him Marc. And that he doesn't deserve a break. But years ago, remember he said it himself, he will not accept charity from anyone. Therefore we won't give him charity." she said gloating.

"Chris is a survivor. I'm willing to put a wager on it that when he puts his mind to work, he'll be a success. You'll see."

Marcus had overheard only half of what she'd babbled. All-the-while engrossed in deep thought thinking about how he'd treated his brother so unfairly, he sat choking back tears. Tears from a despicable mood swing that momentarily baffled Pitney.

"Cheer up man," Pitney yelled hoping to forget about why she and Marcus were so rile, "You act as though you're attending someone's funeral. And so do I." she laughed.

"Now that we've eulogized Chris, let's bury him; and head to our latest project."

"The Martinelli Villa deal—yes—" Pitney said smiling. "We'll discuss it over a bottle of crown royal during the plane ride."

"Mexico City—Where the money's at—Let's go—"

When the Kanin's arrived in Mexico City before long Klara had located them and began tailing Marcus around town.

While he visited a female friend of his she had the chance to kill him, but for an unknown reason she held off.

During those nerve-jangling moments, through ponderous fear, she realized that the spin off of the job she suddenly had to perform, it was going to change her life dramatically.

She thought seriously about if it was ever disclosed to Chris that she initiated such a cruel act against his family, there's no telling how he'd have his revenge on the persons whom brought them harm.

When Chris arrived in The Big Apple using the name Diangelo-Lorenzetti Builders—he contacted Kanin Enterprises trying to get in touch with his kin.

However, for security reasons, Marcus' secretary wouldn't give him any information pertaining to the belt where his folks had a task to heed.

He dialed Marcus' home number and no one answered. Rachel had gone to pay some friends a visit.

Excessively fidgety he swilled down a half bottle of gin.

Around 9:30 p.m. he got through to Rachel.

This time quickly identifying himself he questioned her about Marcus' trip.

Rachel became quietly alarmed provoking her to stand mute. She feared with the utmost precaution that Chris wanted to harm her husband like he'd done on his previous visit to their house.

Within a while he'd won her confidence and she related to him that Marcus and Pitney had caught a flight earlier that morning to visit the Martinelli Villa site. She then gave him directions to where he could locate them in Mexico.

Around 11:30 a.m. the trailing morning Pitney and Marcus along with their chief architect—and a building inspector were a spectator there at the site.

Near to his Villa Mr. Martinelli had built a sub division that had homes with price tags beginning at two and a half million dollars upwards of nine million dollars each. Also in the locale he'd built a shopping mall that had a mega movie theater complex that offered everything form automobiles to collectable art for the 21st century shopper. And currently a part of the gym structure was completed there at the private sports arena he was having constructed; because of his sixteen year old son's interest in athletics. Housed and situated on the adjacent grounds, there were baseball diamonds; tennis courts; and golf courses for his son's friends to further be entertained; if by chance they grew tired of playing hockey—basketball and ice skating inside the arena.

After playing a quick game of tennis with his architect Marcus, Pitney and the rest of their coalition headed towards the gymnasium.

Once inside the building while inspecting its electrical units there was a loud whack on the front door.

Pitney rushed to open it and a man progressed with great speed past her moving in the direction where Marcus and the building inspector were standing.

Pitney chased after the figure.

"What is the meaning of—" Marcus' words were unstated when momentarily he realized that the unidentified man trudging near him was his brother Chris.

"Marc, I've got to talk to you," Chris yelled out of breath.

Marcus stared at him rapt in wonder not knowing what to make of such a seemingly demented intrusion.

"I'm serious—" Chris shouted again.

While casting his eyes watchfully around the building he checked out what appeared to be a single anatomy concealed behind some building materials that sat on a deck of the bleachers.

Fast Chris strove to try to save his brother by tackling him ultimately forcing the deuce's weight thumping into Pitney and such an impact sent them accelerating to the floor.

Unimaginable gunshots rang out from an automatic weapon—and they came in rapid succession—which frightened the individuals inside the gym. Also mortals who was angle half upwards felt the hot air and in a free agent act—they made strides for cover beneath anything that was attainable.

Frigid interior fear engrossed the association as they lay silent; hoping that whatever evil force that'd attacked them, it would disappear.

A brief moment of silence fell.

Contacted in the upper shoulder and thigh was the building inspector.

From a bullet that had ricocheted off the wall then touched his head Chris lay a few feet away—screaking in pain.

Still laying psychologically in a catatonic stupor Marcus and Pitney lay cuddled clinging tightly onto each other.

Suddenly upon realizing that her attempt to snuff out Marcus' and Pitney's life had failed—and observing that Chris was immediately there, what ensued next, Klara foolishly reacted by turning the weapon to her head and fired.

After things had calmed down a bit en route back to the air terminal Chris who'd decided not to take hospital treatment for his superficial wound again pleaded with his family members to subcontract him a part of their work.

". . . Why—Chris—darling—how can you discuss such an unimportant matter—at a time—when everyone's—in such a mood of despair?" Pitney said with a disparaging temper. "You were there—and witnessed the worst work of evil that a human could ever be exposed to. We all need to get over this. So how about we discuss your little gripe over dinner tonight?"

For whatever her reason might be seemingly she's grown set at defiance. And all screwed up. Chris' heart pounded thinking of what to do next.

She has a lot of balls thumbing her nose at me.

Now there's TWO DEMONS in this family.

Why my family?

There are so many influential people who—just—let—satan—possess—and control—them.

But the huge question is when did she become so materialistic? An angelic person like she once was?

Now she's sharing the same ideals and geared toward being a force to reckon with, like Marc.

Currently the situation looks grim. Very grim. Chris was agonizing quietly.

4:00 p.m. that evening.

Inside the partial rec and entertainment room of The Kanin Estate Pitney and Marcus were joined by friends who'd heard about the adventure and had come over to console them.

For what seemed like a full hour they were laughing from time to time; tipple booze; did drugs and held conversational interchange aloud about the incident that had impermanently threatened their lives. The contingent deliberately evaded giving any matter of praise to

Chris the person who saved his kin's life.

At once Pitney and Marcus began arguing. What had become a broadening problem between the eristic kin—when friends were around—escalated on this evening.

Pitney ridiculed Marcus about his insecurity to function as a businessman.

Publicly she became more and more indignant toward him.

Amid the clashing related duo's contention their clique once again directed their attention back to discussing the incident that had occurred at the gym.

Chris quietly left the crowd and sought a snug harbor in the reading room.

Staring grievously with his head inclined toward the ceiling he again recalled the draining work that he finished up out in the field with his father. The hard shock when the lives of his three brothers were taken. His status and slamming sentence at home and the love his mother had for him. And the spot of trouble that led to her too early death.

He saw the sensible relationship that he had with his first girlfriend whom was found dead washed up on the beach.

His father denouncing him in his will. His adverse circumstances in France and his attempt at trying to get himself established in England.

He remembered his first introduction to Klara and how they'd sparked a romantic relationship and how they'd dreamed about becoming enormously rich.

And he saw how in the end she'd taken her own life to spare his; and the lives of his blood relatives. Two aliens. Individuals who didn't care whether or not a Christopher Kanin ever shared the same space with them on this planet.

Within hardly any more moments of brawling with his conscious, the argument accelerated with him listening to voices interrogating himself—then fast—he concentrated his efforts on the whole federation who was getting their groove on in the living room of the estate and by surprise, they lay sprawled dead, from wounds they'd suffered after Chris' mind had violently exploded—and his independent out of control activism was over.

At hand, after the incident had occurred, Dan Throbs arrived at the house to arrest Chris.

In the drawing room, Chris was at it; motivating himself meticulously, arranging module blocks.

As he moved them from position to position established somewhere in his psychic apparatus, he was listening at inner voices—that were those of his vicious—evil minded—occasionally mentally ill—father plainly bitching at him.

Chris—what—in—the—hell—are—you—doing? Why—were—you—sent—home—again—today....

I. I. I was—

So—you—don't—have—an—answer—huh? Get—your—rear—end—inside—the—house....